MW01228875

Ambiguous

The Sin Series – Book 4

Jay and Annette

By C.D. Blue

All Rights Reserved © 2017 by C.D. Blue

Join me on Facebook @ C.D. Blue
https://m.facebook.com/cdblueauthor

Follow me on Twitter @
https://twitter.com/CDBlue5

Join me in The Sin Series Group on Facebook
https://www.facebook.com/groups/TheSinSeries

Cover Design by: Jamie Lee – Mogul Focus

Editing: Jelicia Manuel-Blue & Amber D. Kelley

ISBN-13: 978-1548867034

ISBN-10: 1548867039

<u>Acknowledgments</u>

First as always, I want to thank God, for everything!
My husband, Shawn, for his continuous support and dealing
with the mood swings when the characters have taken over.
My family, for being the best family in the world! I love you
guys!

I have the best team! Jelicia, your edits and feedback
made this book the best it could it be. We have come a long
way and we will continue to grow. The Sin Series would not
exist without you. Thank you so much! Amber, thanks for
your expertise, friendship and support. Your expertise
helped take The Sin Series to new heights! I will always
appreciate you and I just hope that I can be there for you as
you have been for me.

Jennifer, Calandra, and Peggy, without each one of
you, I'm not sure if The Sin Series would have made it this
far. Your feedback and support means the world to me, it
also keeps me motivated to keep going. Never think that I
take your support for granted because I don't. Jamie Lee,
thank you for turning my words into a vision! Your covers
are the best.

The local Sin Series group thank you for seeing my
characters as real as I do. We have grown in number, but
with each new addition comes new friendships and I
appreciate each one. It has been a joy to be able to talk
about The Sin Series characters as extended family members
with others who understand.

The Sin Series Facebook group, thanks for joining me
and it has been wonderful getting to know you. And finally,
every reader that takes a chance, continues to read, and tells
someone about my titles. You guys are the best and I never
take you for granted. Your support and love humbles me! I
hope you enjoy this title!

Note from the Author

Thank you for choosing Ambiguous Sins! This novel symbolizes growth. Growth for me as an author, growth for The Sin Series characters, and growth for the wonderful team of people that help me in this publishing journey! This novel was an emotional rollercoaster and I hope that I conveyed the emotions enough for you to feel what the characters felt.

Once again thank you for taking a chance on an indie author and I hope you enjoy your read. Please check out the Sin Series titles and they can be read in any order.

C.D. Blue

Growth is the sum of adversity and heartbreak.
C.D. Blue

Chapter 1

Jay itched to leave the office. Usually it was his sanctuary, but today it had turned into his prison. His life was in turmoil, and he needed to put it back together. The first thing on the agenda was to talk to Annette. He hadn't realized how much he had messed up until the day before. Whatever it took to repair their relationship, he would do. If he needed to lay on hot coals butt-naked for an hour, it would be done with a smile on his face. He leaned back in his chair and thought about how he got to this point.

Jay met Annette innocently enough, it was at the bowling alley. At the time, he was married to Elaine, unhappily, but he never cheated. When he met Annette, everything changed. There was something about her that he could not get out of his head. She was beautiful with a great body, but it went so much deeper. There was something inside of her that shone around her like a halo.

Once they connected, his life changed and he knew that he wanted her in his life. They fooled around for a while and when he made the decision to leave Elaine, he never told Annette. Eventually, Annette left him. As he reminisced he realized that those were his darkest days, before he got to this point. He left Elaine and waited until things settled with her, then he went back for Annette. His life was now complete, well almost complete.

Elaine worked hard at making their lives miserable. Jay put up with her because he wanted his son, Malik, transition to be as 'normal' as possible. He kept the peace with Elaine, gave her extra money when she asked, and made sure that everything in their home was kept up. He now knew that only festered the hatred in Elaine's heart. The two fears that he tried to eliminate were: becoming a replica of his dad, and Elaine poisoning Malik against

Annette. Not only had she tried it, she used his fear of being a bad parent against him. And he fell for it.

He shook his head. He went from a man on top of the world in every area of his life, to his business being the brightest spot. A small chuckle escaped as he thought about how he almost sent that to hell also. He had expanded his business, and the expansion included partnering with two computer geniuses that were brothers.

Jay owned Auto-Tech, a computer networking/programming company designed just for automobile dealerships. His business did well, but he knew he needed something extra for expansion. That extra came when he met Omar Rives, Annette's best friend fiancé. Omar was in the security business, more so private investigations, but also was a computer whiz. Jay's idea was to enhance his accounting/floorplan programs with a security program. Omar and his brother Xavier were the perfect pair for it. Omar was good with code, but his brother's skills were amazing! He created security data with impassable encryptions in a few days. It would have taken Jay months to do half of what he did.

After he found out that Elaine was the reason his personal life had crumbled, he was so mad that he listened to the murmurings of his best friend Carl. Carl was his lifetime friend, he was more like family, and was embroiled in a nasty divorce. He planted the seed in Jay's head that it was possible that Xavier had gone after Annette while they faced their problems. His emotional rollercoaster led him to believe it. He was glad that Xavier hadn't been there when he confronted Omar.

His anger at Elaine had caused him to lash out at Omar. After Omar looked at him as if he was crazy and seemed clueless about Xavier and Annette, Jay apologized. He had let his emotions get the best of him. Once he calmed down he realized how foolish he had sounded. Usually Carl was spot on with his advice, but Jay realized that Carl's emotions had gotten the best of him too. The last thing he needed was his career to take a dive. Although the brothers owned the patent and he had licensed it for the dealerships he managed; he wanted to expand. He needed them for that. There were a few dealerships in California interested and if there was a rift, the brothers could decide not to let him license it.

Omar was cool, he and Jay got along from the beginning. Xavier was a different story. He was friendly enough, but somewhat standoffish and quirky. Xavier had dated Jay's sister for a brief time, but she had recently broken it off. She said he was too hard to read and he was too close-mouthed about his life. Jay was secretly glad. As smart as the guy was, there was something off about him. He knew that his imagination along with his personal feelings about the guy had gotten the best of him.

His phone startled him when it rang. It was his mother, René.

"Jay what the hell is going on?" She spoke loudly. "Elaine called me and said you almost assaulted her!"

He usually kept his mom out of his business, but he was tired of Elaine's games. "Mom, nothing happened, but I wish I had beat her ass. Elaine is a bitch and I don't care what she says."

There was a brief silence before his mom spoke. "I've been telling you that for years, but she's not worth getting in trouble. What is going on now?"

Now that she realized that he hadn't snapped she was back in her normal nosiness mode.

He sighed heavily, "I'll tell you all about it later."

"Okay, I'll be home this evening." He knew she meant that she needed to know sooner versus later.

"Not today Mom, I'm going to Annette's this evening. I'll see you tomorrow."

René's voice perked up, "That's fine. Is the wedding back to the original date?"

Her words made his heart hurt. Annette had postponed the wedding because she was tired of dealing with Elaine. He felt like a fool now that he knew that had been Elaine's plan all along.

"Not yet, we haven't talked about it yet." If he didn't end this call soon, his mom would pry all the information that he planned to tell her later.

Her voice dropped an octave. "Don't think that you will get out of letting me know what is going on. If I don't see you tomorrow, I will come to you."

He promised that he would be there and hung up. As the day drew on he stopped in the computer room before he left. Omar sat at the back monitor, on the phone.

"I just hope you know what you are doing. I don't think that you have…" Omar turned and spotted Jay. "Let me call you later."

"Sorry man, I didn't mean to interrupt." Jay still felt foolish from earlier.

"No problem. What's up?" Omar's face was calm, but he seemed tense.

"I just wanted to make sure we were cool after I showed my ass earlier." Jay said with a sheepish grin.

Omar shrugged his shoulders. "Don't worry about it. You've been under a lot of stress. Like I told you earlier, if something was going on between Annette and Zay, that's a conversation to have with them. You and I are cool."

Omar stood and gave Jay a man-hug. Jay felt better, but still hoped that Omar wouldn't think that this was normal for him. He left soon after because he needed to get home to shower and shave. He wanted to look his best when he saw Annette.

When he got to Annette's, her baby sister Ashley let him in and gave him a tight hug. He took that as a good sign. Annette was in the kitchen and the aroma of whatever she'd cooked filled the house. He felt like he was home! Annette came out of the kitchen and when he saw her his heart tripled its beats. She had on jeans and a crew neck striped shirt. This had to be the way children felt on Christmas day.

"Hey." He approached her slowly.

"Hey yourself." She walked up to him and looked up.

He wanted to ravish her right there, but instead he pulled her close and kissed the tip of her nose. "It smells good in here. Did you cook enough for me?"

When she looked at him to answer, he leaned down and kissed her. He felt her arms as they looped around his neck and he pulled her closer. Forget dinner, he wanted to go straight to the bedroom.

"Umm-hmm." Ashely cleared her throat and reminded them she was there. "I promise that as soon as I eat, I will go straight to my room."

They laughed as they pulled apart. Dinner was scrumptious, but Jay barely took his eyes off Annette. As they talked and laughed about a variety of subjects, he realized how much he missed nights like this. In the past they would eat, spend some time with kids before their bedtime, then they would go to the bedroom. There was never a moment that he didn't want to be here. He wanted his life back.

Ashley, true to her word, went to her room after they ate. She hugged Jay again and told him that he had been missed. He helped Annette in the kitchen before they finally settled on the sofa. He wished he had told her everything on the phone, so that they could go to their sanctuary. As she settled in next to him, he grabbed her hands.

He told her everything, well almost everything. He still did not admit that he slept with Elaine, even though she had drugged him. He kept hearing Carl's voice in the back of his head. Carl told him if he told Annette, she would leave him. So, he omitted that part. When he told her about what Elaine had done to Malik, Annette's eyes filled with tears and she stopped him.

"Poor Malik! Why didn't he tell you?" She wiped her tears with her hand.

Jay's heart filled with love. Regardless of what she had been through, her first concern was Malik. Her compassion was one of the many reasons he loved her so much. He told her how Malik thought if he told Jay, it would be confirmed that they didn't want him full time. He said it as softly as possible.

Annette stood. "Everything we have gone through recently was orchestrated by Elaine?" Her tone was incredulous.

He nodded his head slowly. "I have to accept the part I played in it too. I allowed her to come between us, and I'm so sorry about that. I promise it will never happen again."

He stood and wrapped her in his arms but she wiggled away from him. She faced him. "Maybe if you had included me in your life completely this wouldn't have happened. Maybe I could have offered or suggested something that would have brought this to light. Or maybe if she saw that you included me in your son's life she wouldn't have taken it this far."

Everything she said was true, there was nothing he could say to dispute it. He eased over to her again.

"Annette, I thought I was protecting Malik and I thought I was protecting you." His hands remained at his side even though he desperately wanted to reach out to her.

"How were you protecting me Jay? By excluding me?" Her hurt rang through her tone.

"I didn't want you to deal with Elaine's nasty mouth and I didn't want her to poison Malik against you. I know now that I was wrong, baby I'm so sorry. I never meant to hurt you, I thought I was making it easier for you." Jay rubbed his face, and this time he did touch her. He placed his hands around her waist and pulled her to him. "I just want to make things right for us, forever."

It hurt him when he saw the indecision and hurt in her face. She wasn't through.

"Jay, I told you that we needed to tell Malik the truth about how we met. If we had maybe he would have known how much we wanted him." She looked at him but didn't pull away.

"I know you did, and you were right. I should have listened to you. Everything you have said is true, and I have beat myself up for being such a fool. Can you forgive me?"

He tried to convince his body not to react, but as he felt her body pressed against his, and looked into her eyes, he felt his nature rise. It felt so natural to lean in for a kiss and as she pulled him closer, his desire overtook his mind and body. His hands roamed over her body, as he felt what he had missed so dearly. As he touched every curve and contour of her body, it was more than familiar. He knew her body better than he knew his own. He inwardly groaned as she pulled away.

"Of course, I forgive you, but did Elaine promise that she would give up?" She peered deeply into his eyes.

She moved slightly back as his silence surrounded the room. "She's not giving up, is she?"

"It's not that she wants me, she just doesn't want me to be with you." He let out an exasperated breath.

"Jay that is the same thing. It still means that she will try to interfere in our lives. And now she's including Malik in her shenanigans? That's just too much." Annette pushed her hair back from her face.

"I'm working on getting full custody of Malik. Once I get him, we won't have to deal with her."

"Why not? She will still be his mother." She stepped out of his embrace. "Jay, I love you, I truly do. But I am so confused right now and it's not all Elaine. Some of it is me. So much has ha—, I don't like the hatred I feel towards her. That's not who I am or who I need to be."

She looked down briefly before she finished. "I can't marry you right now, or even be engaged…"

"Baby, don't do this." He cut her off as her words sliced through his soul.

"Jay, I can't. I need my soul, heart and mind to be aligned together before I can promise you anything. I love you too much to let you think that everything is fine when it's not!" Tears ran down her cheeks. "I just think that we should continue our break until we are both sure of what we want and how we want to live. I'm sorry if I hurt you, but you deserve the best I can give, and I can't give that right now."

Jay was stunned. It took him a minute before he went to her and covered her in an embrace. "Now wait a minute! Let's not make any rash decisions right now. I don't want to lose you Annette."

She looked at him sadly, "I hate to lose you too. But what you just said pretty much sums it up. Elaine is not going away while we are together. Even if you get full custody of Malik, she is still his mother. You getting full custody is not going to make her accept reality, it will probably make her worse."

She softly caressed his face, "Besides that, I need to get my head on straight. I know I love you, but I'm not sure our relationship is strong enough to weather all storms. This past month has shown me that it isn't. Maybe once everything becomes clearer we'll be stronger than ever."

"And if we are not?" Before she answered he kissed her long and deep.

While Annette clung to him he reached under her shirt and freed her breasts from the confines of her bra. She moaned in his mouth as he rubbed his palm across her nipples. Her moan sent tremors through his body. He sighed in frustration when she pulled away.

"Jay, I don't want to think about not being with you, but we can't continue as we have been. Elaine's outburst had become so commonplace, I don't think we realized how much it damaged us. It made it easier for her to drive a wedge between us."

Jay thought about Elaine's threat and realized that this was a blessing in disguise. This would give him the time he needed to get that video from Elaine and get her out of his life for good. He understood that Annette was tired of her, hell, he was too.

"Baby I respect your opinion, and I can give you the space you need, but I still want to spend time with you. I love you and I know that you don't believe me, but I will fix this." His hand moved back to her breast, as he kissed the side of her mouth.

Since she hadn't turned away he enveloped her lips under his as he moved her to the sofa. As they kissed his hands became adventurous and unbuttoned her pants, when his finger rubbed her wetness, he almost came in his pants.

"Annette I've missed you so much. Please let me make love to you." His voice was hoarse, from the huge lump in his throat and in his pants.

His finger traveled deeper amidst her heat and when he slid his digit inside of her he almost cried. Annette unbuckled his pants and when she stroked his hardness gently, he stopped her.

"Don't." He grinned at her shocked expression. "A few more strokes and I will come all over your hand."

He stood, "Let's go to the bedroom. I don't want Ashley to come up here and I'm making love to you on the sofa." He noticed her slight hesitation. "Please?"

He turned out the lights as she led him to the back. Once they were out of their clothes and in the bed, he moved slowly. He wanted this night to last long as possible. He kissed her slowly, savoring the taste and feel of her essence. As he made his way down her body he suckled on her nipples as if he was a nursing baby. She rubbed her fingers through his hair and tugged at him to move up. Before he entered her, he gave her a serious look.

"Will you give me time to straighten things out?" Before she answered his body of its own volition delved inside of her softness.

She felt so good, he barely hung on. He watched as her eyes widened and then became hooded as she moved against him. Annette's body weaved him deeper inside and as his strokes increased in tempo, her body heat did also. His balls tightened as he tried to slow his pace but he lost the battle. When her body clutched his hardness, he nuzzled in her neck as his vibrations rocked his core.

Barely recovered, his body reacted when she nibbled on his shoulder. She always had this effect on him! She moved her hips in time with him as he once again asked her to wait on him.

"Jay, I can't promise you anything. That's why I said we need to take everything in consideration." She propped up on her elbows, her face constricted slightly as he went deep. "I love you dearly, but I can't give you all of me right now. Umm, hmm…"

Her body hummed against his and though her words said something different, her body didn't lie. He knew that it would take some work, but the song her body sang told him that her heart belonged to him.

He rubbed her hair, "It's okay Annette, I'll give you your space. But tonight, I want to love you as if nothing has changed."

She nodded as she pulled him close and that's exactly what he did.

Chapter 2

Annette drove home and thought about her week. It had been crazy. She had almost given in to Jay, when he told her what that awful woman had done. All thoughts of a broken engagement and a canceled wedding flew from her mind. Two things stopped her. First when she knew that Elaine hadn't given up and then the most important, Xavier. She admitted to herself that she was not ready to let whatever they had go.

Xavier was the older brother of Omar, her best friend Bianca's fiancé. Omar and Jay worked on a computer program for Jay's business when Omar called for Xavier assistance. When Annette met Xavier, she noticed that he was drop dead gorgeous and fine, she wasn't blind, but she didn't look at him like that. At the time, she was happy with Jay and Xavier seemed to have his eyes on Jay's sister Damita. She was happy for them, and it seemed as if the people closest to her had found love. Then Damita stopped seeing Xavier, while she and Jay began having problems.

When she and Jay went through their trials created by Elaine, Xavier had been there for her. As a friend and lover. She recognized when her feelings got involved, but had no idea that his had too. He had planned to go back to Texas because he thought her life would be easier without him. He was so wrong. Shivers ran down her spine as she thought about their last time together. It had been amazing!

Her thoughts turned to earlier this week with Jay. She felt a little whorish having slept with Jay after she spent so much time lusting after Xavier. But since she was a newly single woman, she hadn't cheated on anyone. Xavier told her he would be back in three days, it had now been five and she missed him. His quirky personality became quirkier long distance. She found out he wasn't much of a phone talker, he only texts a few words at a time, and she only heard from him once a day if that.

Earlier that week, he did tell her some things came up and he might make it back by the weekend. It was Friday and she hadn't heard from him at all. She was bored without her children. Her parents had taken them for the entire summer but she talked to them every day and she missed them like crazy. If they had been home she might not have gotten in so much trouble this summer. She smiled as she thought about how they sounded as if they were having the best of times.

Her parents had taken them on an extensive vacation. They had gone to Tennessee, Kentucky, North and South Carolinas. The only one who mentioned coming home was Anthony Jr. He might have his dad's name, but he was the spitting image of Annette, and had a similar personality. Ant was shy, much shyer than she had been and she worried about that quite a bit. Jolisa was the oldest and the only girl, but she was outgoing and full of personality. Corey, her youngest wasn't shy either, he was her daredevil child.

The ring of her phone interrupted her thoughts and music. She hadn't grown accustomed to the modern technology, as she had driven her old Honda until the wheels just about fell off. Jay bought her an Audi, and the memory of when she asked him if he wanted it back made her smile. An unknown number glowed on her dash, if her children weren't in another state she wouldn't have answered.

"Hey, what are you doing?" It was Xavier!

"Driving home. What are you doing?" She knew he heard the smile in her voice. She was grinning from ear to ear.

"Just sitting here wondering if you want to go to dinner tonight?" His voice filled her car.

She squealed, "You're back? When did you get back?"

Xavier laughed, "We'll talk about that when I see you. Do you want to go out?"

"Yes! Of course, I do!" The one thing she adored about him was she could always be herself. She never worried about seeming too anxious, or if he looked at her differently about anything.

He gave her the time and told her to "dress up some." She laughed as she hung up, her day had gotten brighter. When she arrived home, Ashley met her at the door, with a backpack slung over her shoulder. Her sister's current boyfriend lived in Opelika, they alternated weekends visiting one another.

"Are you sure you don't want me to stay?" Ashley looked worried. She'd cried when Annette told her that she was no longer engaged.

"No, I'm fine. I'm going out to dinner tonight, I'm good." She toned her million dollars smile down to a thousand watts.

Ashley narrowed her eyes but only nodded her head. They hugged before she left, and as soon as the door closed Annette ran to her room. She took a long shower which included shaving and a body scrub, then she looked in her closet. Ten minutes later six different dresses draped her bed. She finally decided on a red, sleeveless lace sheath dress with a neckline that plunged halfway down.

The time glared at her from her cable box, and she hurriedly pulled her hair up in a chignon, put on her make-up and perfume. The doorbell rang right when she got one shoe on. She hopped to the door and swung it open, only to see her ex-husband Anthony!

It was hard with only one shoe to stand indignantly, but she pulled it off.

"Anthony! The kids aren't back."

His eyes swept over her from head to toe before he answered. "I know. I came to check on you."

"Check on me for what?" She kept the door opened just enough to stand in. He was not coming in.

Anthony grabbed her free hand, "I heard that you and Jay had broken up, so I was worried about you."

Before she asked how he heard, a shadow fell over them. Annette stood slightly over five feet two, Anthony was five feet ten in shoes, and Xavier at six feet four or five towered over both.

"Hey what's up?' Xavier's voice was deep and boomed as he pointedly looked at her and Anthony's hands.

"Hey!" Her million-watt smile was back.

Anthony frowned as Xavier somehow managed to maneuver himself beside Annette. She tried to get out of his grip, but he fiercely hung on.

"Nette who is this?" His frown deepened as she finally snatched her hand away.

"Anthony this is Xavier. The kids will be back next weekend." She smiled and hoped he would get the hint.

He didn't. Instead he looked Xavier up and down, noticed that he never acknowledged him and leaned forward to reach for her arm. "Nette, let me talk to you for a minute."

It happened so fast, it barely registered with her how he did it. Xavier moved between them and left Anthony's hand hanging as he reached for her.

"You might have to speak with her some other time. We are headed out." Anthony might not have caught her hint, but he picked up the steel in Xavier's tone.

"I'll be back tomorrow Nette to talk to you. Privately." Anthony mean mugged Xavier once more before he trudged off.

Xavier stood and watched him until he got in his car, then he turned to Annette. When Anthony looked her over, she felt dirty, Xavier's look made her panties moist. She stepped back and allowed him in. He looked good. He had on charcoal slacks and a grey pinstripe shirt, neither hid his muscular form. He glanced down at her feet.

"I would have been ready if Anthony hadn't interrupted me." She grinned at him mischievously.

He nodded, as he tried to hide the smile that lit the corners of his mouth. "I was just going to say you look beautiful. But since you brought it up, was that your ex-husband?"

She looked at him as he sat on the sofa, his arms spread out across the top. "Unfortunately, yes. But don't judge me. I was young and inexperienced

"Is he a problem?" Something in his voice made her turn, but he still gazed at her innocently.

"No, not for me anyway. I'm sure he is for somebody. He's an idiot." She finally got her shoe on and she turned to him with a smile.

Xavier stood and held his arms out. She melted in his arms. This was what she missed, the feeling of security. He kissed her cheek as his hands ran over her body until they stopped at her butt. Once more he softly kissed her cheek, before he moved to her lips. Her body flushed with heat as his tongue became her lifeline. Thoughts of food left and her clothing became a major hindrance as she yearned for this man.

He lightly tapped her butt as he pulled away. "Come on let's go before we start something we have to finish."

She stroked his erection through his pants. She had eaten earlier, food could wait. When she looked up her smile was frozen in place by the desire in his eyes. His hand covered hers and stopped her in mid stroke.

"I missed you Xavier." Her desire overwhelmed her and cracked her voice. She knew from the beginning that the way he made her feel was dangerous.

He simply nodded and moved her hand. One of the many things she learned about him was that it was hard for him to express his emotions. Since she understood she knew his nod meant he acquiesce.

When they made it to the restaurant she was surprised to see it was a small place nestled in one of the oldest neighborhoods in Montgomery. It was also not far from Bianca's and Jay's moms' homes. They were shown to their table by a man in a tuxedo. There was no hustle and bustle seen as in other restaurants. Their table was covered with a white linen tablecloth, the lights were dim, and the room lit mainly by candles. Other than the tinkle of silverware and glasses there was little noise.

15

Once they were seated she looked at the menu, which was sparse but expensive. After a few minutes, she glanced up and found Zay looking at her.

"What do you want to eat?" The variety of salads caught her eye, the ones without the onions.

"You." His eyes danced under the candlelight.

Trapped by his gaze, she sat in a puddle of her own moistness. Forget the salad, she could eat a side dish if that would escalate them to the bed.

"I was thinking either the scallops or the snapper. Probably the snapper since it's been a while." He smoothly moved on to the original answer as if he hadn't caught her in his web of desire.

The server ruined the moment or saved her from jumping in his lap. Xavier ordered the snapper and she ordered a steak salad.

"Are there any other exes I need to know about?" His voice interrupted her lustful thoughts.

"No. Remember we talked about my limited experience with partners, Jay and Anthony are it."

He cocked his head, "I thought you said three."

As she looked at him she felt quite amorous, "I did." She pointedly looked at every inch of him she could see, without getting under the table. "Jay and Anthony are it, as far as exes."

Xavier eyebrows raised and he sipped his water. "I was included in your count?"

When she nodded her head, he sat back with a stunned look.

"Well damn!"

Xavier had a heavy voice and even though it wasn't at its highest decibel, it was loud for the setting. She chuckled at his response. The server brought their food, but he still sat there and gazed at her.

"Why are you so shocked?" The candles and the gleam in his eyes made her squirm slightly.

"I don't know, I guess I thought I was an even number." With that, he picked up his fork and began eating.

During the meal, he told her why it took him so long to come back. He moved some furniture from Texas, and he shipped his cars.

"Cars? How many?" Xavier seemed to be very frugal, she imagined that the car he drove was the only one he had.

"Three, just like your number." When he grinned, his dimples showed and she almost missed her mouth with the fork.

Zay reached over with his napkin and wiped her mouth, at the same time she tried to reach it with her tongue. When her tongue grazed his finger, an electric shock went through her body. He stopped in mid-wipe, and she turned her head slightly and gently sucked the tip of his finger. When she was with him she felt reckless, free and she liked it. Xavier slowly removed his finger but never took his eyes off her mouth.

"Are you finished eating?" There was no trace of a smile on his face.

She shook her head as he signaled for the check. While she ate, he drummed his fingers on the table, and when she stood he put his hand as low on her hips as he could and still be decent. Her entire body blushed.

Before they left the restaurant, Xavier turned to her, "Do you need to go home first?"

She patted her purse, "Nope. I came prepared."

He chuckled as they pulled off. When they got halfway to his house he reached over and placed his hand on her thigh. The sexual tension was high before, but this amped the ante!

"Do you have plans for tomorrow?" His tone was sensuous and his hand moved up slightly.

Her original plan of shopping for groceries changed instantly to spending the day with him. "No, not really."

Xavier cleared his throat, "I have to go to the security office in the morning and I was wondering if you would hang around until I returned."

"Why do you have to go on a Saturday?" She tried to keep the whiney sound out of her voice and failed miserably.

"Omar is not organized and each time I leave him for a minute, he acts as if everything is out of whack. It shouldn't take more than a few hours."

She nodded and knew that with the heat his hand caused, it would have taken an act of God or Congress to make her leave him. If he let her she would have gone to the office with him.

When they got to his house there was a car under a tarp in his driveway and two cars in his garage. One was a fixed up red Chevy Chevelle and the other was a rusty Mustang. Inside the house everything looked the same. Xavier had a serious OCD for neatness.

"I thought you brought furniture from Texas?" She looked around nothing seemed different.

He led her to his extra bedrooms. The three empty bedrooms were now filled with furniture and his bonus room was a miniature office. There wasn't a box in sight and even the beds were made. She turned on the lights to one of rooms amazed at how he could put things together so quickly. She thought of the dresses she left on her bed and smiled.

"I have a question." She peered at him as he grimaced. "Why did you buy a house this size when it's just you?"

Xavier flipped off the light and led her to his bedroom. He removed his clothing as he spoke.

"Once I saw that Omar and Bianca were serious, I knew that he would make this his home. I bought this house in case I start a family." He glanced at her. "There will be no need to move."

He walked behind her as he spoke and unzipped her dress. Annette felt flushed and very hot. She swooned as his tongue traced her spine, while his hands worked their way to the front of her body. His breath was hot on her back and he trapped her nipples between his fingers, gently tugging them. When her dress hit the floor, she turned around, only to find that he retrieved her dress and threw it on the chair.

His hands and mouth were all over her when they made it to the bed. She felt his hardness as he sensuously rubbed against her, but never allowed her to stroke him. He teased her unmercifully as he coated his head with her wetness. When he leaned over and grabbed a condom out of the drawer, she sat up surprised.

"I thought after last time…" The last time they were together was the first time they had unprotected sex, and she loved it. She had thought of little else since.

"I know, but until we decide what we are doing…" He slid it on with ease. "I don't want to take any chances. I can't have another man raising my baby."

Her pout became ecstasy when she felt him inside of her. He moved slowly and captivated her mind with a slow kiss. She grabbed his shoulders with each long stroke, and she almost cried when he stopped. He held her and kept her from moving as she felt him throbbing deep inside of her.

"I want to feel you on top." He rasped.

Once they changed positions he directed her body with his hands while he grazed her nipples with his teeth. As he alternated between grazing her nipples and rolling them between his lips, she felt a sensation she never experienced before. She was on fire! Sweat popped up and rolled down her body and she felt lightheaded. Tears of frustration rolled down her cheeks as he held her back with his hands each time she tried to increase her rhythm. He moved her slowly across his hardness, as he thumped across her spot each time. When her body contracted, she grabbed his shoulders and with each contraction harder than the first her nails moved down his chest. As her body settled down she felt his vibrations which caused her to once again clutch his hardness tight within her. Wave after wave assaulted her as she snatched at his forearms and released her heart. She slumped on top of him and welcomed his embrace as he held her tight.

He kissed the top of her head and softly murmured, "I missed you Annette."

Chapter 3

Jay sat on his balcony with Carl as they talked about sports and women. They had met in middle school and became life-long friends. Carl was separated from his wife after he found out she had cheated on him for quite some time. Since Jay was now officially single, they had spent more time than usual together. When he told Carl about the broken engagement he of course asked if someone else was involved. Jay knew what he hinted at. He hoped that his friend would find someone soon. He was tired of Carl seeing the ghost of his wife in everyone.

Jay stretched and knew that Carl wasn't the only one who needed to get his life together. He was in the same boat. Elaine had wrecked his life and until he and Annette were back on sure standing he would not rest. He occupied his mind and time with work. He had gotten two more dealerships to buy into their program, one was the largest in Birmingham. This dealership wanted the program, but with a few modifications. Modifications that Xavier could have done in a day or less, but it had taken Omar and Jay the entire week.

Carl got up to replenish the beer and before he made it back the doorbell rang. Jay heard his sister Damita before he saw her.

"Where's Jay?" She sounded excited or upset.

Carl must have pointed to the balcony, and Jay saw Damita as she charged at him with Carl at her heels.

"Jay! What the hell is going on? Why was Annette on a date with Xavier?" She placed both hands on the table as she leaned over.

Jay shook his head as Carl's eyes widened. Damita stared at him with anger in her eyes.

"Hold up! What do you mean a 'date'? Maybe they were just out to eat, or ran into each other at the restaurant." Jay's words belied the increase of his heart rate.

"It wasn't that type of restaurant. Do you think that I would have cut my date short if it seemed innocent? We were at Vantage Point! You don't run into someone there!" Damita finally sat down.

Jay thought about it, Vantage Point was a very upscale restaurant, perfect for a date. He tried to rationalize it in his mind, but his heart knew that there was something in what Damita said. His face flushed as anger tried to overwhelm him.

"Instead of asking me what is going on, tell me what you saw. To make you think it was a date." His frustrations released as he snapped at his sister.

Damita wasn't one to cower or easily offend, so she ticked off what she had seen, with her fingers as props.

"Let's see, he was wiping her face with a napkin when I passed them. Neither one of them noticed me, because they were so into one another. And finally, when they left his hand was damn near on her butt! Now do you see why I thought it was a date?"

Before Jay responded Carl uttered his two cents. "I told you man! You will learn one day to listen to me."

"You knew about this?" Damita screeched at Carl.

"No, I didn't know but I sensed that old dude had his eyes on Annette. And when we were at Bianca's get together he was looking at her like he was her man! I tried to tell your brother but he didn't believe me."

Jay cut Carl off before he went further. "Are you sure it was Xavier and Annette?" Although in his mind he knew it was true, his heart did not want to accept it.

Damita lowered her voice, "Yes. You know if there was a chance I was mistaken I wouldn't have told you."

Jay looked in her eyes and stood as the blood rushed to his head. "That slimy bastard!"

"I told you sometimes it's the ones in your camp that you have to watch out for." Carl mumbled into his beer.

Jay directed his question to Damita, "You really feel as if it was intimate? I mean do you think they left and…" He couldn't complete his thought.

"Jay I'm just going to keep it real, as much as I hate to. It looked as if they have been intimate before tonight. That's why I came to ask you, I thought maybe you knew." Damita looked down.

"Hell no, I didn't know! Shit! I can't believe that Xavier did this shit! He waited until she was most vulnerable and took advantage of her!"

"That's how some of these bastards' work. All the time they want what you have and once they see an opening, they run for it. I told you there was something about him I didn't trust." Carl shook his head.

Damita cleared her throat. "Annette didn't look as if she was being held hostage. It's not all on Xavier. He couldn't have gotten to her if she didn't let him."

Jay looked at Damita as if she had grown horns. "You know that Annette wouldn't have even talked to the guy if we hadn't had our problems. I was consumed with Malik's supposed problem and I hurt her. This asshole saw an opportunity and took advantage of it."

"I'm not saying that she would have slept with the guy if y'all hadn't had problems. But she has a part in this too. Beyond the problems, you work with the guy and I use to date him! She could have thought about that." Damita grabbed his untouched beer and took a swig.

Carl watched their interaction as if he was at a tennis match. After a few minutes of silence, he interjected his thoughts. "I understand what both of you are saying, but I agree with Jay." He held his hand up to silence Damita. "Listen to me first. I'm sure that Annette was so upset, that she wasn't thinking clearly, and didn't consider everything. Xavier on the other hand, knew what was going on from both sides of the fence. He knew what Jay was doing and he probably knew how hurt Annette was. But I don't think it was just an opportunity."

"But..." Damita started to speak but Carl was on a roll and cut her off.

"Wait a minute let me finish. Jay, I told you after that night at Bianca's it made me remember that this guy always watched her." He looked at Damita. "No disrespect to you, but I think he always had his eyes on Annette. Excuse my language, but that's what pussy-hounds do. They scope out the women and then find out who's single and who's not. I'll bet my last dollar that he asked his brother about Annette in the beginning! And I'm sure Omar told him that she was taken. Then this shit with Elaine happened and he saw his chance to get inside her head and panties."

Jay and Damita were silent as Carl's words marinated in their heads. Of course, once Carl saw that he had their attention, he continued.

"I'm surprised that you two never noticed. Xavier only came to events that Annette would attend. There have been many times that Jay, Omar and I would go out for drinks, he never showed. But if your momma had something he was there. The more I think about it, I can think of a few instances when Annette would go to another room or inside, and he would find a reason to go inside too." Carl finally sat back.

Stark silence met the three friends as each one seemed lost in their own thoughts. Damita broke the silence.

"I do remember that at first he seemed to have asked a lot of questions about Annette. But he never said anything negative about you, Jay. This shit just seems fucking unbelievable!" She sipped from the beer that had become hers.

Carl got up to go inside. As soon as he disappeared Jay leaned over and spoke quietly. "What did he ask about Annette?"

"I can't remember everything, but it was broad questions. Like how long had you two been together." She looked embarrassed. "I probably messed up when I told him how the two of you got together." Her eyes lit up, "But when I told him he did find it hard to believe, because he said she seemed to have such a gentle spirit." Damita rolled her eyes and did the air quotes.

"Who has a gentle spirit?" Carl approached them as he juggled three beers.

"I was just telling Jay what Xavier said about Annette." Damita rolled her eyes as she reached for a beer.

"Yeah right, he cared about her spirit! That dude thinks he's slick. I wonder what he will have to say when he realizes you know." Carl smirked.

"I'll find out tomorrow." Jay's anger bubbled as he thought about how Xavier had talked to him, was supposed to be looking for dirt on Elaine, and all the while he plotted to get with Annette. That bastard!

"Maybe you shouldn't say anything just yet." Damita looked at him nervously.

"Why the hell not? There is no way I'm going to let that son-of-a bitch continue to think he is getting over on me. Hell no!"

Carl nodded his head as Jay spoke. "He's right. Xavier needs to know that the gig is up. Ain't no way Jay can keep looking in his face knowing what he knows. Nope."

"Carl, I let you speak, now I want both of you to hear me out. I say let it ride because it's not going to last." Damita looked around the table at the two men. "Xavier is too quirky…"

"You mean weird." Carl mumbled.

'Whatever, but I promise you it will not last. Jay, you are right, Annette is sweet and very naïve, but she is also use to you. An even keeled guy, you are the same pretty much all the time. Annette also likes to ask a lot of questions and you know how she always has something silly to say."

Jay nodded his head as Damita's words caused him to realize how much he stood to lose. Everything she said was true, but those were some of the main characteristics that made Annette so lovable. His heart felt heavy as he thought about her.

Damita continued, "Xavier will not want to deal with that, and I can't see Annette dealing with his ways. It's only a matter of time." She nodded.

"Oh, I know it's only a matter of time, because Annette is my woman, and he is going to have to step off." Jay gulped his beer.

"I don't know Damita. You would be surprised." Carl looked as if he wanted to say more but he glanced at Jay and kept his mouth shut.

"Okay, but what about Annette? Xavier is not the type to keep in touch, he's moody, and damn near rude! You know how sensitive Annette is, after he makes her cry a few times she'll snap out of it." Damita was determined to prove her point.

Jay stood up and looked down to the street. "All that might be true, but I'm still letting him know. I'm not trying to give him all the time he needs to make Annette cry. I've hurt her enough." Jay looked at his sister, "Sorry, but I can't sit on this one. This shit was lowdown and there is no way in hell I'm just going to sit back and let it play out."

Damita spoke softly, "Just be careful."

"You might need to save that sentiment for him. Because if he hurts Annette…"

Jay's night was restless, each time he closed his eyes he saw Annette, without him. The rest of the time he thought of everything he should have done differently. Once he rose, he fixed some coffee and tried to call Annette, but she never answered.

After he dressed, read the paper, lied to Damita and Carl that he was fine, he got in his car and headed to her house. When he saw her car in the drive he felt reassured, until he rang the bell and received no answer. Jay rarely entered Annette's house with his key, but he thought that desperate times cause for desperate measures.

He walked in and the silence made him sad. Everything looked in order, but his heart dropped when he saw the clothes strewn on her bed. She had spent the night with that bastard! The blood rushed to his head and he wanted to hit something or someone. Unable to look at the chaos that represented his life he stormed out. Before he got in his car he paced in front of it. He needed a plan.

He realized that he had no idea where Xavier lived. Jay kicked his tires. It wasn't as if he could ask Omar. Then he remembered Omar mentioning that he and Xavier were working at their security office this weekend. Jay jumped in his car and headed that way.

The security office looked deserted, except for the lone car in the corner of the lot. Xavier's car. Jay took a deep breath and tried to pull himself together before he walked in. The door chimed as he walked in and saw Xavier as he sat behind the desk. He looked up at Jay.

"Hey what's up? Omar's not here, but he should be here sometime this morning." Xavier went back to the papers he fed to the shredder.

"I'm not here to see Omar, I came to see you." Jay kept his tone even.

Xavier grunted as he glanced up, "I just got back in town, I haven't had time to do anything else about your case."

The brothers had put a surveillance on Elaine, and Xavier was supposed to have looked deeper into her world to find some dirt. Jay grimaced as he thought about why he hadn't had any results.

"I'm not here about Elaine, I'm here about Annette." He finally had his attention. Xavier looked at him and narrowed his eyes. But he said nothing.

Jay sat in the chair opposite of Xavier and looked him dead in his eyes. "I know you fucked her, but I want to know why?"

He waited for Xavier to say something foul like Annette came on to him, or even to apologize.

Xavier never flinched or looked away. Instead he raised his eyebrows, "Man, shit happens." He then proceeded to feed more paper into the shredder.

Jay's anger burned through his soul. "Shit happens? What the hell are you trying to say? She tripped and you fell on her with your dick out?"

Xavier leaned forward, his eyes cold. "No. What I am saying is that you hurt her bad, and I was there when she needed someone. And then shit happened."

Xavier had laid his forearms across the desk and Jay noticed the scratches on them. His ears roared and he saw streaks of red. He wanted to kill this guy! He took a deep breath and stood.

"That is so fucked up. But I have accepted the role I played in this. Whatever I did was no reason for you to take advantage of her just because you knew she was hurting. That's some low-down shit, but two facts still remain." Jay leaned over the desk. "Annette loves me and she is still my woman. So, if you want to play the side piece a little longer try it, because I'm coming back for what is mine."

Xavier leaned back in his chair and stared at Jay. He rubbed his chin, "Yours? That's funny because I just..."

"Zay!" Omar cut his brother off as he walked in the office, Carl right behind him.

Jay's glare never left Xavier. "You just what?"

Xavier looked between his brother and Jay. "I just nothing. But Annette is free to see whomever she chooses. And right now, that's me." He smirked.

Before Jay knew it, he had propelled towards Xavier only to be stopped by Carl and Omar. As Carl dragged him out he left with a parting shot. "She might be with you now, but once she realizes you can't give her what she needs or treat her the way she is used to being treated; you will be a fucking distant memory. You aren't good enough for her."

"Come on Jay, let's go." Carl pushed Jay out the door.

Once they were outside Carl let him have it. "What the hell are you doing? That could have turned real nasty, it's a good thing I know your ass. Do I need to follow you home?"

"No, I'm good. I'll be alright. That guy in there..." The vibration of his phone cut him off. It was Elaine! This was the tenth time she had called. Jay waved Carl off and answered as he stepped in his car.

"I need to see you Jay." Elaine whined in the phone.

"No, you don't, I'm not coming over there. I'm too busy trying to clean up the mess you made." Jay knew if he saw Elaine right now he would hurt her.

"Oh, so you want to do this on the phone. Okay. Let's see how you will clean this up, I'm pregnant."

Jay looked at the phone and dropped it on the seat. His day had just gotten worse!

Chapter 4

Omar looked at his brother. Xavier leaned back in his chair with his eyes closed and he pinched the bridge of his nose. Omar waited, he knew his brother well enough to know that he was deep in thought and needed to decompress. He remembered when he was in high school, each time Xavier was called to the school, he would sit with his eyes closed, pinching his nose. Omar caught hell once they got home.

When Xavier finally opened his eyes Omar spoke, "What the hell happened?"

"Hell, if I know. I thought he was looking for you, then he started going off about Annette." Xavier rubbed the back of his neck.

Omar told him what Carl had explained to him. "You could have shown a little compassion. You know that shit wasn't right, and what he's been through."

Zay pinched his nose once again. "I did show him some compassion."

Omar's eyebrows raised as he asked, "How? I didn't see any compassion. I think if I hadn't walked in when I did you were about to say something real nasty."

"I showed him compassion by not cleaning this floor with his ass. Shit!" Xavier stood.

"Look, I told you there would be some shit if you pursued Annette. Are you sure it's worth it?" He knew that Zay didn't do drama well, and he had stepped in a landmine.

"I don't know." Xavier closed his eyes. He sat back down when he opened them and locked his hands together. "Omar, she is different. But you are right, some decisions need to be made. Some real decisions. But my gut is telling me to give it a try."

These two brothers had been stuck to each other like glue all their lives. Omar could not think of a time when his brother was not there for him, and vice versa. They had always been straight with another and as much as he hated to do it, he had to be straight with him now.

"But is Annette going to want to continue to try once she knows that Jay and Damita know?" Xavier looked at him intently as he continued. "Most of what Jay said was out of anger, but one thing he said that was true, they have a bond. When I first met them, I would have never believed that they wouldn't be together."

The whir of the computers seemed loud in the silence. Omar knew that even though Zay hadn't responded, he was taking it all in.

"Then you should think of the Damita aspect, she and Annette are friends, but she was with you first. That's going to affect their friendship."

Xavier held up his hand, "I never touched Damita. We were friends and we hung out sometimes. It was no way near the same."

"But she was attracted to you. And I don't know Annette very well, but what I do know is that she is very sensitive to others. Bibi says that she will sacrifice her feelings for others. Do you think she can withstand this type of upheaval in her life?"

"You asked me if I thought it was worth it. I can't tell you what she thinks. But if it's too much for her I know how to walk away. I'm not in that deep." Xavier smiled.

Omar knew that Xavier was fooling himself, but he left it alone. He would check on him in a few days after Annette disappeared from his life. His brother was a good guy, but Omar felt as if the demons he held on to kept him from finding love. He shook his head, maybe he would find someone one day.

Xavier stopped him before he walked out of the office. "What did Bianca have to say about this?"

"She wasn't home, I'll let you know later when I tell her." Before he took two steps Zay stopped him again.

"You can go home, I've got this squared away. You should stop keeping so much paper around. I told you before if you scan it, then shred it, you won't get so disorganized." Xavier shook his head as he shredded more documents.

Omar thought about what almost happened and decided to stay. It took Xavier another hour before he was ready to leave.

♨♦♧♨

Bianca was home when Omar arrived. He hated to tell her about his morning. She was almost sold on the idea of letting whatever Annette and his brother had play out. After this morning, that would probably never happen.

He called her name when he walked in and she yelled that she was in the bedroom. His heart stopped when he saw her in the closet standing on a step-stool. As he hurried in to keep her steady, he realized that he would probably be dead from a heart attack before their baby was born.

"Bibi! I thought we talked about you doing things like this. You could have fallen!" He held her arm as she stepped down.

"It's barely a foot off the floor Omar! I'm not even showing yet! Calm down." They frowned at one another. She smiled at him first and gave him a kiss. "It's sweet that you worry so much, but you are getting on my damn nerves! Where have you been anyway?"

He told her about Carl's visit and the subsequent visit to the office. They moved to kitchen as he spoke and Bianca sat down heavily at the island.

"So, the shit has hit the fan. Did you say Damita saw them together?"

"Yep, then she went and told Jay and Carl." Omar rubbed his nose as he shook his head. "Maybe this needed to happen to make them stop seeing each other."

Bianca brushed her hair back, "That is probably what Damita called me about. Poor Annette, I bet Jay went straight over there when he left. She didn't have a clue what she was about to be hit with it."

Omar cleared his throat, "Bibi, Annette was at Zay's place. He said that he would tell her when he got home."

Bianca's head jerked as if she had been physically slapped. She was aware of Xavier's quirks, like his extreme neatness and his need for privacy. As far as they knew the only two people that had ever been allowed to stay at his home without him was Omar and Liberty, Omar's daughter. No woman had ever been left alone in his home.

"Well damn! That says a lot, a whole lot. Shit as much as your brother gets on my nerves I hate to see him get hurt. Did you tell him how Annette hates to hurt people's feelings? And we are not talking about just 'people' this time, we are talking about Jay! What a mess!"

"And Damita." Omar reminded her. "Yes, I told him, but he said that he would have no problem walking away."

They sat in silence, the hum of the refrigerator their only companion. Omar stood and stretched.

"I don't want to see him hurt either, but it seems inevitable. He knew what the risks were before he came back. He should have stayed in Texas." Omar reached up and swiped at the ceiling fan.

Bianca shrugged as she got up and hugged Omar from behind. "Who knows what will happen, but I do know that you will be there for him. As always."

He sighed heavily, "But I don't know if that will be enough this time. I think that this is Zay's first foray into matters of the heart."

Chapter 5

Annette had gotten up with Xavier, and fixed him an omelet before he left. Once he was gone she cleaned the kitchen, went to the guest bathroom and took a dump. She would have been mortified if he made it back before she finished. Then she cleaned the bathroom, sprayed and took a shower. There wasn't much to do, so she turned on the television and went back to sleep.

When she awakened Xavier stood over her. She had no idea how long he had been there or even what awakened her. As she stretched the smile in her heart never reached her face as she noticed his expression. He looked at her stonily.

"Come on and get up, I'm taking you home." He fiddled with his keys as he looked at her.

"Huh? Why are you taking me home? I thought—, wait, what's wrong?" This was not the same man that left this morning.

"Nothing, I'm just taking you home." He never broke his stare.

She searched his face for clues, and was met with a hard glare. Annette sat up and tried to think of what could have happened while she slept.

"You asked me to stay, now you want to take me home? This doesn't make any sense. I'm not ready to go home." She leaned back on the pillows.

Xavier gave her an exasperated look, then the bed shifted as he sat on the edge. "Jay came to see me this morning."

"For what?" The only thought that crossed her mind was that Jay had mentioned that he spent the night while Zay was gone.

Xavier told her what transpired and how Jay came to know about them. Annette closed her eyes as she imagined

Jay's hurt. This was not how it was supposed to have happened! She opened her eyes to Xavier's cold gaze.

"I'm sure you need to get home to reassure him that you still love him and that you guys are alright." His gaze swept over her body, not in a sensuous way, but with a derisive look.

"I can't tell him we are all right. If we were all right, I wouldn't be here with you." Annette spoke softly.

He turned his back and just sat there. She gingerly sat on her knees and hugged him from behind. "I'm sorry, I should have been the one to tell him."

Xavier stood suddenly and she almost fell off the bed, but he caught her before she did. "What the hell are you apologizing for? Even if you had told him I'm sure he would have still run his ass in my face."

His tone was brusque and she willed her tears not to come. "I apologized because you are mad at me. So, I thought that maybe if I had told him, the result would have been different."

Her tears didn't fall but they filled her voice. Xavier looked at her and sat back down. When he spoke again his tone was softer.

"I'm not mad at you, but I think it's best if we let this go. I'm too old for this shit." He wrapped a tendril of her hair around his finger.

"Wait, you just said last night that we…" This time the tears did fill her eyes.

Zay turned so that he could hold her. "Annette, I'm not mad at you, but I know that you are still unsure about your feelings. I realized today that I need to walk away, before someone gets hurt. If I'm going to be with you it needs to be just me and you. You aren't ready for that and I'm not pushing it on you."

She inhaled his scent loving and hating it at the same time. She hated it because she knew he was right. Intellectually she knew that his point was valid, but her body fought the logic of his words. He kissed the side of her face, and she was proud that her tears had not fallen.

"But we talked about this, I thought we were going to play it by ear." Before the left side of her brain formulated a response, the right side spoke up.

Xavier sighed, "I know we did, but I'll be honest with you, it won't be too many times that he can confront me like that. Without getting hurt."

She paused as she thought about what he said. "Xavier, I don't want anyone to get hurt either. But I don't think if you walk away it will change my feelings."

A hard glint entered his eyes. "Yeah, but if I'm not in the picture maybe you and he can get back together so that you can decide what you want. As far as Jay is concerned you still belong to him, and you were the only reason I didn't clock his ass today. He won't get too many passes like that. You can't sample us and decide who you want. One of us needs to be completely out of the picture."

This was the dark side that she felt existed, but she had never seen. She saw more than anger in his eyes but she couldn't decipher what it was. Her body's reaction to his dark side surprised her, she was turned on beyond belief. She was unsure if it was because she saw his dark side or the knowledge that he shared it with her so honestly. She decided it was both.

Her nipples hardened under his thin undershirt that she wore and they ached with need. The need for this man. As they sat in silence, the room was thick with quiet desire. Annette slipped out of his shirt and bared her arousal to him. Xavier gently moved her over, the brush of his hands only added to her heat.

"Come on Annette, that won't change anything. Put your clothes on." His face was lined with frustration.

"I know and I am, but I need you to touch me." She grabbed his hand and placed it on her breast.

The anger cleared from his eyes as he rolled her nipple between his fingers. Her fire flamed from his simple touch and she moaned softly as his hands expertly quenched her thirst. She felt his other hand as it rubbed under her nipple and then she heard his intake of breath.

"Did I do this to you?" Concern was the only emotion she detected from him as he examined her breast.

Annette had left whelps and scratches on Xavier, but he had also left his mark. Her shoulders, breast and stomach were marked with the love marks left from his nibbling and sucking. She nodded as his tongue flitted over the marks. The heat from his tongue and sensations he created with his hands had her in a frenzy. Cool air assaulted her body as he lifted his head and she closed her eyes to slow her body down.

"Zay I think…" The words stuck in her throat as her body began to tremble.

"Damn." He said seemingly to himself.

Annette's vibrations turned into a mini eruption when he dipped his finger inside of her. Once she stopped shaking, the reality of what occurred hit her. She covered her face with her hands in shame. Within a span of a month, she had turned into a freak! Who else could have an orgasm without penetration? The left side of her mocked her as she pictured him running away from her instead of walking.

"Annette?" She heard him, but ignored him as she turned on her side.

The bed sunk in from his girth as she felt his body next to her. He ran his hands over her body as he sucked her shoulder.

"Annette what's wrong?" His breath tickled her ear.

"That was so embarrassing! I don't know how that happened." She kept her back to him and spoke into the pillow.

Her sensitive sore nipples perked up when he ran his fingers across them. "That was sexy as hell. Damn! I might have to rethink my decision." He chuckled softly.

Her retort was lost when he entered her heat with his magic wand. His thrusts began slowly, slow enough for her to wonder when he had put a condom on. With each thrust he became more aggressive, and her body once again fired up. He pushed her forward slightly as she aggressively met his pace.

"Shit! I don't want to give you up." He muttered, desire slurring his voice.

"You. Don't. Have. To." She managed to spit out as goosebumps covered her flesh.

He pulled her up and held her body trapped against his. "Yes, I do. Because I want you to belong to me, I'm not borrowing you anymore." He whispered in her ear.

His hand clasped her stomach as his finger snaked down to her wetness. He rubbed her softly and her body reflexively clutched his hardness and held it tight. He grunted as her walls contracted tightly around his hardness. It was bittersweet as he jerked inside her and tears fell from her eyes as she shook softly against him.

"Annette, if you come back to me, I want that asshole completely out of your life. I promise that I will do whatever it takes to make you happy."

Later she questioned herself if his words in her ear were real or imagined.

Chapter 6

Jay's original plan had been to go to Annette's and wait for her to come home, no matter how long it took. Elaine's phone call changed that. He was sick of her! Shortly after Malik was born, Elaine had gotten her tubes tied, she must have thought he had forgotten. It was time to end her games once and for all.

Malik was at his mothers' and he knew he had to reign his anger in before he approached her. He took the long way to the house. When he arrived, Elaine met him at the door.

"What game are trying to pull now Elaine?" He spat out as soon as he entered.

"No game. Would you like to see the test?" She looked at him slyly.

"No! You probably got that test from one of your girlfriends. Did you forget that your tubes are tied? Or were you just thinking I had forgotten?" Jay still stood because he didn't want to spend a minute more than necessary around her.

Elaine sat in the recliner and crossed her legs. She wore shorts and a crew neck silk shirt. "See, when we got divorced, I thought I might meet someone who wanted children, so I had my tubal ligation reversed."

All he could do was clench and unclench his hands. Elaine reached over and picked up a pregnancy test off the coffee table. She walked up to him and flaunted the positive sign in his face. A cold fear snaked up his spine.

"I guess you will be a single parent. I'm not falling in this trap again." The fear he felt was hidden in his anger.

Elaine squinted her eyes and smirked. "I might be but you will have to take care of your child. But before we get to that point, how do you think your damn trophy girlfriend will feel about it? Does she love you enough to help you take care of your new baby?"

Jay stared at her unable to believe that he had been married to this monster. "Why the fuck are you doing this?" He bellowed.

Hate radiated from her pores as well as her mouth. "I gave you the best years of my life and you threw me to the side for that simple whore. You weren't happy enough to just fuck her and keep her in the dark. No, you humiliated me! I've been with you since we were teens and you think this whore can just come and take my family?"

Jay took a step back as she advanced on him. Spittle popped from her mouth as she spoke. "It wasn't enough that you left me and hooked up with her, but you wanted my son to leave me for her too! Did you think that I would sit still and let you do that? Hell no!"

Elaine's face was mottled with anger and she seemed to glow with her outrage. Jay got right in her face.

"I don't give a shit what you do, I'm never coming back to you. And I will do whatever it takes to get my son away from your crazy ass. Until I hear an official announcement that you are pregnant, I don't believe this bullshit!" The doorknob was at his fingertips and he swung the door open. Her voice stopped him.

"But will Annette believe it without a note from the doctor? Like I told you before, if I find out you and she are playing house with my son, I'll put the video on blast and tell her about our baby early." She smacked her lips, "But she will find out eventually anyway, you can't hide a baby."

Jay stormed out of the house before he hurt her. He had driven two to three miles before he somewhat calmed down. There was no way Elaine was pregnant! If he told Annette, hurt her and this turned out to be part of Elaine's games, he chanced losing her forever. But if he didn't tell her and she found out, he would still lose her. He didn't know what to do.

Something had to be done because along with everything else that damn Xavier hung around like a vulture. As his thoughts moved to Xavier, he knew he needed to talk to Annette. If she had spent the night with him, things had already gone too far. Before he decided how to handle the situation with Elaine, he needed to get Annette away from Xavier.

A few minutes later he pulled in her driveway. He took a deep breath and tried to look as normal as possible. This had been a morning from hell! His heart settled down a little when she answered the door. Her eyes were filled with sadness as she let him in.

"Hey." He got choked up as he thought of everything he had put her through. He felt ashamed.

"Hey yourself." As she looked at him imploringly he realized that Xavier must have told her that he knew.

"I guess you know that I found out about you and Xavier." That was the hardest thing he ever had to say.

With a slight nod of her head she turned and led him to the den. The sway of her hips captivated him even though he knew she had spent the night with that guy. He couldn't bring himself to think of his name. It hurt too much.

Once they settled on the sofa she turned to him. "Jay, I should have told you about Xavier. But I never meant to hurt you."

His eyes closed and he felt her hand on his face. When he opened them, he was struck speechless by the tenderness reflected on her face. Within seconds all his anger drained from his body. The combination of her touch and the love that shone in her eyes soothed him.

"Annette it's not your fault. I created this mess with Elaine and by trusting the wrong people. That guy took advantage of you because he knew you were hurting and vulnerable."

"No Jay, you can't take all of the blame and you can't shift it to Xavier either. We all played a part in it, including me."

As Jay looked at her he felt a shard of his anger return. Annette was so sweet and she always saw the best in everyone and that guy took advantage of that! He glanced at her and took in her beauty, it ran much deeper than her appearance.

There was an innocent quality about her and it angered him that he hadn't been there to protect her! She wouldn't even blame that asshole when he just used her for fun! Instead of lashing out at her he stood.

"I have a responsibility in this mess that Elaine created, but that guy played a major part in this too." Images of Xavier's hands touching her shaded his vision.

"I wasn't forced. I'm not going to stand here and make it his fault for decisions I made." Annette remained on the sofa.

Jay felt his anger as it surged back to the surface, as he heard her take up for that jerk. He spoke harsher than he intended. "Annette, you don't understand how guys like him operate. If you hadn't been so emotional, he would have never tried it! Because he knew it would have never happened. I wouldn't have let it."

Annette rose and came to him, "Jay let's be realistic. Elaine put this into motion, but if our love had been as strong as we thought it was we wouldn't be in such turmoil."

She quickly closed the gap between them. Even though he knew where she had spent the night, his body responded when she placed her hands on his waist.

"Jay, I love you and I never meant to hurt you, but we need to figure out what we both want." She laid her head on his chest.

His arms wrapped around her and he held her close. There was one thing he needed to know but he was scared to ask.

"Is he a source of the confusion you spoke of before?" He whispered the question in her hair.

With each slight nod of her head, the fear he felt earlier returned with a vengeance. She shifted, but he held her tightly, as if she could mend his heart.

"Are you going to continue to see him?" His voice broke.

Annette pulled away and looked up at him. "No, I need to get myself together. I'm no good for either of you right now."

His body sagged from relief. Her lips beckoned him so he leaned down and hesitantly tasted them. Every emotion he had felt in the last twenty-four hours was released in that kiss. Annette kneaded the knots out of his back as she returned his kiss. As his manhood hardened against her, she stepped away.

"I can't tell you I'm not glad to hear it. That guy is just out to screw whomever he can." His hand traveled to her butt and pulled her closer. "We will work out whatever we need to."

His phone cut off whatever she started to say. It had rung insistently since he got there.

"You should probably answer that." Annette grimaced as she stepped away.

Disgust lined his face as he saw once again it was Elaine. He turned his phone on silent before he slipped it back in his pocket.

"Jay, I don't think I should be with you or Xavier right now. I need to get myself together by myself." She crossed her arms.

"You seemed to be together okay before he stepped in the picture." He snapped.

"Obviously, I wasn't if he was able to step in. And apparently, you haven't solved your problem either." She glared at him.

"Touché. You are right, I haven't, but I am close." He stepped closer to her. "I love you Annette, and no matter what, I will always love you. Can we try to work on us? I promise that Elaine will not be a problem. Maybe going through this was meant to be, it has shown me how much you mean to me."

He moved her hair off her shoulder and kissed her forehead. Annette hugged him and he felt tears burn the back of his eyes.

"I love you Jay." Big tears rolled down her face. "But how can you promise that? She's calling you right now. I just don't know."

"Just trust me one last time. I know that recently I have made some terrible mistakes, but I'm not going to do it again. I won't pressure you, but I want us to at least work on things. Whenever you need time to yourself, I'll give it to you. I'm willing to do whatever it takes."

Jay removed her key off his ring and handed it to her, he wanted to show her that she wouldn't be crowded, but he needed to be back in her life. When he handed her the key he held her hand and once again embraced her.

"Please baby, just give me a chance to make it up to you." Annette looked at him, and unable to resist he kissed her slowly. The response of his body was fierce and at that moment he knew that there was no way he could let her go.

As he broke away, she looked at him solemnly, as she stepped away. "Okay, we can work on us. But Jay, I need you to include me in decisions and what's going on in your life, before I'll even consider being engaged again."

"Okay baby, I promise." Relief flooded his body. It hit him so strong his knees almost buckled.

He walked to the door with a smile. Her words stopped him.

"But Jay if we start dealing with the same crap from Elaine, I'm through. I can't deal with her anymore."

Jay closed his eyes before he turned back around. "Annette I'm taking care of that this weekend. I'm done with Elaine other than to get Malik, and I'm asking my mom to pick him up on my weekends. I'm serious this time."

Anger blurred his vision when he got in his car. When he moved Annette's hair off her shoulder he noticed the ridge of a hickey on her. That low-down bastard! His phone was lit up when he took it out of his pocket.

"I was just about to call you." Jay looked back at Annette's house before he pulled off.

"Where the hell are you? This is my third time calling you!" Carl sounded excited.

If something else had happened Jay was moving to a deserted island. "What happened now?"

"Nothing I just wanted to make sure you hadn't gone off the deep end."

Jay reassured him that he was fine as they planned to meet back at the condo. Carl bustled through the door when he made it.

"Jay man what's going on? As long as I've known you I've never seen you act like you did this morning." Carl looked at him as he stood at the bar.

Jay fixed a drink and took a swallow before he answered. "Man, that guy didn't even have the damn decency to act ashamed. He is fucking crazy!"

Carl wiped his face with a cocktail napkin before he answered. "I told your ass that there was something wrong with Xavier."

Carl jumped back when Jay slammed his hand down on the bar. "Damn! Look I need some advice and help."

He told Carl about Elaine and Annette. By the time he finished Carl was on his second drink. His friend's face reflected how he felt.

"Elaine is pregnant? Man, you went from good luck to good grief in ninety seconds! What the hell are you going to do?"

"I'm not worried about Elaine; her ass is going to get an abortion if it's true. My concern is how to keep Annette from finding out." Jay filled Carl in on what he told Annette.

"Wait a minute! You told her that shit, but didn't tell her that Elaine says she's pregnant? I don't know Jay. I know I told you not to tell her about having sex with Elaine, but if Elaine is pregnant..." Carl's voice trailed off.

"She can't find out! Not only will she leave me, but with that dickhead hovering around like a vulture, I can't take any chances. Maybe if he wasn't around." Jay gulped his drink.

"I thought your shit was fucked up when we found out about Xavier and Annette, but this takes the damn cake! You need to worry about his ass finding out about Elaine. He will definitely be at Annette then."

Carl's words barely penetrated, Jay was so caught up in his own thoughts. "I can't figure that guy out. And now Annette thinks she's catching feelings for him." He gave his friend a hard look. "That's why she can't find out about this last game that Elaine is playing. If I tell her that I might as well give her to him on a platter. His ass probably wouldn't even say thanks!"

"The only thing working in your favor is Annette is naïve. This is a mess! How the hell are you going to get Elaine's ass to calm the hell down?" Carl shook his head.

Jay told him what Annette said about getting herself together and that they would take things slow.

"Whew! That's good news. Maybe in the meantime you can drug Elaine's drink and take her to the abortion clinic. That's the only way I see her getting one." Carl shrugged his shoulders.

Jay looked determined. "She is not having that baby if she's pregnant. I promise you that."

Chapter 7

Annette felt good! The past three weeks had been just what she needed. Instead of worrying about men, she spent time getting to know herself. She realized that she spent too much time pleasing others, worrying about what others thought, and beating herself up for everything. She wanted to keep her basic personality, but those things had been learned.

Her parents, especially her mom, always acted as if nothing she did was good enough. She spent many years trying to live up to their standards. If what she did was good enough for her she realized that was all that was needed. If they weren't pleased with things she did, it was just too bad.

She also realized that whatever people thought of her she could not change. She tried to change who she was, not only to please but to change the perceptions of others. No more! She could only be who she was destined to be. She was also not responsible for what people did to her or themselves.

These revelations came through reflections during long walks, journaling, and looking inside of her soul. But it still didn't help her decide what her love life should look like. The time alone had been so enjoyable, she almost decided to be by herself. But not quite.

Jay made sure he gave her space but he also made his presence known. He called and text every day. He even brought Malik over to see her children. She was glad because she missed them both. While the children played, they talked and ate. It felt good. He was a perfect gentleman and he never brought up their issues. With their daily talks and when she saw the kids together it brought a sense of familiarity to her. She realized how much she missed her life with him. But something was off.

She knew that most of it came from her, but there was something with him too. One thing was that she didn't want him to spend the night until they were back one hundred percent. He was okay with that, too okay. Then there was the matter of Malik. He tried to hide it but she noticed that when he had Malik, he had excuses for her not to come to the condo at night. She thought he felt as if she hadn't noticed, but she had. Even though it only happened once. That was enough for her radar to go up.

There were other problems that came from her. Xavier had ruined her sexually. She still craved for him, her drug of choice. When she and Jay made love, it seemed to be the same for him, but it wasn't for her. Hell, she hadn't even scratched him! Of course, because of their living arrangements and trials, it wasn't as frequent either. Which sadly was fine with her. But slowly she seemed to be getting back in the groove of their relationship.

Then there was Xavier. He said that she needed to be completely without him, but she wasn't. She saw him at the gym in the mornings, and they managed to talk twice a week. And he still sent flowers once a week. Then unexpectedly he asked her to lunch, she smiled as she thought about that day.

He had asked her the day before and when he entered her workplace, all heads turned. He looked good. But the funniest reaction came from her boss Greg. They bumped into him on the way out and when Annette introduced them, Greg's eyes widened and he stammered. Xavier, odd as usual, never shook his hand or anything, he just smirked and said something weird.

Their 'date' went quite different. She sat across from him because she didn't trust herself next to him. They talked, laughed, and never mentioned the past. The only uncomfortable moment was before they left he gave her that lazy, sexy look of his.

"You look good Annette. Is everything going okay for you?" A flicker burned deep in his eyes.

"Everything is good. I'm getting reacquainted with myself and I like it. Jay and I are working on things slowly but…" She felt trapped in his stare.

"But what?" His voice was a smooth caress.

"I still miss you." She mumbled.

He grabbed her hand and caressed her palm. "How can you miss me when we see each other all the time?"

His simple touch made her flushed and moist! "I know, but it's not the same."

He kissed her palm with a little tongue. "Ahh, I understand. But I'm sure that will pass."

Not like this! Somehow, she refrained from voicing that thought. But instead she stupidly blurted out, "But when? I mean it should be less now, shouldn't it?"

She hated the whiney tone of her voice, but couldn't have helped it. It was hard to speak normal when she sat in a puddle. She forgot about not beating herself up as she mentally kicked herself. Surprise was written on his face as he looked at her. To make up for her gaffe, she stood, ready to depart.

Xavier put his hand on the small of her back as he whispered in her ear, "It's been hard for me too."

This was not lunchtime conversation. His hand, along with the heat that radiated from his body made her dizzy. When he said "hard" all types of titillating thoughts crossed her mind. She tried to recover maturely.

"Hopefully it will pass soon." She whispered, although they were now at his car.

She turned as he opened the door and saw his lips had tilted in a small smile. He kissed the top of her head before she got in.

"I hope so too *la amante*, I really do."

That memory still made her warm when she thought about it. Especially when she got back to her desk and looked up what *la amante* meant. Very little work had gotten done the rest of the day, because memories of their salacious moments filled her head. Not just that day either. But overall, she was proud of herself for not giving in to her desire.

She interrupted her musings to finish dressing for dinner tonight. This would be the first time that all the girlfriends had gotten together. Since Damita ratted her out. Oops! Another character flaw to work on, she just hadn't gotten to it yet.

She had dinner and conversation with both Bianca and Tonya, but she had only talked to Damita briefly. Damita had called when she found out that she and Jay were working on their relationship. She missed her, when she wasn't angry at her for being a tattle tale, and since she only called when it seemed as if Annette was back with Jay. It was time to mend that bridge and she thought that was why Bianca suggested tonight. No matter what happened she wanted to remain friends with Damita.

Tonya, of course had gotten there first, and she looked great! Tonya finally thought about leaving her husband, Fred, who was a serial cheater. Omar and Xavier's security company had taken on the job and last Annette heard they found some things but not the smoking gun. Tonya had on plaid crop pants that only skinny people seemed to be able to pull off, and a sea-green spaghetti strapped top. Annette was surprised because Tonya rarely showed skin. Her thick hair was curled, make-up was impeccable, but it was her eyes. They glowed with happiness.

They hugged but before she got any info Bianca showed up. Bianca's hair was slicked back into a high ponytail and she wore a sleeveless red jumper. Jumpers were usually not meant for shorter people, but Bianca of course wore it well. The main thing Annette noticed was that she looked tired.

As they hugged and tried to find Bianca's baby bump, Damita showed up. She looked gorgeous! Damita's hair was straightened, it was the first time any of them had seen that, and she wore a royal blue wrap around dress. She wore three-inch heeled sandals but since she was the tallest of the quartet, she towered over them.

Once they were seated, Tonya and Damita sat across from Bianca and Annette. Annette noticed because usually Damita and Bianca sat together, but tonight Bianca made sure that she sat next to Annette. She shrugged it off as nerves.

After they ordered Bianca told them the plans for her wedding. Instead of going to the justice of the peace, they opted for a small wedding and reception. She explained why.

"The courthouse only allows eight people, and since my grand mom, mom, uncles, brother and such want to come there was no way." She glanced around the table. "And I want you guys to be there too."

"Aww, that's so sweet! We want to be there too." Annette squeezed her hand.

"Does this mean we will be in the wedding?" Tonya peered at Bianca.

"No, we aren't doing all that. It's a place down the highway, past where Zay lives." Bianca looked at Annette, then quickly turned her head. "Umm, and the wedding portion will be a small, quick affair outside, but it has a facility for the reception, and in case it rains."

Bianca had recovered quickly, but Annette felt Damita's eyes boring into her before she looked and met her glare.

Annette cleared her throat, "Is that why you look a little tired? You and Omar have been running around looking for a place for the wedding?"

Bianca laughed, "That and some land to build a house. Of course, he wants to move close to his brother, but he really wants to wear me out."

"Why?" Tonya asked as she grabbed a mozzarella stick that the server had just left.

"He's trying to convince me to stop working. Everything else he's tried has failed, so I guess he figures if I get tired enough, I'll quit."

Damita who had been strangely quiet spoke up. "Humph, it might not be possible now since certain business deals have gone to hell."

She never looked up, but Annette felt the sting of her words. Bianca spoke up before she could.

"If I wanted to stop working I could, business deals or not. Omar doesn't put all of his eggs in one basket." Bianca's words were harmless, but there was a bite in her tone. "But as much as my job stresses me out, I actually love what I do."

Their food came and everyone got lost in their food or thoughts. It was obvious to Annette that Damita had a bug up her ass, but she couldn't think of how to approach it to resolve it. Damita solved that problem for her.

"Speaking of Xavier, I've decided to give him another chance. We've been talking, spending a little time and we are going on a date soon." She smiled behind her napkin.

Annette felt a burn that started at her neck and worked its way up. Her food had gotten caught in her throat and she sipped her soda to wash it down.

"Damita! Now you are just being petty." Bianca spoke sternly.

"How am I being petty? You brought him up and I was just sharing." Damita looked at Bianca innocently.

Ever since Damita brought up Xavier, Tonya looked stricken, but after Bianca spoke she lowered her head. Tonya had been caught in the wrath called Bianca many times, so she realized how this could end.

Bianca took a deep breath, "We are all aware of the previous situation, you don't have to make sideways comments about it. That's what's petty."

"We all did not know about it, because I was clueless." Damita's eyes glittered angrily.

"Well we did and obviously we didn't tell you for a reason. And if you knew you were still salty…" Annette cut Bianca off.

"It's okay Bianca, I don't mind. I know Damita is upset with me and I understand. If you have something you want to say to me, go ahead and say it." She looked at Damita.

Tonya glanced at her, shook her head and mouthed no.

"No, let's clear the air. I want all of us to remain friends and as friends we should be able to resolve our issues." Butterflies in her stomach depleted her appetite, but Annette knew it needed to be done.

"Yes, I am salty, and not just because Jay is my brother. The whole thing stinks! Not only is Xavier doing business with Jay, the love of your life, supposedly, but he is also the guy I was dating. I thought there was some type of friend code."

Annette was caught in the cross-fire. Tonya looked down and Bianca pressed her leg against Annette's but said nothing.

Damita wasn't finished. "I understand that you were tired of Elaine's crap, hell, we all are. But couldn't you have found some other man to fool around with?"

Annette refused to cry. She reminded herself that she was stronger now. "I didn't look to fool around on Jay. What happened with me and Xavier, just happened. It's not as if we had been looking at each other before then."

Damita smacked her lips, "I can't tell."

"Come on Damita, let's not do this here." Tonya pleaded with her.

Annette's ire had risen. "No, let's. Obviously, you blame me for everything since you have decided to give him another try. If we hadn't both been involved it couldn't have happened. So why does he get a pass, but I still get the business?"

Damita looked startled by her outburst. Annette was not finished. "I was wrong, I admit. But if your brother had done what he is trying to do now and put Elaine in her place, involve me in his life more, none of this would have happened. Yes, Zay and I went a little to the left, but the most important thing is that he was there for me as a friend when I needed one the most."

Tonya and Bianca gaped at her. Had she not been on the inside of the booth, she would have thrown her napkin down and made a grand exit. Damita still refused to back down. Annette thought about how Jay always said that she and their mom could not let go when they got on a subject.

His actual words were that they were like pit bulls with a bone.

"A little to the left? Okay maybe I have given him a pass more so than you, because men will never turn down a piece." Damita looked at Tonya as she coughed out her drink. "It's true. I guess I expected you to think about more than that. You know like Jay or our friendship." She looked over the rim of her glass as she sipped her drink.

"Don't sit here and act as if I didn't think about Jay." Annette sat back and crossed her arms. "But Jay was the one who wanted the break. And for your information, it's not as if I offered Zay a *piece*." She let that settle before she continued. "Furthermore, you said that you and Xavier had just been friends. If it was more than that to you, then you should have said something. I don't think there is a code for friends."

Damita narrowed her eyes, but Bianca jumped in before she said anything. "Okay that is enough! What happened, happened, and we have moved forward. We are all friends, Jay and Annette seem to be back on track, and everything else is in the past."

Tonya nodded her head and she looked at Damita for confirmation. Damita swung her hair and tried to give one parting shot.

"I might have said that we were just friends, but you knew in the beginning I was interested in more than a friendship. That should count for something."

Annette leaned forward, "If that counts for something, then since I was the one who actually fuc— slept with him, maybe you should be the one applying your damn friend code."

Everyone sat in stunned silence. This time Annette did throw her napkin on her plate and she looked around the table.

"I'm sorry Bianca for spoiling your good news." She glanced sideways at Damita. "I guess I'm not ready for these types of dinners. I hope y'all have a good night."

She scooted closer to Bianca to let her know she wanted out.

"Annette don't leave!" Tonya begged her.

"No, I think that enough has been said tonight." Annette slid out when Bianca rose and as Annette tried to give her money for her meal she shooed her away. Bianca hugged her and whispered that she would call her later. Annette reached down and hugged Tonya, then left.

When she got in her car, she sat there for a minute. She realized that most of her anger came from Damita talking to and going out with Zay. If it hadn't been for that she would have been more charitable in her reaction.

She glanced at her phone and saw that she had texts from Jay and Xavier. She left them unopened because she had no intention of responding. She was tired of being treated like a game of chess.

Chapter 8

Once Annette left there was an uncomfortable silence. Bianca picked at her food because she was mad. She was mad at Xavier, she was mad at Damita, and she was even mad at Omar. Just because she knew that he pulled for Xavier and Annette. If he had tried to convince his brother harder to stay in Texas, they wouldn't be sitting here now tongue tied.

Damita broke the silence. "I'm sorry. I guess I should have waited until it was just me and Annette. I shouldn't have done that here."

"You think?" Bianca noticed that Tonya was about to placate matters. Not tonight! "I understand that Jay is your brother, but he wasn't totally innocent in this."

"I didn't say he was. But if Annette wanted to have a fling, did it have to be with Xavier?" She looked at them for understanding.

"I don't think Annette planned to have a fling." Tonya finally found her voice. "I don't know all of the details, but I know Annette, she is not a fling person."

"Right! And not to throw more salt your way, and I can't say for sure, but I'm almost certain that Xavier did more pursuing than Annette." Bianca rolled her eyes. "Because he is not the type to just accept any piece that comes his way. They both got caught up."

Damita looked down, "I didn't mean to come at her the way I did. I just hated to see Jay hurting." She looked up, "He was devastated when he found out about Xavier and Annette. He's had so much thrown at him in such a short while."

A thought pricked at the back of Bianca's subconscious. She felt as if Damita didn't know everything. "How about how devastated Annette was when Elaine sent her that picture?" She continued after noting Damita's look of surprise. "Or the nights that she drove by Elaine's and saw Jay's car there? All night! You should have gotten all of the details before you just shot her down."

"What picture?" Once they filled her in, she dropped her head. "Jay didn't tell me about that."

"There is a lot that Jay doesn't seem to tell." This came from Tonya.

"What do you mean?" Damita asked.

"Jay still hasn't admitted that he slept with Elaine. There is no way in hell that he was naked in her bed and nothing happened. You and your brother have jumped all over Annette and Xavier but he still hasn't come clean to the woman he supposedly loves." Bianca's nostrils flared.

Damita looked stricken, but she had no response.

Bianca continued, "I'll be the first to admit that Xavier was wrong, but Jay is not innocent, hurt or not. Annette was hurt and he barely called her for a week after Malik returned home. Why do y'all expect Annette to keep sitting around and dealing with Jay and Elaine's shit? I'm glad they are trying to work it out, but if they hadn't I wouldn't have been mad."

"Bianca!" Tonya looked shocked. "You don't mean that."

"I do. I'm sick and tired of the shit she has dealt with from Elaine. She might try to fool herself that she's not, but she must be. And it's obvious that Elaine is not going anywhere."

Damita was back on her track. "Why does everyone treat Annette like she is so innocent? Sure, she was hurt, and certainly Jay was wrong, but it's not as if she fell asleep and woke up with Xavier. Elaine drugged Jay, he wasn't in his right mind. Annette was."

Tonya nodded, "You are right Annette wasn't drugged." She waved her hand at Bianca, who frowned at her. "But sometimes hurt can be worse than being drugged, Annette wasn't in her right mind either. By the time she was coherent she had gotten caught up. We are not saying that Annette is innocent, but we understand that a certain level of hurt can make you do strange things."

Bianca chimed in, "Yes, because she thought that Jay was getting back with Elaine and going to put her back on side-chick status."

Damita face filled with horror. "Jay would have never done that! He loves Annette too much."

Bianca softened her tone, "Annette knows how much Malik means to Jay and that he would do whatever it takes for his son. She thought it was possible."

Damita clasped her hands together deep in thought.

Bianca continued, "Xavier might have taken advantage of the situation, but he was the only thing that kept her sane."

Tonya raised her eyebrows at Bianca, and nodded her approval.

"Why didn't he think of the business side of things? You can't tell me that he's so altruistic that he put his livelihood on the line? Annette didn't think of that aspect either, it's as if she didn't care." Damita stuck to her guns.

Bianca covered Damita's hand with hers. "I'll let you in on a little secret. If Xavier doesn't receive another penny from Jay it will not affect his livelihood. That man works all the time for people all over the country. That's probably why it wasn't important to him. You also know that Jay is not hurting either. If you and I know that then I'm sure that Annette knows it too."

Damita sighed heavily, "I guess I was jealous. Carl and Jay made it seem as if Xavier had his eyes on Annette even when he was with me. That hurt my feelings along with when I saw them, I know he never acted that way with me."

Bianca was never known for biting her tongue. "I figured that's what it was. Sometimes the most unexpected people have the biggest attraction." She pulled her wallet out. "Anywho, I'm going home to my love. I just hope that y'all have reconciled your differences before my wedding. Or one of you won't get invited." She looked pointedly at Damita.

Omar was sprawled across the bed, knocked out when Bianca arrived home. He was bare-chested and wore shorts, his intention obviously had not been to fall asleep because the television was still on. In her eyes, he was perfection. His Hispanic roots showed in his coloring, hair and temperament, although most didn't see it. She walked up to the edge of the bed and still he slept. When she nudged him, his eyes slowly opened.

"Omar, how can you sleep like that?" She sat on the edge of the bed and took her shoes off.

Omar stretched and caressed her butt with his hand. "Like what? I was waiting on you to come home."

"This might have been the last girl's night out for a while." Bianca stood and turned for him to unzip her jumper.

With clothes on her bump was nonexistent, naked it was noticeable. Omar as usual clasped his hands around her waist, and then reached down to kiss her stomach. She swore he acted as if their baby was the first baby conceived. He was so happy and she was too. They both had other children from previous marriages, both girls. Omar had Liberty who was in college at Auburn, and Bianca had Marisa who would soon be going off to Florida for college.

"Wait Bibi, don't move! I think I felt him kick." Omar still held her around her waist.

Bianca had frozen because she thought he saw a bug or something on her. Once she realized he was being ridiculous she swatted him away.

"You did not feel him or her kick! Why do you keep saying it's a boy?" She moved to the mirror to contain her hair.

Omar chuckled, "I just think our baby is a boy. Zay thinks so too."

"Humph, well I guess if he said it, it must be true. What will little Ome call him? Pop-Unc or Unc-Pop?" She chuckled at her own joke.

Omar laughed, "You know he asked me about you calling him my Bro-Dad."

"You told him that?" Bianca's eyes grew wide.

"Nope. Annette did, but don't worry he thought it was cute." Omar smirked.

"That girl has a big mouth. I wonder why she told him that? It seems as if they would have had enough to talk about other than us." Bianca looked in her drawer for her scarf.

"She asked him why was he called that. I think she thought he knew about it."

"Wonder what fantastic story he came up with? Or did he do his usual and deflect?" She tied the scarf around her two long braids.

"No, he told her the truth. All of it." Omar met her startled gaze through the mirror.

Shock kept her from responding. Xavier barely spoke of his upbringing with Omar, and he told Annette. No wonder she was all confused, they had done much more than screw around. Omar gave her that 'I told you so' look.

"Speaking of your brother, he is the reason that there will not be a ladies' night out again soon." She turned and joined him on the bed.

"He showed up?" Omar sat up and looked worried.

"No!" Bianca told him about what occurred. She laughed at the myriad of facial expressions that crossed his countenance.

"Damn! I'm not surprised that Damita approached it from that angle, but I'm surprised that Annette didn't cry. I feel bad for her."

Bianca laughed, "You know Annette has been on this self-awareness kick, and after tonight I think she is aware that she has a backbone. I wanted to laugh but I didn't because I have never seen her like this!"

Between her laughter she managed to choke out Annette's remarks about the friend code before she left. She laughed harder at the shock on Omar's face before he laughed.

"Annette said that? I can't imagine."

"Yes! She almost said fucked him, but she caught herself. It was hilarious, especially coming from her. You should have seen Tonya's face." Bianca had another fit of giggles.

"You know what this means don't you?" Omar smiled as he kissed her on the cheek.

The gleam in his eyes alerted her that this would not be good news. With a deep sigh she asked, "What does it mean Ome?"

"Xavier has a chance. I think Annette has more feelings for him than she realizes."

"You think because she had an argument about the 'friend code' that means she has feelings for your brother? No. Annette is just tired of being so damn nice all the time." Bianca huffed.

"Bibi, come on, you know that wasn't about a code. Annette was mad because Damita is going out with Zay. You've known her longer than I have. Have you ever seen her act like that?" Omar tried unsuccessfully to hide his grin.

"No, but I think it has to do with this whole Zen thing she is doing. In case you have forgotten, she and Jay are working things out." Bianca sounded unconvinced.

Omar pulled her close as he turned off the television. "I haven't forgotten, but you know the Baudoin's aren't the only one with magic. The Rives men are known for getting what they want by any means necessary." He chuckled in her hair, "It's called a pipeline."

She elbowed him in the ribs, and then relaxed in his embrace as all thoughts of others ceased to exist for both.

Chapter 9

The rays of sun that reflected off his sunglasses, did not match his mood. Jay was on his way to meet Elaine at her doctor's office. He wanted to get there early enough to make sure she didn't have the chance to run some type of scam. That's how much he distrusted her.

When it took so long for her to tell him about an appointment, he knew that she was lying. He worked more on regaining his relationship with Annette. Thoughts of Annette made him sad. The only bright light in that situation was that she was not still involved with that guy.

Jay had only seen Xavier once since their confrontation at the security office. The glitch that he and Omar thought they had fixed had come back. The customer had gotten frustrated with the problems it caused, and Omar urged Jay to let Xavier come fix it. It only took that bastard four hours to rectify the problem!

Before he left he told him it was fixed and then turned as he reached the door. "How's Annette?"

Jay stared at him because he wanted to swipe the smirk off his face. Xavier chuckled and left. But he realized that if nothing else he would have to deal with him for business purposes. The dealerships in California had called him and would let him know within the next two weeks if it was a green light. Xavier held the major portion of the patent, and if he chose, he could refuse to let Jay license it for them. So, he held his tongue and thoughts.

Jay parked at the doctor's office and waited in his car for Elaine to pull up. Once she got there, he never left her side. When they called her to the back, nausea rose in his stomach as they declared her pregnant. She looked at him and smiled. When the doctor examined her Jay sat in, but answered emails from his phone, the entire time. Elaine glanced his way as the doctor proclaimed that she was in excellent shape and everything looked fine. Jay looked up and scowled.

Once they were in the doctor's private office, Jay wasted no time and got to the point. "Is it too late for an abortion?"

Dr. Weatherly looked at him in surprise while Elaine looked at him in anger.

"Umm, okay, I wasn't expecting that. Is there any reason you don't want the baby?"

"We are divorced, and this was a huge mistake." Carl's advice about not telling people he didn't remember having sex hummed in the back of his mind.

Elaine jumped in, "Dr. Weatherly please excuse Jay. I'm not getting an abortion."

"We'll see about that." Jay muttered.

Dr. Weatherly was clearly uncomfortable. "You have time to weigh your options, and umm, if you decide on abortion, let me know. I can refer you to the best places."

Elaine cried and Jay ignored her. "Is there a way to test DNA before birth? Just in case the abortion route doesn't work out."

Elaine's snivels stopped. "You low-down bastard! How dare you?"

If the doctor tried to hide his discomfort before, it was impossible to now. He cleared his throat, and moved papers around on his desk. "I'll let you two talk about your options and maybe by the next appointment we can discuss things more calmly."

"You didn't answer my question Dr. Weatherly. Is there a way to test for DNA before the child is born?"

The doctor looked between Elaine and Jay. "Yes, there is. But she is not far along enough for that test. Also, it usually is not covered by insurance."

"Can you please make note that it needs to be done? I don't care how much it costs." Jay stood.

Before he walked out he turned, "How soon can it be done?"

Dr. Weatherly looked up from the notes he made on Elaine's chart. "About two months. Mrs. Darrington caught her pregnancy very early, which is good. But I would like to wait another eight weeks before we administer that type of test."

Jay nodded and walked out with Elaine on his heels. He stayed ahead of her because he did not want to hear her mouth or even see her face. When he got to the lobby he walked right into Omar and Bianca!

"Jay? Hey, what are you doing here?" Omar stopped in front of him as Bianca signed in.

"Umm, I…" Jay could not come up with an answer. He didn't have to because Elaine had caught up with him.

"We are expecting!" She beamed at Omar.

Omar raised his eyebrows, then looked down.

"Expecting what?" Jay heard Bianca before she materialized beside Omar.

"A baby! Why else would we be here?" Elaine rolled her eyes at Bianca, then she grazed Jay's arm as she waved goodbye with three fingers.

"Jay what the hell is going on? Please tell me that she is lying." Bianca had lowered her voice as she noticed people watching.

Jay pulled them over to a corner in the waiting room. "It's true, but hopefully she will get an abortion, and I also don't believe it's mine."

Omar's face was lined with concern, but Bianca looked at him coldly.

"Obviously there is a chance it is yours or you wouldn't be here." She said through gritted teeth.

Jay rubbed his face. "I know this looks bad, but just let me tell Annette. I think it will be best if she hears it from me."

Omar still looked stunned. "Yes, sure. I mean it's your place to tell her not ours. Man, I sure hate this for you."

Jay always believed that Omar was a good guy and considered him a friend. The sincerity he heard cemented that fact. He clapped Omar on the back, thanked him, and glanced at Bianca while she glared at him. He glanced back when he made it to the door, he met Bianca's glare and it frightened him.

When he got to his car, he pulled his mirror down and wondered how he could be besieged with so much bad luck. He knew that Omar wouldn't tell Annette, but he was certain that Bianca would. He knew he would have to catch her before Bianca did.

To keep his mind occupied, Jay went back to the office and before the day ended he called Carl to meet him at the condo. Before he went to Annette's he needed to be coached.

Carl came shortly after Jay had showered and changed. After Jay told him about the doctor's visit Carl was more subdued than Jay had ever seen. When the doorbell rang he made Carl promise not to mention it to Damita. She was the only person who popped over without calling first.

Jay's heart fell when he opened the door to Annette. Her hair was in a messy bun on the top of her head and her nose was lined in red. He knew she had been crying.

"Elaine's pregnant? Really Jay? I thought we were working things out and you conveniently forgot to tell me that small bit of news?"

"Annette listen! I was coming to tell you. We just went to the doctor today." He tried to embrace her, but she slipped through his grasp.

"How did you know to go to the doctor? Did she send you a text and ask you to secretly meet her there this morning?" Her eyes were red and her voice carried.

"No, but I wasn't going to tell you until it was confirmed." Jay grabbed her arms. "I didn't want to upset you any more than necessary, you have to believe me. I'm so sorry baby, I'm not trying to hurt you. I don't know what else to tell you."

Annette's eyes bulged and she put her finger on his chest. She punctuated each word with a jab, "How about the truth? You promised me that you would not keep shit from me! As a matter of fact, you never even told me that you slept with her. You said that you woke up in her bed alone. Remember that?"

Jay hung his head but he held on to her. "I know, I was ashamed, but baby she drugged me. I don't even remember it. It would have never happened otherwise."

He tried to hug her but she pushed away, "I know you were drugged, Xavier told me. But you didn't, all these things have happened, but you never shared them with me. I also know that you spent more than one night over there, because I rode by every night and saw your car." She stepped back and he saw her face was wet with tears. "I believed in you once again and you keep hiding things from me. Had you included me in the beginning she wouldn't have done these things. Because I would have been right beside you, regardless of her insults and name-calling."

Jay realized she was right and he felt like an ass, because while he thought he protected her, he never thought of her feelings. He tried to pull her closer, but she stepped away and shook her head.

She swiped her face with her hands and stared at him. All her words swiveled around in his head. Jay stepped closer and talked fast. "Yes, I was over there but I was there for Malik." He dropped his head, "I only slept with her twice. That's why I feel pretty certain that it's not mine."

"Twice! Now we have gone from zero to twice? This is too much. I love you Jay, and I trusted you, but you keep treating me like a fool. I'm done. I can't do this anymore with you. Elaine has just guaranteed another eighteen years in your life. I can't do it."

A cold fear snaked around his heart. He heard the finality in her voice, but he had not given up. "Annette no, baby. Elaine is either going to get an abortion or if not, the doctor said he can do a DNA test in two months. There is no way that baby is mine."

"What if it is? What am I supposed to do?" He felt her as she came closer and spoke softly.

He looked her in her eyes, "I don't know."

Annette looked at him with tears in her eyes. "I love you Jay and I hate that she has done these things to you. You should have told me. If you had been honest in the beginning, this wouldn't have been so shocking, and maybe I would feel more inclined stay beside you. Instead you lied. You lied even after you promised not to keep anything from me. I can't deal with this anymore."

As she turned and walked out, Jay felt his heart break.

Omar was pissed off. Bianca had meandered to the bedroom while he fumed in the den. When the doorbell rang, he didn't move. He knew it was one of her girlfriends or someone looking for Marisa, and he didn't want to scare anyone away. The big bulk of his brother entered the room.

"What's up? You don't have any food around here?" Zay's voice filled the room. He opened the oven door and peeped in.

"Nope. I have half of a Five Guys hamburger on the stove." Omar had lost his appetite while arguing with Bianca, she had eaten all of hers.

Xavier bustled around in the kitchen and when he entered the den he must have seen something in Omar's expression. "What's wrong with you?"

"Nothing. Bibi pissed me off." Omar peered over Xavier's shoulder to make sure she wasn't behind him.

"What? The honeymoon is over before you guys get married?" Xavier laughed.

Omar ushered him outside as his brother munched on his burger. He told him what happened earlier at the doctor's office. He was surprised when Xavier chuckled.

"Man, where did he find that woman? He has the ex-wife from hell!" Xavier chuckled and chewed.

"But he asked us to let him tell Annette. And what does Bibi do? As soon as she gets off work she runs her ass to Annette's and tells her! That's what pissed me off!" Omar puffed on his cigar.

At the mention of Annette, Xavier stopped chuckling and grew serious. "How did she take it? Man, I know that knocked her off her feet."

"Not well at all. She's doing some Zen thing, but it didn't seem to work." They leaned against the railing around the patio and gazed in the backyard.

Xavier gave him a strange look. "Zen thing? Oh, okay. Well bro, Bianca probably told her because she knew that his ass wouldn't."

"Exactly." Both brothers were startled to hear Bianca.

Omar turned around. "But Bibi, you didn't give him a chance to tell her. We told him that we would let him handle it."

"Omar, it takes anywhere from three weeks to a month to get an appointment with Dr. Weatherly. He had plenty of time! And I didn't agree to anything, you did." Bianca sat at the patio table.

"In case you don't know, when my brother agrees to shit, everyone with him agrees." Xavier's shoulders heaved with laughter.

He looked pensive as he addressed Bianca. "How is Annette?"

She pulled at her nose and closed her eyes before she answered. "She was upset, she didn't fall out or anything, but she cried. She was angrier than anything. I guess Jay had promised her that he would be more open and honest. I stayed with her until she calmed down. I think the children being there helped. She didn't want them to see her upset."

Omar noticed a hard glint appear in his brothers' eyes. "That stupid ass! If he knew this shit before he should have stayed away from her. Instead he just continues to mess over her."

Omar nodded, "That's true in hindsight. But it still wasn't our place to tell her." He rolled his eyes at Bianca.

A small smile touched Bianca's lips. "Omar she's my friend. What if Elaine had told her first? Then I would have to say that I saw them at the doctor's office. He had no right asking us not to tell."

"She has a point. You guys go ahead and make up, I have to run." Xavier fiddled with his phone, then he gave Omar a hug, and he whispered in Bianca's ear when he hugged her. She nodded her head and looked at Omar defiantly.

Omar pulled Bianca's hair and kissed her forehead as he watched his brother disappear. He wondered where he had to go in such a rush.

Chapter 10

Annette pulled over at the first gas station she saw. With her head on her steering wheel, she cried her eyes out. Once she felt as if there were no tears left, she lifted her head and saw a beautiful sunset. There were beautiful orange rays tinged in red, with spots of yellow. She was so enthralled by its beauty, her tears dried as she soaked it in. Just as the sunset turns into night, her mood shifted from hurt to anger as she thought of the day's events.

Bianca stopped by shortly after she arrived home. Since Bianca never just dropped by, she felt a bad vibe. When she told Annette about Elaine, a pain speared her heart and seared her soul. Her tongue became heavy and stopped her from speaking as her tears spilled down her face. Bianca held her as hurt wracked her body. Once she calmed down she felt numb, but asked a few questions. Bianca explained as much as she could as she told her that she wanted her to hear it from someone who loved her.

Not many people saw Bianca's soft side, Annette was one of the few. She appreciated and loved her friend for it. Annette knew that Bianca told her before Elaine could. Thinking of Elaine, her body flushed with anger. Her thoughts warred against every self-help book and all that she achieved in the last month. Her thoughts won.

She hated that bitch! Elaine was a bitch, Jay was a punk-ass when it came to her, Xavier was an asshole for taking Damita out, and Damita was petty for going out with him. Forget all the books she read about positive thoughts, and being the best she could be.

"Fuck it!" She yelled to the interior of her car. If she wanted to, she would go home and write 'I hate that bitch Elaine' one hundred times and send it to all the positive thoughts assholes she knew. She smiled with that last thought and headed home.

Her children bombarded her as soon as she arrived. It was movie night and she was cooking hamburgers and potato wedges. Once she got them settled and agreeable to baths before the movie, she got busy and cooked. It helped somewhat.

As the last batch of wedges fried the doorbell chimed. She steeled herself determined to stay strong if it was Jay. After she took a deep breath and stood ramrod straight, ready for battle, she opened the door. Xavier was draped in her doorway.

He wore a charcoal short-sleeved button-down shirt and black denims. He looked good, but her bad attitude kept her from acknowledging it.

He held his hands up, "Can I come in?"

She shrugged, opened the door wider and walked back to the kitchen. He followed.

"Damn! It smells good in here. Do you have extras?" He gave her that smile that under normal circumstances would have melted her panties.

"I might. What brought you out my way?" Unintentionally her words came out harsher than she meant. Of course, he seemed not to notice.

"I heard about what happened and I came to check on you." He lowered his voice about ten decibels.

Annette's heart thudded in her chest, but she couldn't let go of her anger. "So, you thought I had fallen apart and you came to rescue me?"

Xavier brows knotted together briefly. "No, I came to see if a friend needed someone to talk to."

That made her feel small, but she still hung on to her anger. "I'm fine. The kids and I are watching a movie in a few, and then we will go to bed."

"Okay. I can stay if you need me." He looked so deep in her eyes she felt as if he could read her mind.

"Don't you have a date tonight? I wouldn't want to be held responsible for interrupting that. Since I seem to be responsible for everything else." She snapped.

Xavier cocked his head and gave her his funny look. "Okay I'll leave you alone. Can I have a burger before I go?"

This guy had the sensitivity of a bull in a bullfight. She waved her hand over the food and nodded. Ant and Corey ran to the kitchen and surrounded him.

"Mr. Xavier!" They yelled his name like he was famous or something.

Jolisa walked up and shyly waved at him. Zay sat down at the table and asked about their trip as Annette fixed their plates and seethed. He left shortly after he inhaled two burgers, Annette breathed a sigh of relief and felt a flash of anger.

She knew that tonight was his date night with Damita. She and Damita had somewhat made up. Damita intentionally slipped and told her that she was going out with Zay tonight. She told herself that she didn't care, but the rush of anger she felt for them both determined that she did.

Once the kids rushed through dinner to get to the movie she decided that she would reflect on her feelings later. She knew that sleeping would be impossible tonight.

Less than five minutes into the movie her doorbell chimed. Aggravated she snatched the door open and there stood Xavier again.

"I brought popcorn and butter." He smiled mischievously.

Corey and Anthony jumped up and even Jolisa smiled, there was no way out. After he popped the popcorn, they rewound the movie back to the beginning and everyone settled in. They watched some PG-13 comedy that Annette felt still showed and said too much, but it was funny. The laughter removed some of the lead off her shoulders, especially since Xavier laughed the most and the loudest.

She looked around the darkened room as they were engrossed in the movie. Corey sat with her on the loveseat, while Zay, Ant, and Jolisa occupied the sofa. Lately Jolisa had that pre-teen attitude, but tonight she seemed to be her old self. They were all upset when she told them that she and Jay had broken up, but they seemed to adjust. She knew that came from seeing the barrage of women that their dad broke up with monthly. Break-ups were a part of their lives.

As soon as the movie ended, Corey jumped up and reminded her that they could play the game for a brief time. Since he didn't realize that was before her world had crumbled, she agreed. Two things surprised her: Xavier was still on the sofa and Jolisa hadn't gone back to her room. Xavier glanced at her as she moved to the kitchen, but he didn't say anything.

The usual noises came from the den as she cleaned the kitchen. Ant and Corey arguing about moves. She knew when the game ended because Corey cried out.

"You cheated!" His voice was laced with tears.

Not in front of company, Corey! She wanted to scream.

"I did not! You are just a sore loser!" Ant had laughter in his tone.

This was the same argument every time they played. Annette walked out of the kitchen about to give her usual speech which included turning the game off and them going to bed. She was shocked when Xavier spoke.

"No, I watched the whole match. He just knows more moves than you do, but it was a fair match."

She heard Corey began to get whiney again. Zay cut him off.

"Do you want me to beat him in a match?"

Annette watched this interaction from the doorway of the den.

Corey looked down, "Nobody can beat Ant but Jermaine. He's too good."

Ant's chest puffed out and Xavier laughed as he took the remote from Corey.

"Well let me try. If I win, I'll show you some new moves later. Deal?"

Corey nodded, his expression switched to excited. He was the first to notice Annette.

"Can we play a little longer Mom? Please? Mr. Xavier thinks he can beat Ant!"

Both of her boys looked at her with hope in their eyes. Annette laughed as she agreed. Soon her den was filled with game talk. Ant, her shy child, came alive when he played video games, and he was lit tonight. When she finished the kitchen, she walked back in just in time to hear:

"Damn! How did you do that?" Xavier looked at the television with a smile.

She cleared her throat. Her boys looked down with smiles while Zay looked guilty.

"Sorry. Was I too loud?" He looked at her sheepishly.

Corey rolled on the floor with laughter. "Mr. Xavier, you said a bad word!"

The kids laughed as he realized his gaffe and apologized again. "Sorry about that. You hit me with that move, and I thought I was playing with a grown man."

A few minutes later, the game was over and since Xavier won he was a hero. Corey and Ant swarmed around him as they asked how he did this move and that move. Annette broke up the party. They hugged her and high fived him as they trooped off to bed. Xavier leaned back on the sofa and closed his eyes.

She stood and looked at him. His legs were stretched out and as she gazed over his form she realized he looked as if he had lost weight. When she reached his face again he stared at her, but didn't move.

She sat beside him timidly. "I didn't realize you were a gamer."

He looked at her and pulled a tendril of hair back up to her bun. "I'm not. I haven't played in a long time, I usually only play when Horatio comes around."

His words registered but she was so busy trying not to get lost in his gaze. His voice caressed her ears while his eyes pulled every need she had from the depths of her soul.

"Who's Horatio?" Was all she managed to say.

Xavier looked at her funny. "Bianca's brother? Wow! She really kept her family under lock and key, didn't she?"

"Yes, she did." Annette murmured. She was glad her cycle was on, because her body had the hot flash reaction she always got when she was around Zay. Then she remembered that she was mad at him!

"Didn't you have a date tonight?" She blurted.

Xavier chuckled, "I can't have any secrets in this town."

His laughter made her angrier, it was not funny. She rose and he grabbed her hand.

"Sit back down Annette." His chuckles dwindled.

With her arms crossed over her chest, she stood and looked at him.

"Yes, I was going out with Damita tonight. I don't know if you would call it a date. We were meeting up with some of her co-workers to shoot pool. I was going because I didn't have anything else to do." His eyes swept over her body.

Damita had lied to her! What was going on with her friends? She sank back down on the sofa.

"Why did she tell me that y'all were going on a date?" She looked at him doubtfully.

Xavier shrugged his shoulders and still held on to her hand.

"Why didn't you say anything earlier?" She needed to remove her hand from his, but couldn't.

"I just thought maybe down here when you went out with a group of people it was called a date." His dimples showed.

She laughed, grabbed a pillow to pop him with and somehow during the horseplay ended on top of him. His body heat molded her body in place. The hardness of his body felt familiar and alluring. The laughter stopped and a magnetic force pulled her to his lips. He stopped her.

"If I start, I don't think I'll be able to stop." They were centimeters apart, and his breath tickled her lips, while his eyes dared her to come closer.

"I guess I should get up, since my period is on." The shock factor of her statement was lost with his response.

"I don't think it would matter at this point." His hand which had hung loosely on her waist tightened.

A small tingle reverberated in her spine. She felt strangely licentious. Zay moved her over.

"But I wouldn't want your children to catch us." He smiled dangerously.

She sat up properly chastised, somehow this man always made her lose her mind. As she pushed her hair back she tried to regain her sensibility. "Yeah, right. I think I should be celibate for a while anyway." If her condition had been different she would have said for a minute.

As they sat up he pulled her close to him and then he cut his eyes at her. "Is that part of the Zen thing you are doing?"

"What Zen thing?" Did he think she had become a Buddhist in a matter of weeks?

"I don't know. Omar said you were doing some Zen thing."

Annette laughed so hard her sides hurt. Her laughter sliced through the sexual tension and they spent the rest of their time talking and watching television.

After a lengthy silence, she turned to him and realized that he had fallen asleep. It took three nudges to wake him, which was odd since he was a light sleeper.

"Damn I'm tired!" He yawned.

After a brief tug of war between body and mind, she offered him the sofa for the night, he stretched out and smiled. She was gently jerked back as she tried to get up and was met with a chaste kiss on her cheek.

When she returned with a light throw as cover, he was back fast asleep, she placed it over him and went to bed.

Chapter 11

Saturday mornings usually meant sleeping later, housework, and finding something for her children to do. In her not too past life the activities included Jay, he always had an idea even if it was just to go to his moms. An ache hit her heart like a thunderbolt. It didn't last long because she heard Corey's laughter from the front of the house. Those boys and that game! It took them forever to awaken for school but the weekends and summer gave them life. She closed her eyes determined to get a few more minutes of sleep. They flew open when she heard the rumble of Xavier's voice. Damn! She had forgotten.

Any other time they were quiet as mice when they snuck to play the game early. Poor Xavier! She ran to the den and if she hadn't been in mom mode she would have laughed at the scene in front of her. Xavier, Ant, and Corey all sat on the sofa with baseball caps on, turned to the back. Xavier and Ant played, while Corey watched Zay's hand motions on the remote.

"Ant and Corey!" At least they looked guilty. "You both know that you are not supposed to play the game this early! And you awakened Mr. Xavier which is just bad manners."

The boys hung their heads, but Xavier's gaze stopped her short. A flush spread over her as his eyes swept over her body. She still had on the tee-shirt and very short shorts that she slept in. His gaze was openly lustful and as her body responded she turned and went back to her room. She heard Corey and Ant as they scrambled behind her, probably to make-up their beds.

When she reappeared in the den she had freshened up and changed into sweats and a shapeless tee shirt, but her body still burned with desire. Xavier remained on the sofa with his head back and eyes closed. She approached him cautiously. He opened his eyes as she stood between his legs, and once again looked her over.

"I guess I should make it home." He sighed and she heard disappointment in his voice.

"You don't want to stay for breakfast?"

She laughed as his eyes lit up and he agreed. She led him to her bathroom to brush his teeth and whatever else he needed to do. As he glanced around her bedroom she felt guilty. This had been the sanctuary for her and Jay.

Before she finished cooking, Jolisa came out of her room and she was startled to see her fully dressed and her hair was combed. As Jolisa smiled shyly at Xavier, Annette hid her smile. Another female infatuated with him. Annette had wondered if a penis was her birthmark, but there was no doubt if it was Jolisa. She obviously needed to have a talk with her daughter.

It always amazed her how quiet her house became when everyone ate. She nibbled at her food in the kitchen. She had been surprised at how well she slept considering, but her appetite hadn't returned. She jumped when she felt a hand on her hip.

"I'll clean the kitchen." Xavier's voice was low and his hand stayed dangerously low on her hip.

"You don't have to. The kids and I will get it." She smiled through her hot flash. Her heart was broken, but her body seemed to be fine.

"They can help me. It's the least I can do to thank you for such a delicious breakfast." He leaned down and kissed the top of her head.

She thought of numerous ways he could have thanked her and none of them had anything to do with the dishes. His hand disappeared as her children migrated to the kitchen.

As she moved to the other room, she heard the clatter of dishes and the murmur of their voices. The sounds comforted her but were also so disconcerting. Her children adapted too well. They should have mean mugged Xavier and begged for Jay to come back. Instead they seemed happy. To prove her point, Ant ran in the den, excitement written all over his face.

"Mom! Mr. Xavier told me to ask you if we can come to his house later today. Please Mom?" Ant's eyes were bright.

Ant was her shy, reserved child, who never got excited about anything. He was the reason their time with her parents had been cut slightly short. He wanted to come home. Now he hopped with happiness.

"Ant, I don't..."

"I'm putting some meat on the grill, Omar and Bianca are coming over too." Xavier smiled.

Corey barreled into her and told the whole story. "Please Mom? Mr. Xavier has a PlayStation 4 at his house."

Xavier's cough sounded suspiciously like laughter.

"Go clean your rooms and let me talk to Xavier." The boys ran out while Jolisa settled on the sofa. "You too Miss."

Finally! A taste of her usual attitude emerged. There was no doubt that she would be talked to. Annette saw the makings of another Andrea.

Once they cleared the room, she looked at Xavier. She knew what he tried to do and she appreciated it, but she wanted to stay home and mope. She also knew that her children would be so disappointed if she said no. With a huge sigh, she got the details and after he told them good-bye Zay left.

The day rushed ahead and before she knew it they were in route to Zay's house. To say she was surprised when Tonya came with Bianca and Omar would have been an understatement. The look on Tonya's face told her that something was wrong. As Tonya's boys joined hers in the backyard, they sat at the patio table.

"I left Fred." Tonya said simply.

"What!" Annette looked from her to Bianca. Bianca tried to cover her smirk, but couldn't.

"Girl that man was doing too much. Not only was he cheating, he has a baby with someone else!" Tears crowded Tonya's eyes.

Annette felt her friend's pain, she hugged her tightly. "Someone just had a baby by Fred? Oh my, that's terrible."

Tonya's eyes glittered, "Child please! The 'baby' is almost two years old! He had hidden the child from me all this time. And she's not the one he's cheating with now, it's a new woman."

Her words sunk in as each woman reflected. Annette knew that if Fred had pulled that deception off, Jay would have too. Maybe not because Elaine would have flaunted it in her face. She told Tonya about Jay and Elaine, and this time Tonya's tears fell.

"Oh no! So, he did have sex with her. What are you going to do Nette?"

She explained what he told her about being drugged and the DNA test. Bianca looked disinterested, while Tonya clucked and held her hand.

"I'm done. I can't deal with Elaine anymore and Jay refuses to clue me in on anything. But this time he outright lied! I'm tired of it. But enough of my sad story. What are you going to do?"

Tonya's eyes looked tired and were red rimmed. "Right now, we are staying with my mom until we find a place. He can have the house."

Bianca looked at her with dismay, "Why the hell should he keep the house? Girl you better keep your house."

"I can't afford it. I'm not looking for more stress." Tonya's voice shook.

"You have proof of what he did, make him pay for it. He can afford it. Fred had you living like y'all were struggling because he used his money elsewhere." Bianca sipped her juice.

Tonya looked as if she was thinking, but never answered. She moved back to Annette's business. "Are you going to start back seeing Xavier? I see the kids have taken to him."

"No, it's time to work on me. But you are right he is their hero." Annette looked around and saw Corey was in the yard with Tonya's sons, while Ant looked under the hood of the beat-up Mustang with Zay and Omar. Jolisa was in the house with Liberty, Omar's daughter.

Tonya laughed, "Damita was upset before, she will hate that she missed this!" She looked playfully at Annette, "You might want to skip the next girls' night."

Annette shared what she learned about the 'date,' Tonya was upset, but Bianca was annoyed.

"Why would she tell you that anyway? I understand if she is upset about you and Xavier for Jay's sake. She's mad because he's more into you than he was her, and that's not right." Bianca stood. "If she keeps this up, she won't be invited to my wedding."

Bianca walked in the house. Tonya looked around and then lowered her voice.

"I think you might need to get with Xavier. It seems as if since I left Fred I can see clearer. I'd never noticed how fine he is until today!"

Annette laughed and didn't know how honest she wanted to be. "He is fine, but I don't know. Look what happens every time I try love. I'm tired of making bad decisions."

Tonya nodded knowingly and they talked more about their failed relationships. Annette grabbed her third cooler, it was what she needed as a part of the broken dreams club. Bianca walked back out to the patio with another plate.

"I told Nette that it might not be a bad idea if she gets with Xavier." Tonya blurted out. Maybe she needed to put her wine cooler down.

Bianca raised one eyebrow while she chewed. Annette broke in before she could speak.

"I told Tonya I don't want to rush into anything, too many bad decisions. And not to mention every time I think of Jay I just feel empty." She took a swallow of her wine.

Bianca wiped her mouth, "Jay wasn't a wrong decision, I don't think that any of us thought that Elaine was that damn crazy. But she is a lot of baggage." She bit into her burger. "But Zay? Maybe he shows you a different side, but he has baggage too."

"He has an ex-wife too?" Tonya's eyes bulged out.

"Hell no! Nobody married his crazy ass. He's just…" Bianca stopped as she noticed the men and children as they approached.

"You are feeding my nephew again? That's going to be a big ass baby! Omar, you might need to get a bigger crib." Xavier laughed as he hugged Bianca.

She slapped his hands away, "If he or she is big then we will know that he takes after you."

Xavier laughed as Omar shook his head, then the boys wanted to go inside to the game. Corey chattered to Tonya's sons of how Xavier beat Ant multiple times. Tonya and Bianca gave Annette a look.

"Did I hear Corey correctly? When did this happen?" Bianca still munched on what was left in her plate.

"Last night. But you never told me about your brother." Annette tried to deflect the conversation.

"There is nothing to tell. He's weird, he and Zay are close friends, so go figure. Birds of a feather flock together." Bianca rolled her eyes.

"Wait a minute! He was at your house instead of out with Damita?" Tonya couldn't drink her wine cooler because she laughed so hard. "Uh-oh, that's the end of our foursome friendship. Bianca can you see the next time we get together?"

"Hold that thought." Annette left them in a fit of giggles. She went to the bathroom and ran into Zay in the hall.

"Are you okay?" He asked quietly.

"Yes! Why do you ask?" She giggled.

"I just noticed you were drinking." Concern lined his brow.

"Oh! No, I'm okay. They're just wine coolers." She breezed by him. As she almost fell in the toilet she knew that had been a slight exaggeration.

As she washed her hands she looked in the mirror, she looked a mess! Her top knot had fallen apart, her eyes looked bleary, and her complexion looked washed out. She giggled as she thought of Xavier's concern. He probably thought she was an undercover lush. It took a few minutes to wipe the smile off her face and straighten up, just in case he was still in the hallway. It was clear when she breezed out of the bathroom. Bianca and Tonya looked guilty when she got to the table.

"Back to what you were saying. Damita has no need to know that Zay was at my house. Unless one of you plan to tell her?" She looked at them defiantly.

Omar stepped out and motioned for Bianca to come inside. He whispered in her ear and she looked resigned. When she stepped back out, she looked curiously at Annette.

"I'll be right back. Omar wants me to go to the store with him." She sighed heavily.

Since Tonya and Annette were a bit tipsy, they barely noticed how long Bianca was gone or when she came back. When she showed up again it was to inform Tonya that it was time to leave. Jolisa ran to Annette.

"Mom can I go with Liberty? She said that she would do my hair." Jolisa had beautiful curly hair that she always complained about.

Before Annette shut her down Bianca said that it would be fine. Annette felt as if her world spiraled out of control. Her sons were content as they played a video game, they hadn't bothered her once; and her daughter was eager to leave her for the night. It seemed to be irrational for her to think that way, but she knew her children. She had to get back on track and out of this slump.

After they left she wandered back into the house, intent on going home to get her life in order. Xavier met her before she made it to the bedrooms and her boys.

"Thank you, Xavier, everything was great. But we need to get home." She fell into his eyes when she looked up.

"Corey is asleep, you guys can stay here tonight."
Xavier's tone was final.

Tonya's words came back to her, he was a fine glass of
water and she was thirsty! "No, thanks, but no. We need to
go home."

Xavier walked closer to her, "Annette you have been
drinking, I'm not going to let you drive. If you want me to
I'll drive you, but there's no way you are leaving here
driving."

She felt his heat, remembered his warmth and comfort.
If he kidnapped her right now, there would be no complaints.
Then she thought about her vow she made, and the numerous
hurts she had all in the name of love. No more.

"I just had wine coolers! I'm fine really." Just let me
sit down for a few minutes and I'll be okay." When she
flopped down on his sofa it felt good.

The next thing she knew she woke up, in a bed,
undressed and sunlight beat through the window. At least it
felt like it beat through when she opened her eyes, for a
second. Two things hit her olfactory at once: food and
Xavier's cologne. Since the food smell didn't agree with her
stomach she pulled the tee-shirt over her face and wallowed
in the scent of Xavier.

It seemed as if as soon as her eyelids closed, she felt
the bed dip. Not sure if it was the bed or her head she laid as
still as she could.

"Are you going to stay in bed all day?" Since Zay's
voice was loud anyway, in her condition, it was magnified.

She rolled over slowly. Embarrassment flooded her,
she knew she looked awful, and it was too painful to make
sudden moves.

Laughter filled his eyes. "Just wine coolers huh?"

Her eyes once again closed because her head was too
heavy to lift. A strong breeze blew over her as the comforter
and sheet were swept off her body.

"Come on get up, the boys have asked about you."

Ant and Corey! To add to her failures in her love life
she also added bad mother to the list. Consumed with self-

pity it was a few minutes before she realized that other than the tee-shirt, she only had on panties. With her pantyliner! Would her shame never end?

"I'm sorry Zay. I didn't mean to drop the kids on you. I'm getting up right now." She pulled the sheet over her lower extremities.

A strange look crossed his face as he moved her hair off her shoulders. "Don't worry about it. They're good kids and I enjoyed it." He paused as he traced her collarbone. "You've done an excellent job."

Hungover or not her body responded to his touch, which ended too soon. He abruptly stood and handed her a tumbler of a thick red liquid from the nightstand. "Drink this, it will make you feel better."

After she took it from him, he walked out. The drink whatever it was tasted gross, but she held her nose and gulped it down. Once it settled she timidly sat on the edge of the bed. Her purse sat on the chair, she reached for it and extracted her phone.

Jay had called her six times! As everything came back to her she grimaced. He was no longer Jay to her, he was Elaine's baby daddy.

She jammed her phone back in her purse and wobbled to the bathroom. When she exited she felt a little better, Bianca had left her a sundress and some new panties. As she walked down the hallway, the boys played the game, and she heard Xavier talking. She figured he was on the phone but when she wandered to the kitchen, Damita stared at her from the table!

Chapter 12

Jay ran off adrenaline. He was upset, no he was pissed off! More pissed off than he had been in a long time. After Annette left, he moped around with Carl and then he decided there was no way it was over between he and Annette. She needed to know that even if he had to take the abortion doctor to Elaine, he would. There was no way he would have another child with Elaine. When he told Carl what he wanted to do, Carl nixed the idea.

"No, you need a realistic plan. Wait until Elaine has calmed down some and appeal to her logical side."

"What logical side? You think that she will stop being bitter?" Jay remembered Carl's advice to not tell Annette that he had sex with Elaine.

"No, but once she realizes that pregnant or not you are not coming back to her, she might acquire logic." Carl looked at Jay over his beer bottle.

He had a point, this whole pregnancy ploy was meant to get him away from Annette, as if that would make him come back home.

"What do I do about Annette while I wait for Elaine's logical side to appear?" Jay glanced at Carl.

His friend swiped his face with his hand, "Beg. That's all you can do. But you don't need to wait. You should go over tonight, beg, and give her some good loving."

Jay thought about how angry and hurt Annette had been, her words seemed so final. Carl was right! He needed to turn this around quick. He and Carl discussed a plan of action before they walked out to the parking deck together.

"Call me in the morning and let me know how it worked out." They bumped fists and left.

Jay rehearsed what he would say and how he could convince his way into her bedroom. He knew all her hot spots and at least Annette would listen to him. He was ready to beg! When he pulled up he received the shock of his life!

Xavier's car was there! Not just there, but this dude parked in the driveway like he belonged there. He was so filled with disappointment and anger it flowed out of his pores. He swerved off, his anger so great he was even mad at Annette.

How could she say she loved him when she called another man over there before her tears dried? He thought of any signs he might have missed between the two of them. His anger led him to Carl's place. He sat in his car and realized that he knew Annette well enough, that she would not have done that. If nothing else he realized how much she worried about what others thought.

Bianca or Omar must have told Xavier what happened! Confident that's what happened he slowly exited his car and trudged to Carl's door.

"Damn that was quick! What happened? Carl opened the door wider while he talked.

Jay told him and Carl bit the nail of his index finger. Jay knew that meant he was deep in his thoughts.

"I hate to make your bad day worse, but you have some serious trouble on your hands. That fella ain't playing. The worst thing is that he's always there when she needs a shoulder to cry on."

Jay nodded, "I know and it's messed up. But you can tell he can't be good for her. Because if he had a decent bone in his body, he would have felt guilty and left her alone. It doesn't help that I keep giving him ammunition to work with, shit!"

"True that." Carl still bit at his nail.

Jay was frustrated, angry and hurt. The more he thought about it the angrier he became. The only solace he found was that the children were there. He knew Annette well enough to know that if he hadn't been able to spend the night, that jerk couldn't.

"Man, I've got to do something! I can't just sit here with my hands in my pockets while this dude acts like she is his woman. I need some ideas on what to do to get her back." Jay paced the floor.

Carl's eyes lit up. "That's it! You are thinking about this all wrong."

Jay was incredulous, "I'm wrong to want to get Annette back? What the hell are you talking about?"

"No, you want to get her back, but sometimes you have to fight fire with fire. We need some dirt to spread on his ass. As crazy as that guy looks there has to be something he's hiding."

"It would be great if it was a wife and three or four kids." Jay muttered. Carl tried to help but Jay had to let him know that he missed the mark.

"We don't know shit about this guy other than he is Omar's brother. It's not as if Omar will give us some dirt. We have no way to find out anything."

"If Omar didn't have Bianca hemmed up, I could throw my charm her way and get some info through pillow talk." Carl mused almost to himself.

"Man, we need a realistic way, not your daydreams." Jay felt disgusted.

"I know! Damita! Hell, she spent enough time with the guy to know something." Carl jumped up.

The wheels in Jay's head turned, and he nodded as he warmed up to the idea. "You might be on to something bro. No matter how small it is we will have to dig. Are you up for it?"

"I don't have shit else to do. Jay, we didn't get as far as we have by being dumb. We can beat this asshole at his own game."

"Hell yeah." They high-fived and Jay felt better than he had in days.

Two days later he was still at ground zero. His life had turned into a damn reality show. Every day he faced drama. Xavier's car was still at Annette's Saturday morning, and the dealership in California was ready to do business, which meant that he had to meet with Omar and Xavier. If that wasn't enough on Sunday he sat at his mother's kitchen table while she berated him.

"I know I wanted more grandchildren, but not from that heifer! How the hell did this shit happen?" René stood with her hands on her hips.

Jay's mom rarely cursed, so when she did they all knew that she wasn't just mad, she wanted to kick someone's ass.

He told her as much as he could without giving dirty details. René had called him early and told him in no uncertain terms that she needed to see him. He knew from her tone that it was bad. Once the DNA had been determined he planned to tell her, but Elaine beat him to it.

"Wait you mean to tell me that you don't remember having sex with her, but you continued to go over there? Without Annette?" Jay swore he saw steam come off the top of his mother's head.

He nodded, "I didn't want Annette to have to deal with Elaine's insults."

"Annette is a grown ass woman! She's been dealing with her! What does she have to say about this mess?" René finally sat down, which made her voice surround sound. "You did tell her, didn't you?"

He told her how that went down and cringed as the decibels of her voice increased.

"Someone else told her that Elaine was pregnant? Jay what the hell were you thinking?"

"I was going to tell her! Bianca got to her first. I tried to explain to her that I don't think the baby is mine." He looked at her for understanding.

"Who else is going to screw that trifling woman? She knows that she has you under her thumb, so why would she chance it?" The look in his mom's eyes was the same one she got before she whipped his tail as a kid.

She nodded absently, "So Annette is done, which I don't blame her. I told you that you were going to lose her behind Elaine's crazy antics." She softened her tone slightly. "Jay, you should have had Annette with you from the beginning of this mess. Then Elaine would have seen that she didn't have a chance."

"Yeah, I know that now." He hung his head and scratched it. "Hopefully I can get her back."

"With a baby on the way? You can't possibly expect Nette to help you take care of baby conceived while you were with her!" René stood and grabbed her purse. "Let me know how that works out for you."

She walked out the house and Jay just sat there. The sausage and toast on the stove called his name and as soon as he filled his plate he heard the door open. He waited for his mom to take his plate and put him out, she was just that mad. His body sagged with relief when Damita walked in.

"Well hey! What are you doing here?" Damita looked surprised and upset.

"I was summoned by your mother." He recounted his sorry tale once more when Damita looked at him in confusion.

She grabbed a sausage off his plate. "Elaine is pregnant? Please tell me that it is not your baby."

Once again, he gave the reasons he believed and hoped it wasn't, but this time it was to someone who listened.

"Does Annette know?" There was a strange look on his sister's face.

"Yes, thanks to Bianca." He had forgotten that portion of the story. Damita stopped eating out of his plate when he told her about the doctor's visit and Annette's visit.

"Now it makes sense." Damita murmured as she shook her head.

"What? That Annette is through with me? We were working things out and then…"

"No! Xavier! Now it all makes sense." He pushed her hand back when she reached back in his plate.

"That dude." Jay shook his head. Damita nodded emphatically as he told her about Xavier being at Annette's.

"That's what I'm telling you! He canceled our date Friday night and she's at his house right now! Now I understand why!" Damita stood and walked to the oven. She hurried back when he choked on his toast.

"What do you mean she's at his house?' Jay croaked once his coughing subsided.

Damita sat back down with her plate and gave him an intense stare. "I went over to his house this morning, because he canceled on me Friday, and I didn't hear from him at all Saturday. I decided to see what was his problem." She looked defiantly at Jay.

Jay thought that was a bit foolish, but he didn't say anything.

She continued, "He told me that something had come up and he had been busy. Next thing I know Annette is coming from the back looking as if she just woke up." Damita's nose turned up at the memory.

"What did she say?" Jay wanted to ask if she was dressed, but he knew that Damita needed few prompts.

"Well, she started to say something, but Xavier cut her off and told me to leave." Damita's face showed embarrassment and shame.

"That doesn't sound right. It sounds a bit controlling to me." Jay wondered what Annette had gotten herself into with that guy.

His alarm must have shown on his face because Damita shook her head. "No, she was not kidnapped and being kept a prisoner. I might have been a flip at the mouth." The last part was mumbled into her toast.

"Dammit! What did you say? Tell me exactly how it went." Jay knew that his sister's tongue could be sharper than any knife.

"I just said something like she couldn't stay away and I asked if you weren't giving her enough or something like that. But I didn't know about your predicament!" Damita's eyes had widen. "Then she said something like it wasn't like it seemed, but Xavier cut her off and told me to leave. So, I left."

They sat in silence for a few minutes. Then Jay thought of something. "You didn't see her car?"

"Nope. It either wasn't there or it was in the garage." Damita's face lit up. "But I don't think anything went on because I did hear the children before I left. It sounded as if they were playing in the back of the house."

This man had stolen his dream and his family! Jay felt his anger rise once again. It was time to get some information from his sister.

"Damita, I'm not trying to get in your business," He decided to use his mother's tactic, "But have you had sex with this guy?"

"What the hell? If that is not getting in my business, I don't know what is." She sat back and crossed her arms.

"Listen, I need to know as much as I can about this guy." Jay leaned forward.

"So, you need to know about his skills in the bedroom? Where are you going with this?" Damita sounded indignant.

"No, but I need anything I can use against him. I'm not going to let this dude just waltz in and take Annette because he wants to sample every woman he can. If he's going around sexing all her friends, she needs to know about it."

Damita looked at him sorrowfully, "Bro, you will have to find another way, because no I have never had sex with him." She clamped down on her sausage, "That was the plan for this weekend."

Jay grimaced, "I still need your help with this. I need to know everything you know about him. I'm not giving Annette up without a fight. And even if we don't get back together, I'll do everything I can to make sure she is not with that jerk."

Damita looked stunned, but they put their heads together while he drilled her for information.

The rest of the day was a blur for Jay. He moped, sulked, the rest of the morning. That evening he did better, he worked out until his muscles ached, each uppercut on his punching bag was Xavier's face. He knew he had to be calm to meet with the brothers on Monday about the business deal. This was one deal he needed, because now his thirst was for power. He needed to be as powerful as possible, in case he needed to run Xavier out of town.

He prepared carefully Monday morning. He text both men after he talked to Damita and suggested the meeting. Both had responded that they would be there. When Jay pulled up to his office, he took a deep breath and reminded himself to focus on the business at hand. Once he felt semi-calm, he walked in.

Omar as usual was already there and they made small talk as they waited on Xavier. When he hurried in Jay took a good look at him. Xavier was a big guy, well over six feet, muscular and his neck was huge. Jay looked at his neck because he wanted to strangle the bastard. But it was his eyes that made dealing with him difficult. They showed no emotion or life. Hell no, this guy was not going to take his woman.

Jay ignored the fact that Xavier didn't speak when he came in, he just sat there and looked at him. Jay walked to the whiteboard and explained what the dealership wanted and needed. He drafted a flowchart on the board as he spoke. Once he finished he turned and looked at the brothers.

"This is how it can work if you let me license your program to them." He looked at Xavier because he realized that he held most the patent. And because they had differences.

Omar spoke first, "It sounds good to me."

Xavier's eyes were cold and hard. He stood and went to the board, wrote some specifications along with other technicalities. This guy was so good with programs that Jay almost forgot he hated him as he watched him work.

"I think it can work." He finally stated as he sat back down.

Jay scooted his chair up to the desk, and noticed in his peripheral vision that Omar stepped closer.

"Okay I'll draw up the paperwork, but before I do there are some things we need to clear up." He glared into his nemesis' eyes, which hadn't flickered or even blinked it seemed.

"I'm not trying to start anything or offend anyone, but let's be real here. I need to know how much of this work can you do offsite. Because as much as I can deal with the business side, I might have a tough time seeing you here every day. Especially since you are still fucking Annette." Jay wanted to hear him deny it.

Xavier's expression never changed. "The program is good to go. But if any modifications are needed, I will have to come in and upload them to your server. I don't have a problem with that. If you pay as agreed, we're good."

Jay nodded, and knew he should have just left it at that. But something had bothered him for a while and he needed to know the truth. "I just need to know one other thing. Is Annette the reason you couldn't find anything on Elaine?"

Xavier looked at him blankly. "Nah man, I never mix business with my pleasure." He gave Jay an ugly grin.

It took all his willpower not to knock that grin off his face. Jay thought about how much this deal would help him along with the promise of future deals expanding to Las Vegas. Before he could rise, Xavier stood, his expression blank.

"If that's all you need, let me get out of here." He walked over to Omar, gave him a half hug, nodded his head at Jay and left.

Jay slumped in his chair. Omar sat on the edge of the desk and looked at him. "Man, I'm sorry things went down like they did. I understand if you are upset with me by association, but I want to let you know that I don't have any issues with you."

Jay looked at Omar, saw reflections of Xavier in his face, but realized that he didn't have anything to do with it.

He sighed, "Omar I don't hold you responsible for any of this. Hell, I created most of this mess. But your brother is a prick."

Omar looked shocked, then he laughed. "Yeah, he can be, but I wouldn't trade him for the world."

Jay stood, "Well, I would." He walked out.

Chapter 13

While most people were excited about the weekend, Annette was nervous. She built up enough nerve to do something that scared her to death. The past three weeks had been good, Jay still called and sent text, but he brought pain. Each time she heard his voice she pictured a newborn baby, and Elaine at his side. Not to mention that nasty picture, now that she knew what she had suspected was true.

She cried as she boxed up all their pictures and put them on her closet shelf. It was necessary because of the memories that came every time she looked at them, but her heart was heavy when she sealed the box. It was as if that chapter of her life was closed.

She had gotten back on track with her self-awareness plan, and she learned so much about herself. It was evident that she took people at face value too much, and she tried to make everyone happy. Which led to her to feel lost in the process. These were things she worked on daily.

When Jay asked to see her, she heard the pain in his voice and it hurt when she told him no. She knew she was not ready and that if faced with his pain in person she would have caved in to his desires. It was the right choice due to the pain of being lied to and how they lost what they had together still angered her. The attitude he adopted lately hadn't helped either. He accused her of being with Xavier, and when she told him that she wasn't she knew he didn't believe her. She forced herself not to care. How the hell could he question her, when he had a pregnant ex-wife!

It also pissed her off because she was no longer intimate with Xavier. He had gotten real comfortable with the friend role. They saw each other on a regular basis, he came over and played the game with the boys, and ate. He wasn't a freeloader eater, he brought groceries, cut her grass, and her children adored him. When they weren't with Anthony, they wanted to go to Zay's house.

Ant Jr. was excited because he helped Omar and Zay work on the Mustang, Corey was happy to explore the expanse of his backyard, and Jolisa… she finally had a talk with her, Bianca had given her guidance. Annette had gotten so sick of seeing Jolisa moon over Xavier, that she told Bianca about it. Each time she thought of that conversation she smiled.

She called Bianca and told her about the problem. Bianca laughed and said she had the same problem with Marisa.

"Marisa had a crush on Omar?" Annette hoped her friend meant when Marisa was younger.

"No! She had a crush on Zay. He spent a lot of time at Grand mere's house, since he and Horatio are good friends. Marisa knew she was in love and ready to get married at the age of eight." Bianca chuckled.

"Wow! So, he's been doing this for a while." Annette laughed.

"Yes! I just explained to her that Xavier was a grown man, and that he looked at her as a child. And that I would whip her ass if she didn't stop. She got over it."

Annette sat Jolisa down shortly after that conversation and told her a similar version. Jolisa surprised her.

"I know that Momma! But he is cute for an old guy, I hope when I grow up I meet someone like him." She looked wistful.

As she twirled her hair, she thought about Xavier's reaction when she told him. He had never noticed! It wasn't surprising though, he was so obtuse, and there was a lot he never noticed. Like that she was tired of being his platonic friend.

If he kissed her forehead or the top of her head one more time she would scream. He hadn't noticed her subtle nor her not so subtle hints that she wanted him. When she wore her revealing or sexy clothes, he looked but never tried anything. She assumed he had fallen in love with her sofa, because he managed to sleep on it twice a week if not more.

The only sign that he might still be interested was the Monday after she got drunk at his house two bouquets of amaryllises were delivered to her job. With a white gardenia in the middle. She went to the restroom and cried.

As she thought of that weekend, her emotions warred between morose and anger when she thought about Damita. It would be a lie if she said she didn't miss her friendship, but she also realized that their friendship hinged on her relationship with Jay. Annette also realized that Damita liked Xavier more than she admitted.

When she walked in and saw Damita she noticed the hurt, before Damita covered it with anger. She tried to explain, but Damita was intent on letting her have it. She accused Annette of cheating on Jay and damn near called her a nympho. Before she set her straight, Xavier with fire in his eyes told her to stop and told Damita to get out. That exactly how he said it! Damita looked surprised, but obviously noticed his glare and ran out the door without looking back.

She made up her mind that it was time to set him straight. Their friendship hadn't lessened her feelings for him, it had heightened it. The time they spent together without intimacy allowed her to see the 'real Xavier.' Hopefully it allowed him to see the same thing and hadn't turned him off. Before indecision stopped her, she called him.

"Do you want some company?" She got right to the point after they greeted each other.

"Not really, but you can come over." That was not the answer she expected or wanted.

The fool that she knew she was, overrode her common sense, which told her he was probably in one of his moods. She ignored the thought and went anyway.

Xavier was on the phone when she got there. He sat down in the den, so she followed suit and sat on the sofa. She tried not to eavesdrop, but since he talked loud, and they were in the same room, it couldn't have been helped.

"Yes, I told him. I've told him every time you asked me to." Zay released a huge sigh.

Annette watched his face as the person on the other end spoke, and he seemed frustrated.

"I don't know why he hasn't called you. Yes, he is doing fine. Hmm-mmm, she is too." Xavier looked away from her, as she tried to conceal her nosiness and failed.

He was quiet for a few minutes and then he stood. "I'm not going through this with you right now. I'll tell him again and the money will be in your account tomorrow. Tell Papá I said hello."

He hung up, sat there and brooded. As he looked at the television he twirled his cell phone in his hand. Annette waited a few minutes, then walked behind him. She never said a word as she began kneading his shoulders and neck. It became a hard massage because his shoulders were so tense. It wasn't until his head lolled back a little and he grunted that she dared to speak.

"Are you okay?" Her lips were right next to his ear. He smelled so good.

Her hands were tired, but he felt so good under her fingers and palm, she continued. It took him a few minutes before he spoke.

"That was my mother. I wonder why I answer the phone sometimes." He leaned forward and sighed.

His momentum carried her forward and she bumped her breasts against the back of the chair.

"Ouch!" She yelped.

"Oops! I'm sorry, are you alright?" He glanced back at her.

She was tempted to ask him to kiss it and make it feel better, but something in his eyes stopped her.

"Yes, I'm fine." She pulled him back slightly and moved her hands down his back. "Is she upset that you haven't visited?"

He gave a strangled laugh. "No, my mother calls me to ask me why Omar won't call her. Then she accuses me of not telling him that she wants to hear from him."

His voice held the undercurrents of pain and it struck her deep in the chest. She laid her hands on his shoulders.

"You shouldn't have to tell Omar to call her. And why doesn't he call?"

"Omar has been done with them for years. The last time he attempted to see them after she told him they were sober, he went and they were drunk. He hasn't been back, he doesn't call, nothing. But it's my fault." Xavier spat out the last word.

He continued, "If she's drunk she tells me that I stole her baby and turned him against her. Usually after she's asked for money."

His anger rumbled beneath her hands, then she realized that his anger was laced with hurt. A deep-seated hurt. She softly kneaded his shoulders again while she listened.

"She never once thinks about if I hadn't gotten him out of that hell-hole, he would have been killed or in prison. I know he would have! I did what I thought was best." Another sigh escaped him.

Without thinking she kissed the back of his neck and when he half-way turned she kissed the corner of his mouth.

"Just because she doesn't appreciate you doesn't mean you are not appreciable. You did the right thing, and that is one of the reasons Omar loves you so much." This time she sighed. "Your mom blames you so that she doesn't have to look at her failures." She barely managed to keep the anger she felt out of her voice.

Annette walked in front of him and sat on his thigh. She wrapped her arm around his neck and whispered in his ear, "You are a great person and a wonderful man. Don't ever let anyone tell you different." She paused. "Not even your momma."

He looked at her with an indecipherable expression, "Annette…"

She cut him off with a kiss. Her heart sang when he kissed her back, hard. Her hands roamed over his chest and she heard violins play as his hands traveled slowly over her body. She remembered the purpose of her visit so she reluctantly pulled away.

As his hands rubbed her thigh, he sucked her bottom lip while the desire in his eyes swept her away. Suddenly what she wanted to say could wait. The tremor of her heart stopped that thought and she pulled away, again.

"Xavier, I wanted to talk to you." She gasped because his hand had made its way under her shirt to her neglected breasts.

She stopped him by holding his hand. There were waves of heat coming off him which made her dizzy.

"Zay, I want us to take our relationship to the next level." She blurted out.

The next few minutes went by in slow motion. Xavier's hand moved from under her shirt to wipe his face, and he barely looked at her.

"Uhh, Annette, I was thinking just the opposite." She felt his breath on her cheek.

Chapter 14

She heard the tinkle of her heart as it broke and drowned out his words. When she focused, and heard him mention her children, she stopped him. "Wait a minute, what did you say?" She blinked rapidly to stop the onslaught of tears she felt.

"We have to think of your children. I've gotten attached and they are attached to me. What if you go back to Jay? I don't want to put them through that confusion. I'd rather stay in their lives like I am now." He looked down.

Annette stood and ignored how his eyes roved over her body. "I just told you that I want us to go to another level, and you think that means I'm going back to Jay? This doesn't make any sense."

"I was talking about your children. Okay, say that you don't go back to Jay, but we don't work out. Then you won't let me a part of their lives. I just don't want to do that." His gaze held her.

She stepped closer, because something in his eyes didn't match his words. "I wouldn't do that. What is this really about? If you have changed your mind, just say that, don't use my children as an excuse."

Her voice had risen and trembled, but it was from a mixture of hurt and anger.

Xavier looked down and when he looked back up, the emotion in his eyes shone through. "Annette, I can't treat you the way you are accustomed to being treated. I'm not that man."

His words hit her like bolt of lightning. This was not the first time he expressed not being enough for her. Her anger melted with each step she took back into his space. She sat gingerly on his thigh again and looked at him.

"How I am used to being treated? Does that mean you won't cheat on me from day one or shut me out of the important part of your life and impregnate your ex?" She inquired.

His eyes widened as he chuckled. "I hadn't thought about that."

Annette straddled him and kissed each corner of his mouth. "Zay, stop telling me what you can't give me and just give me the man you are. That's what I want."

He kissed her hungrily before she finished. The fire that encapsulated her became a need instead of a want. She wrapped her arms around his neck and captured the vibrations of his moan.

He stopped suddenly, "Wait. Your car is not in the garage."

One day she would get to the bottom of his obsession of her car parked in the garage, but there wasn't time for that reflection. Instead she flew out the door and moved her car. When she returned Xavier was in the bedroom. She walked timidly to the bedroom and had an immediate relapse. Xavier was her drug of choice and it had been too long since she indulged.

He sat in the bed, his back against the headboard in his boxers, while her habit stood at attention and beckoned her closer. It actually jumped! Annette dropped her clothes, but remembered to place them in the chair, another obsession of his and straddled his body.

As much as she wanted to jump him, there was something she had to know. Once she got in the bed she kissed him gently before she asked.

"Zay?" The question almost seemed unimportant as he rubbed the palms of his hands against her nipples.

"Hmm?" He scooted up and gathered her hair in his hands.

"Did you have sex with Damita?" Maybe it was simple curiosity, or that friend code, but she had to know.

"No, I was, but I didn't." Once again, she understood why he was single. Then she thought of the lies that she had been fed lately and somewhat appreciated his openness.

"What stopped you?" She gasped as his lips wrapped around her breast.

She sighed in disappointment when he stopped and gazed at her. He pulled her head back slightly with her hair and licked sensuously up her neck to her ear.

"You stopped me."

He sucked her earlobe as his words caused the precipitation of her mind and body to rain down to her love. She pushed him back and worked her kisses down his body. His eyes burned a hole in her soul as she licked his hardness lovingly, before she stroked him with her mouth. He pulled at her hair while he called her name.

"Annette, come here." His voice was gargled but commanding.

As she sidled up his body she noticed his hand as it moved to the nightstand.

"No." She grabbed his arm. He looked at her curiously. "It's just you and me."

With his eyebrows raised, he flicked her hair back. "Are you sure?"

She nodded mutely. Xavier slid from under her and positioned himself behind her and entered her slowly. The relief her body felt was soon replaced with a fire that only he could quench. With each long, slow stroke, her arms gave out and held the pillow as she cried tears of pure joy. They moved in sync as he jerked and jiggled against her walls, before he went deep and reached up to roll her nipple between his fingers. Annette saw stars as her body clenched him so tightly, her legs slammed together. Zay let out a roar as he released his seed with a ferocity that she felt as it vibrated to her heart.

As she slumped forward, he held her body in place, his hardness still tremored inside. Before he released her, he leaned forward and kissed the middle of her back. She cuddled next to him with her head on his chest when he finally laid down beside her.

If things had shifted before they surely were different know. Her heart felt coated with his essence and she never wanted it to come off. Xavier absently played in her hair as he liked to do, and she felt his words through his chest before she heard them.

"Did you mean what you said? Or did you just want it raw?"

His lack of subtlety and tact was part of his charm, a minute part.

"Did you really just ask me that?" She chuckled.

She felt him shrug. "Yes. Did you…"

"Don't say it again." She moved her head and opened her eyes to look at him. A vulnerability was reflected on his face. "Yes, Zay. I meant every word. I want to be with you. And I wanted it raw. Did you mean what you said?"

He looked confused. "What did I say?"

"That I stopped you." She molded her body into his.

"Yes, she had hinted around to it earlier, but I stayed at your house." He said plainly.

This guy! She sighed deeply and laughed. Good thing she hadn't dug deeper before.

Then he continued, "But I doubt if I would have gotten with her anyway. At first, she acted as if she had to wait until she had a marriage proposal, this time it was as if she was pushing for it. I thought you and she had set a trap for me."

"I know you didn't think I wanted to share you with her." It slipped out before she caught herself.

She felt a pinch on her butt as he laughed. Her fingers weaved through the hair on his chest. "I do want to know something."

Xavier took a deep breath. She ignored him because she knew how he hated to open about himself.

"I'm not naïve enough to think that you were just sitting in Texas by yourself. Is there anyone I need to know about?" She held her breath as she waited for his answer. She knew her insecurity was borne from what she dealt with Jay. But she needed to know, she had enough surprises in the past few months to last a lifetime.

"If you are talking about a relationship, the answer is no. But I wasn't a monk. There were women that I hooked up with on occasion. But they understood that's all it was." He ran his fingertip down her spine.

"How do you know that they don't have feelings for you?" With the feelings he had unlocked in her she couldn't fathom just 'hooking up.'

He shifted and sighed heavily again. "There wasn't anything to get feelings from." When she looked at him inquiringly, he sighed again. "We just fucked. There was no deep conversation or quality time."

"Oh. Okay." Her feelings were mixed about that answer. She still wasn't used to his bluntness, but it sure beat the evasiveness that she had become accustomed to.

He lifted her chin, "Listen, there hasn't been anyone that meant anything to me in long time. You don't have to worry about that."

Before she processed what he meant he kissed her slowly, then worked his magic down her body. When he got to her core of her heat he ran his tongue slowly around her pelvis, then he looked at her.

"I want to taste us." She almost came from his words.

When his tongue swept across her lips, her back arched reflexively before he delved inside and pressed the tip of his tongue against her spot. Her hips lifted as her thighs trapped his head and the rest of her body shook. When she settled somewhat he repeated it and she grabbed his shoulders as her body tremored uncontrollably.

She couldn't move, her legs were jelly and her mind disassociated from her body. Zay hefted his body next to hers and gathered her in his arms. Where she promptly went to sleep, or passed out.

She awakened cold. Xavier kept his home freezing, and sometime while she slept, she had kicked the covers off. As she moved closer to him she thought about the cliff she had jumped off. Her original plan had been to ask him if they could work on becoming a couple. In other words, he was partly right, it wasn't that she just wanted unprotected sex, but she wanted him. In the worse way.

But once she arrived everything changed. She always seemed inherently pulled into his essence. It was as if he had a translucent web that captured her and when he wasn't around she felt naked and exposed. As she thought back it was always something that pulled her into the computer room when he was there. When Omar worked by himself she bypassed the room and went straight to Jay's office. She pushed that thought away. If that was true then she had been attracted to him while she was with Jay. She wasn't ready to face that possibility, not yet.

Instead she faced the truth of wanting to be with him, that was a fact. As she dealt with her true inner feelings the past few weeks, she knew that she never wanted to let him go. If she had stayed with Jay, a part of her would have always wanted Xavier. Her eyes roamed the length of his body and she knew what part of her it was. She might have recovered from the emotional attachment, but her body would have still craved him.

But she wasn't sure that she was ready for what being with him entailed. Ashley would have to be told along with Andrea and Damita. Her calls and texts to Damita had been unanswered and never returned. And of course, Jay would find out, but at this point she wasn't worried about him. With his lies and a baby on the way, she was finished.

Tired of her thoughts she closed her eyes and begged sleep to return. Instead she thought about his conversation with his mother. It had been evident he was hurt by the treatment he received from his mother. It also made Annette understand him better. His body was perfect, he kept his home, cars, and land perfect, but he was broken on the inside. She felt closer to his emotions than her own, and it scared her.

Xavier shifted, "Why are you awake?"

She jumped. "Sorry, I tried not to wake you, but I was cold." She had barely moved a muscle!

Zay grunted and disentangled himself to go to the bathroom. Annette shivered because his body took the warmth of the room away. When he returned, she snuggled next to him and felt her body relax.

"I have a question." She placed her hand over his heart.

His arm went up and she knew he pinched his nose, a sign that he was aggravated.

"Are your parents coming to the wedding?" Bianca and Omar's wedding was two weeks away.

"They probably don't know he's getting married. I wouldn't want them here either, since they are drinking again." She heard the timbre of disappointment in his tone.

"How is your mom when she's sober?" She hoped that his mom was only hurtful when she drank.

"Umm about the same. She always asks why I took Omar away." He voice was hollow.

He flattened her hair with his hand before he continued. "I guess she forgets that they agreed for me to take him and how she called constantly complaining about him. When he started cursing them out and running wild."

"Omar?" Annette was shocked.

He laughed, "Yes, Omar. He was angry and thought I wasn't coming back for him. But I got him."

He sounded angry when he spoke again. "I just don't understand why she blames me. It's not as if I wanted that responsibility at eighteen. Shit, we struggled and had I been by myself I probably wouldn't have had to do some things I did to survive."

She looked at him endearingly, "I'm glad you did. For Bianca's sake." When he gazed at her blankly she added softly, "And for me too."

"Bianca! That was the worst part, staying in Louisiana. I hated that place. The weather, the swamps, the bugs, the damn Cajun people, just everything!"

"Why did you stay?" She massaged his torso as he spoke.

113

"Because Omar wanted to go to college there. He could have gone anywhere, but he loved Louisiana."

She thought of all the things he told her about his life, everything he did seemed to be for others. Or at least Omar. "When have you ever done anything because it was what you wanted?"

"When I got with you." Everything stopped, her hand, her mind, and her heart.

She kissed the side of his neck and snuggled closer, if that was possible, to him. "I'm glad you did."

"Me too."

They fell into a comfortable silence and she felt relaxed and safe as her eyelids grew heavy.

"Why did you think I would use the kids as an excuse?" The rumble of his voice pushed sleep away.

"Do you want the truth?" She placed her hand on his stomach.

"I always want the truth Annette." He softened his tone.

"I thought that since you got to see the real me, you realized I wasn't what you wanted." It scared her to express her reality.

There was a complete silence that ticked on for minutes. "No, I like the real you better than I imagined how you were." He absently tweaked her breast as he spoke. "I thought you were a gentle spirit, which you are, but you have some fire to you too. I like that."

"I couldn't tell, because if you had kissed me one more time on my head I would have screamed." She giggled.

"Do you mean like this?" He kissed the top of her head.

She scrambled out of his arms and jumped on top of him and held his arms. "No more kisses on my head." She growled as she leaned over him.

She kissed him slowly and once again allowed that phantom web to enchant her soul. She moved down and ran her tongue across his shoulders. When she reached his Adams apple, she knew that was one of his spots, when his breathing became ragged. She sucked the sunk in area beneath it gently and felt his hands run across her body as he pushed her towards his manhood.

He was hard as a rock! She positioned herself over him and when his hands closed over her hips she pushed them back.

"Close your eyes Zay, I just want you to feel me."

He gave her a long hard look but closed his eyes. She slid slowly down his hardness and watched him. As she moved and shifted her tempo, she never stopped watching his face. She rocked against him and he bucked his pelvis to ground into her. She felt him as he pushed opened the crevice of her soul. When he entered, her soul released an inferno of her love, and she felt him stiffened first before he trembled uncontrollably.

"Ahh, Annette." He moaned softly.

The soft purr of her name from his lips triggered her release as her stomach clenched and she milked every drop of his love.

She laid on top of him as he embraced her tightly, she whispered in his ear, "I want to taste us."

Chapter 15

Omar and Bianca had a productive day. They secured the land they wanted to build their house on, it was less than a mile from Xavier. Xavier lived in a secluded area, that if you weren't looking for it you would never know his house was on the street. It was the only house on it. The previous occupants had been farmers Omar believed and the real estate agents had parceled the land off separately.

Once they finished with the preliminary paperwork, Bianca seemed more excited and wanted to secure a contractor. They spoke to a few and after dinner and fantastic lovemaking, he felt it was the perfect time drop some changes on her.

"Bibi? Can you contact the event planner and have her add a place to the family table?" He turned and waited for her reaction.

"This late? Ome, the wedding is a week away!" She sat up. "Wait, are your parents coming?"

Omar frowned, "Hell no!" Bianca had tried unsuccessfully to get him to invite them. Hell would produce ice water before that happened.

"Who is it then?" She narrowed her eyes.

"It's not anyone new, we just need to add Annette to the family table." He studiously became interested in the television.

"Annette? She's sitting at the table behind... Oh no! What are you saying? Just spit it out." Bianca grabbed the remote and turned the television off.

"Well she's coming with Xavier and he is at the family table." He tried to keep a straight face and failed. "Obviously, they are a couple now."

Bianca jumped out of the bed. "But we have invited Jay and Damita. Damn, this is going to be a mess. It's bad enough that I have to worry about Uncle Luis and Uncle Geoff killing each other, now this!"

Bianca's two uncles had fallen out years ago, reasons unknown, and had not been in the same place at the same time since her father's funeral over twenty years ago. Her Uncle Luis, who was her great-uncle, told her no matter what he would not miss her wedding. Uncle Geoff, who loved Bianca like a daughter promised to behave.

"Bibi, it won't be that bad. Jay has been convinced for some time that Zay and Annette are a couple, and maybe you can tell Damita ahead of time."

She glared at him, then became thoughtful. "Okay I'll do that. And I can put Zay and Annette between my two uncles. Maybe let Uncle Luis sit beside Annette, and Geoff beside your brother."

Omar nodded, "That should work. Zay and Geoff have always gotten along well."

Omar was glad that she hadn't blown a fuse, but it also made him curious.

"You are okay with Zay and Annette now?"

She climbed back in bed and stared into space. "I guess. I was so done with Jay after learning that Elaine is pregnant. He and Annette were so in love though, I hate they are not together. But I must admit, after seeing Zay with her children and how he looks at her, I don't know. He might be serious this time."

Omar smiled heartily, "I think he is. He was so happy when she told him that she wanted a relationship with him."

She looked at him skeptically, "He was so happy? How could you tell? Did he jump up and down? But hold up, did you say she told him? Just out of the blue?"

"I guess. But to answer your question, no, he did not jump up and down, but I know my brother. He's happy," he looked sideways at her, "and he's not going to let her go."

"Humph, I guess that's why he hasn't been eating all our food lately. I'll call the planner tomorrow, but I need to call Tonya and Damita tonight." She grabbed her cell.

Bianca hadn't shown Omar her nervousness but she felt it. It was three days before her wedding and instead of butterflies about not stumbling over her vows, she fretted over drama. The only two uncles she had, hated each other but would attend her wedding and now this. Couldn't Annette have waited until after her wedding to tell Xavier? She shook her head.

She reached her destination and took a deep breath. She had given Tonya a heads up, and was surprised that Tonya felt as if Annette had made the right choice. Now Damita had to be told. Hopefully she had gotten over her anger, because Bianca was not in the mood for any theatrics.

Tonya of course had secured a table, and Bianca had broken her neck to beat Damita there. She had. She sat down, looked at Tonya and admitted silently that separation agreed with her.

"Should we ease into it? Or just tell her?" Tonya asked before Bianca was settled.

"I'm not sure let's see what type of mood she's in first." Bianca sighed. "My family will be here tomorrow, and that's stressful enough. If she can't deal with it I'm going to ask her not to come."

Tonya looked shocked. "Bianca, you can't do that! That will seem as if you care more about Annette than her. No, that will hurt her feelings."

Bianca slurped her water through a straw. "I don't care how it looks. Xavier is family and Annette is his guest, so that overrules feelings. I was also thinking about telling her to tell Jay not to come either."

"Does Omar agree with this?" Tonya still looked disapproving.

"He doesn't know. He thinks everyone will be okay, I'm not taking any chances. But we'll see, maybe she will be okay with everything." Bianca smiled as Damita approached the table.

"Hey!" Damita looked around before she settled in next to Bianca. "Annette isn't coming?"

Tonya and Bianca shook their heads. They ordered and right after Damita received her drink, Bianca addressed her.

"Damita, Annette is going to be at my wedding with Xavier. Will that create any problems for you?"

Tonya almost choked on her beverage. Damita raised her brows, but looked resigned.

"No, I expected as much anyway. I knew with Elaine's pregnancy and when he stood me up to be with her that it was a done deal." She looked at Bianca and smirked. "Were you afraid that I would cause a scene?"

Bianca laughed, "I would hope not, especially with my rowdy family in attendance. I just don't want anyone to be uncomfortable. What about Jay? Can you give him a heads up? Because I know it will be hard for him, and if he can't handle it maybe he shouldn't come."

"It probably will be hard for him, but I think he can handle it. He still does business with Xavier, which to be frank, I don't understand."

"It would be very selfish of him to think that Annette would still be with him, knowing Elaine is pregnant. He should have never been alone with Elaine from the get-go, he knew she wanted him back." This came from Tonya.

"But Xavier and Annette were seeing each other before he found out that Elaine was pregnant." Damita narrowed her eyes.

"Doesn't matter, the damage had been done. He could have forgiven her, just like he wants her to forgive him. No one is forgiving a baby." Tonya stared back.

Bianca knew that once again Tonya inserted her personal problems into how she saw the problems of others. Right before she cut them off, the server saved her with their food.

Damita waved her hands. "Anyway, I'm sure Jay will be fine. Neither of us think this thing with Xavier will last anyway. He's hoping that they will be done by the time he gets the DNA results. If it comes out that the baby isn't his, hopefully they can salvage their relationship."

Bianca looked at her in amazement but said nothing. Oh, well if Omar was right, they would find out after her wedding.

"What makes y'all think it won't last?" Tonya narrowed her eyes.

"Because Xavier is so quirky and—, well I just think Xavier needs a woman with a stronger backbone and Annette needs a more sensitive man." She caught the looks the two women gave one another. "I'm not saying that Annette has no backbone, I just know how sensitive and silly she can be."

They finished their dinner mostly in silence and after Damita left, Tonya looked at Bianca.

"Do you believe her? That they will be okay at the wedding?"

Bianca pulled out her compact, "Hell no. She's still upset and she never even slept with the man. How do you think Jay will feel?"

She slammed the compact closed after she glanced in it. She leaned forward and beckoned Tonya to come closer. She lowered her voice, "I just hope that they both behave at the wedding. Xavier will not make it an easy event for them." Bianca looked around and spoke softer, "Just between you and me, Xavier is a good guy, but he is mean and aggravating. If he knows he can get under someone's skin, he will."

Tonya looked shocked, "He didn't seem mean to me."

Bianca rolled her eyes, "Of course he didn't." Bianca thought about how much she could say before she continued. "Xavier is very over-protective about people he cares about. I think he cares a lot about Annette, and if Jay is thinking that it won't last, he still thinks of her as his woman."

Tonya patted her hand, "Maybe he needs to see her with someone else to face reality. Jay should have thought of all that before he bounced over to Elaine's and made a baby. Let's just hope that Annette doesn't let Jay sway her emotions."

Bianca was lost when it came to her friends. Annette was dating her soon to be brother in law, Tonya was happy about it, and Damita had become an angry black woman. Sheesh!

Chapter 16

The wedding was a few days away and Annette was excited. Her happiness for her best friend overshadowed any melancholy feelings she might have felt. The funny thing was that she hadn't had many. Anytime she thought of her failed wedding plans, memories of Elaine's name-calling, late night calls, and Jay's lies about sleeping with her and her pregnancy came to mind. She thought of Tonya's situation. For all she knew Jay might have convinced Elaine to keep the baby under wraps until it was too late for Annette to get out of it. Everything happened for a reason.

Xavier, of course made the transition easier. His peculiar personality remained but with each day she understood him better. What she hadn't realized was how much he worked. He kept the security business organized, he constantly wrote code for people and companies, and then he worked around his home. Yet he still managed to spend time with her and the children.

He brought Ant out of his shell. Beyond the games, Ant loved working on cars! Who knew? The weekend before school started, her children were upset they had to go to their dad's house. Ant was never excited, because his dad acted as if there was something wrong with him because he didn't want to play sports. Corey was the surprise. Usually he was super hyped about going, this time he whined about it. Then Anthony stopped back by after he secured them with his mother. It wasn't nice. If she hadn't spent a few extra minutes with her hair she and Zay would have been gone when he came. But as it was, Xavier was in the car as he waited on her and Anthony barreled through the door.

"Annette what the hell are you doing?" He blustered as he pushed his way in.

"Anthony, I don't have time for this! Why aren't you with our children?" She was not in the mood for his drama.

"They are with my momma, while you are hanging out with some dude. Weren't you just engaged? I don't understand how you now want to be a whore!" His nostrils flared and he failed to notice Xavier.

Before she could say a word, Xavier's voice boomed. "You need to go somewhere else with this shit."

Anthony turned, clearly surprised, but also smelling himself. "Nah, you need to take your ass on. I'm talking to my ex-wife. This don't have shit to do with you."

A look that scared Annette glinted in Zay's eyes. She tried to diffuse the situation.

"Ant, you need to…"

"That's where you are wrong *tonto*. Now you can leave on your own, or I can help you. It doesn't matter to me." Xavier's voice was quiet but deadly.

Anthony was a lot of things but stupid wasn't one of them. He glanced at Annette, "We will talk later. You are not going to have my children around every Tom, Dick, and Harry you fuck."

He sneered at her before Xavier's arm stopped him from walking out. "My name is Xavier, not Tom, Dick, or Harry." He got in Anthony's face. "And what she and I do in the bedroom is none of your fucking business. You know what type of mother she is. Your best bet is to take your ass back to your children and thank them. Because they saved you from a hospital bill. Understand?"

Annette saw fear in Anthony's eyes before he brushed Xavier's arm out the way and walked out. A few minutes after he left, Xavier's eyes returned to normal as he looked at her.

"Are you ready? Hopefully we won't miss much of the movie." The abrupt change unsettled her, but she nodded and grabbed her purse.

She hadn't seen that side of him since, but she knew it lurked beneath the surface. Each time she thought of it, all the good aspects of him brushed it away. The only fear she felt lately was when she thought of Jay being at the wedding. He knew that she was with Xavier because she felt it was only right to tell him. He wasn't harsh when she told him, but as a parting shot he said that he doubted if it would last. His exact words were: "That guy is no good for you, I'll be here when you realize it."

As much as she was upset at the choices Jay made, she had always trusted his opinion. It would be a lie if she said that his words hadn't bothered her. That realization made her remember that she was living life according to her rules and discretion now. As she drove to Bianca's to meet her family and Zay, she shook off all negativity. Corey and Ant were loud in the back, excited to be out of the house. They should have been with Anthony, but he had a sudden emergency and couldn't get them until in the morning.

Cars lined Bianca's driveway and street. Nice cars! She parked across the street, three houses down. Xavier met them at the end of driveway, as the boys plowed into him, he kissed her cheek and led them in.

There weren't as many people as the cars led her to believe. Bianca's mother and grandparents were there. Along with a great uncle and a few great aunts. After the introductions were made, Bianca pulled her into the kitchen where Tonya and Damita sat.

"Hey!" Annette stopped short, unsure of the reception.

They both spoke, then Damita stood. "Annette girl come here. I'm not being petty tonight and our friendship means too much to me to let it go."

Annette felt tears as she and Damita hugged. She sat down and they talked about the wedding while Bianca was in and out with her family. Xavier came inside and with no compunction about Damita he wrapped his arm around her shoulders and whispered in her ear. Even with the truce, Damita rolled her eyes.

Annette stood and followed him down the hallway. He found an empty room and pulled her inside. He wrapped her in his arms and kissed her slowly.

"I didn't want to be too obvious in front of Damita. I thought this was your ex's weekend?" His hands trailed down her back.

Annette frowned and told him about Anthony's last-minute call. His eyes darkened momentarily, but then he shrugged.

"I might have to sneak in your room tonight. I don't know if I can wait until tomorrow." He gave her his rakish grin.

After another kiss, they slipped out of the room amid cries of someone's arrival. Xavier turned to her and whispered, "Stay close to me, Omar, or Bianca. There are some dangerous folks in this house."

He cut off her laugh with a sideways glance, "I'm not kidding. If that's Bianca's other uncle that just arrived we might need to leave."

They almost bumped into a man as they walked back to the kitchen. The man stopped, looked and broke out into a radiant smile.

"*Primo*, what's up?" He grabbed Xavier in a man hug.

Annette stood back and looked. The newcomer was much shorter than Xavier, but not short. He had a slim build, and he was what her grandma would have called a 'pretty boy.' He wore cargo shorts and a tee-shirt, which showed a runner's physique. Xavier seemed happy to see him too, so she chuckled silently that he must be safe. Then the stranger's laser beam fell on her.

"Well, hello." He said smoothly while he grabbed her hand.

Annette spoke and when she looked at him she realized that he was the male replica of Bianca. His next words jarred her.

"You must be Annette. I'm Horatio, Bianca's brother, I've heard a lot about you." He swiftly kissed her hand before he moved into the kitchen.

Annette noticed how Damita's eyes lit up when she spotted him. He grabbed Bianca, and swung her around before she introduced him to Tonya and Damita. He repeated his hand routine with each one, then he and Xavier went outside with the rest of the men.

Horatio obviously made Damita forget her pettiness about Annette and Xavier. She gushed to Bianca, "Girl, is your brother single or what?"

Bianca looked at her with a frown. "He came to Marisa's graduation! Didn't you see him then?"

"Nope, I would have remembered him. But back to my question." Damita's eyes looked bright with anticipation.

Bianca gave a tired sigh. "Once again you have set your eyes on the wrong type of guy." She glanced surreptitiously at Annette, "Sorry, Annette, nothing against your choices. Anyway, no, he is not married but I have no idea if he is in a committed relationship."

Tonya laughed, "Now what is wrong with him?"

Bianca glanced around and lowered her voice, "He's weird, and he spends too much time with my uncle, who I love to death, but is stranger than him."

"We know what you call strange, might not be strange to me. Give me the stats and I'll determine if I think he is weird." Damita looked more alive than Annette had seen her in a while.

Tonya snickered, "Do you mean your uncle that I just met? I'll have to side with Damita on this one. He's seems to be a sweet old man."

"Humph. That shows how off your meter is. But that is not the uncle I'm talking about. All I can tell you about my brother is that he is a professor and he plays video games all the time. If you want to hook up with him you will have to do that yourself." Bianca was summoned to the den by her mother.

Ant and Corey rushed in to Annette. "Momma can we go to Mr. Xavier's when we leave here? Please? We want to watch Mr. Horatio play the game. Please Momma?"

Annette glanced at Damita who was studiously staring at her fingernails. Xavier and Horatio walked in and suddenly Damita looked interested. Bianca walked back in and huffed.

Xavier raised his eyebrows and hid his smile as she agreed. Bianca turned to her brother.

"How did you get here? I thought you were coming with Uncle Geoff?"

Horatio frowned as he looked back towards the patio. "I did, but you know he wasn't coming over here. I dropped him off at the hotel."

Bianca mirrored his frown. "How long are y'all staying? Please remind Uncle Geoff that I don't want any shit at my wedding."

Bianca's brother smirked and held up his phone. After a slight pause, he spoke into the receiver. "Hey Unc, do you need your truck?" He listened intently, before he informed his uncle of his plans. "Oh yeah before I forget, Bibi says she doesn't want any shit to go down at her wedding."

Bianca's eyes widened as large as her brothers smile.

He nodded his head, "Okay I'll tell her." He put his phone back in his pocket.

Omar chose that moment to come in with Bianca's great-uncle and step-granddad. Horatio glanced at them and grinned. "Geoff said as long as Luis stays in his own lane, you shouldn't have any problems."

Uncle Luis looked startled then he snarled, "Fuck that psychotic bastard." He glanced around, "Excuse my language ladies."

Annette covered her smile with her hand because she had not expected that from the distinguished looking older man. Uncle Luis was slightly under six feet, with salt and pepper hair that was slicked back, and he had a gap between his front teeth. He swept out of the room with Bianca's step-granddad, Sonny, right behind him.

Bianca looked mortified, "Why would you say that in front of him? And why did you tell him what I said?"

Omar moved behind her, it was obvious he tried to calm her down.

"Because you told me to. Stop tripping they will be fine. I think a reconciliation is soon in the works for them anyway." Horatio looked at Bianca dismissively.

Fire was in Bianca's eyes, "Get the hell out Ray! Right now." She hissed.

If Bianca hadn't been her best friend, Annette would have laughed. Horatio looked unbothered as he moved to the den and kissed his mom and grandmother good-bye. When he passed through the kitchen again, he stopped at Bianca's chair and squeezed her arm.

"I hope you have a better attitude tomorrow, Bibi." He nodded at everyone and walked out.

During the commotion, Xavier had forgotten about Damita and Annette's reconciliation as he moved behind Annette and absently moved his fingers across her shoulders.

Everyone soon cleared out, Annette, Tonya, and Damita stayed behind with Bianca. Omar went to his condo, since Bianca's mom and grand mom said he absolutely could not see her until the wedding. Xavier left with her boys and Jolisa hung out with Marisa in her room.

Tonya spoke first, "Wow are you and your brother always this intense?"

Bianca snorted, "He gets on my nerves! There is a long-standing secret feud between my uncles, and everyone in the family knows about it. He was being a class A jerk to say that when Uncle Luis walked in."

"It seemed as if your uncle took it in stride. I'm sure they will do fine tomorrow." Annette tried to soothe her friend.

"They better. I wish we had gone to the courthouse and told them later." She moaned.

"It will be okay. I'm sure your brother was just having a little fun. When is Omar's family coming in?" Damita looked around.

Tonya looked curious, while Bianca and Annette looked at one another.

"Umm, it's just Xavier. We thought one of his cousins was coming but they cancelled." Bianca yawned.

The women took that as their cue to leave. Annette gathered Jolisa and Damita stopped her at the door.

"Your children have really taken to Xavier, haven't they?" Damita touched Annette's arm cautiously.

Annette looked at her for any signs of malice or pettiness and answered truthfully when she saw none. "Yes, they really have."

Damita looked thoughtful, "That's interesting. Oh well, children are resilient."

Annette would later think about that comment.

spublish, but hewas close to it. He was great with the

Chapter 17

Her reflection showed an elegant woman who wore a chignon on her neck with impeccable make-up. The struggle of that last hairpin was nary in sight. Annette sighed in relief as it finally went in, without scraping her scalp.

She had dropped the children off early, she wasn't giving Anthony a chance to ruin her day. Her ex-mother-in-law answered the door with her nose in the air. She had been with Anthony for the past few months, so obviously she had moved in with him. Annette didn't care, she was free to prepare for the biggest day in her best friend's life.

Once again, the children bemoaned the fact that they had to go to their father's house. They had no idea how much she understood. Surprisingly Anthony wasn't a bad father, he had been a terrible husband, but she couldn't knock him as a father. Well, she probably could a little but she wouldn't.

Her dress hung on the back of her closet door. Her budget had been somewhat compromised by it, but she loved it! It was champagne colored, maxi length, off the shoulders, with a dip in the back. If she hadn't tried it on she wouldn't have bought it. It fit perfectly. Bag lunches would be in order for a couple of weeks, but it was worth it. After meeting Bianca's family, she was glad she made the choice.

Annette always knew that Bianca lived well and liked nice things, but she never knew that she came from money. She was down to earth and so budget conscious, it seemed as if she had faced the struggles that Annette and Tonya had financially faced. Bianca's great-uncle and grandmother reeked of money, but it was her brother that made it reality.

When they went to Xavier's she studied him while he and Xavier played the game. Horatio was preppy and carried himself the way most privileged people do. There was an air about him, she didn't want to say that he seemed snobbish, but he was close to it. He was great with the children, they reveled in his skills with video games. As she watched them it was obvious that he and Xavier had a close bond. Which surprised her, because other than Omar, Zay didn't seem to be close to anyone.

She threw on her robe when the doorbell rang. She looked at Xavier in surprise when he walked in clothed in khakis and a button-down.

"Why aren't you dressed?" She silently drooled over his casual look. He had a fresh cut, shave and smelled divine.

"My clothes are in the car." His eyes swept over her. "You look beautiful."

He followed her to her bedroom and dropped across her bed as she looked in the mirror.

"Tell me a little about Bianca's family, like who are the dangerous people you spoke of. I only saw some well-off older," she coughed, "and younger people."

When she glanced through the mirror she caught his desire filled gaze. Her robe had been chucked to the side as soon as they made it to the bedroom. He finally caught her glance as he shifted his position on her bed.

"They are wealthy, but it's not all legitimate. I think Luis has foregone most of his 'dirty' business, but I would never want to get on his bad side." Zay sat up. "From the history that I heard about it all started with Bianca's great-grandfather. He was a hard worker, but he also had five or six mouths to feed. So, he did whatever it took. That part of the business has been passed down. But Geoff is the ruthless one." He paused briefly. "Geoff and Luis fell out years ago and as far as I know, they never speak to one another. I think this will be the first event they have attended together in years."

"It's hard to believe that Horatio and Bianca are brother and sister. Even though they look just alike." She grabbed her lotion as she spoke.

"Why do you say that?" His voice deepened.

"Bianca is so down to earth and he seems so preppy." Annette chose her words carefully.

Xavier chuckled, "I can see why you would think that. Once you get to know him, he is very down to earth. He is just a little weird."

Annette listened and she followed her usual routine and opened the drawer of her dresser, propped her foot on it to bend over and moisturize her legs. The lotion dropped from her hands as she felt Xavier's heat when he tugged at her hips and kissed the middle of her back.

"Are you intentionally trying to drive me nuts? I can't wait until tonight, I just need a little piece of heaven right now."

His voice was filled with so much desire and need, it made her knees weak. As she straightened he wrapped his arms around her and pulled her close. His fingertips, though close to her panty line never dipped lower. It was the nibbles on her shoulder that made her dizzy.

"Zay, I just finished my hair and make-up. I think you might have to wait." There was zero conviction in her voice which came out hoarse.

"I promise I won't bother your hair or make-up." His fingers slid under the waistband of her panties and he slowly moved them down.

She turned her head in protest and was met with his delicious lips. As he ravished her mouth, she felt his pants as they dropped and then his skin against hers. When he moved from her mouth, small kisses were planted across her shoulders, but she almost lost it when she felt his hot tongue run the length of her spine. She ached with a need that overtook her body, soul and heart.

Xavier hoisted her up and she exhaled a gasp as he entered her. Each stroke synthesized every cell in her body. She lost herself in the feeling, as she felt him grow harder inside her, she curved her knees around his waist. She closed her eyes as she held on to her dresser, but they flew open at his expletive.

"Shit!"

Annette peered through the mirror to see Xavier as he looked down. To know that he watched as their bodies blended together, increased her ardor and she felt her toes tingle. The voyeuristic experience created sensations within her that overpowered all previous feelings. Unable to tear her eyes away, her body grew weaker as she saw the emotions that flitted across his countenance.

"Zay?" She managed to croak as the tingles hit her hips.

He eyes met hers through the mirror and without her saying another word he held her core against his chest. Before she breathed in relief he gave one long hard thrust that sent shivers through her scalp. His eyes scorched her essence as they never wavered from hers.

Her body released paroxysms of shudders as she felt him explode inside of her. It seemed as if each of her convulsions captured every seed that jerked inside of her. To sever the connection, Annette closed her eyes as she tried to contain the wealth of emotions that entered her heart. Her eyes opened as the room moved.

Xavier moved backwards toward the bed. He tapped her leg so that she could unravel them from around his torso. Ever so gently he leaned back on the bed as he held her still trembling body. She gently removed her body from his and laid beside him. His nostrils flared and his eyes were closed. Consideration for her hair and make-up led her to place her chin on his chest.

"Are you okay?" She broke the silence after a few minutes.

"No," he opened his eyes and gazed lazily at her, "Annette I have never…"

"You never what?" She traced his eyebrows with her finger.

"Nothing. I guess we need to get ready." His eyes held a longing that she couldn't read.

"I was thinking. They've been living together, maybe we can just skip this formality. I'd be happy to stay in bed with you for the rest of the day."

Xavier's laughter bounced against the walls. "I wish *mi amor*, but I think my brother would kill me if I missed him marrying the love of his life." He kissed the tip of her nose.

Somehow, they squeezed in her tub together for a bath. She was not re-doing her hair and make-up!

When they arrived at the event location Annette was glad she chose her dress. They were early, but Bianca's family was in attendance and they were dressed to the nines. As she went in search of Bianca, she found her in a dressing room with her sister and mother. Annette was reintroduced to them and Bianca's mom left to check on the elders. As soon as she left Bianca and her sister Angel broke out in giggles.

Annette smiled at their silliness while she took in the scene. Bianca was beautiful in a silver dress that was a midi/maxi. The shell was the maxi, but it opened in the front to show the fitted sequined shell, her tiny bump showed. Her sister on the other hand was just as gorgeous! Angel had straight black hair and where Bianca and Horatio could have been twins, Angel looked more like their mom. Her dress was also a silver maxi that crisscrossed at the top and had sequins in the middle. It flowed loosely around her frame. She wore it well with her above average height.

Bianca pulled her close, "My baby will have a cousin close in age. But we are keeping it under wraps until after the wedding. Angel will call Grandmére once she gets back home."

They both giggled hysterically as Annette tried to give her congratulations. Once they calmed down she asked, "Why do you have to keep it a secret? Does your grandmother not want any more great-grandchildren?"

Bianca smacked her lips, "She doesn't care for my brother-in-law Rod, who happens to be a great guy."

"No one cares what little Negative Ninny thinks anyway. But to keep the drama down I'll hold on to my news." Angel smiled broadly. "But she might change her tune if Rod gets this coaching job in Florida. If she does…"

Angel rolled her eyes as they laughed. When she heard Florida, it jarred Annette's memory.

She leaned in close and spoke softly, "I'm coming to help get Marisa moved in." Xavier had asked her on the way over.

Bianca and Angel looked surprised. Then Bianca nodded knowingly. "You are coming with Zay, aren't you?" She pursed her lips together.

"Omar's brother Zay?" Angel looked at Annette, "You're dating Xavier?"

Annette knew that Xavier had a reputation and since Angel sounded shocked she wondered if she would be looked at as one of his notches. She knew what she had gotten into from the beginning, so it was time to face the music. She nodded shyly. To her surprise, Angel grabbed her in a hug.

"Yay! So, if you guys get married you will be practically family! My uncle and brother love Xavier just like family."

"Really Angel? They are just dating, no one said anything about marriage." Bianca scoffed.

"Yes, but Xavier needs a good woman. I can look at Annette and tell that she is perfect for him." She nudged Annette softly. "You know we are witches, so we can sense these types of things."

Annette and Angel laughed at the look of horror on Bianca's face. Tonya and Damita burst in and interrupted their moment. She stood back and looked at her friends while they cooed over Bianca. Damita wore a fitted plum midi dress that had a plunging neckline, but it looked superb on her. Tonya was more subdued in a maxi royal blue dress, that had a vee neck and cinched her tiny waist with a sliver belt.

After she finished her inventory, she glanced at Angel, who stood with a strange look as she watched Bianca and her friends. Bianca's mom Cecile came back and shooed them out. When they stepped into the courtyard, Xavier materialized beside her.

"You need to sit on the second row." He whispered in her ear after he spoke to the rest of the women.

"Why?" Annette smiled as memories of earlier caused her stomach to fill with butterflies. Memories and the fact that he looked delicious in his dark grey suit with vest and deep maroon tie.

"I don't know that's just what Omar told me. I guess Bianca wants it. Her family will fill the front row and some of the second. I guess you, umm, and your friends will fill in for our family." He led them to their seats.

She turned and placed her hand on his face to straighten his eyebrows. The urge to kiss him overwhelmed her, but her lipstick and Damita stopped her.

"Humph!" Damita breathed loudly.

Xavier glanced at her, and gave Annette a chaste kiss on the lips. When he walked by Damita he whispered loudly, "You need to chill."

"I'm not the only one!" Damita shot back.

Tonya shushed Damita as people filled the courtyard. They were pushed back to the third row as cousins and other relatives filtered in. Annette looked around. Bianca's grandmother, mother, and uncle sat in the front. There were two empty chairs, one beside her grandmother and another beside her mother. She spotted Angel's husband, Rod, because he sat one down from Bianca's mom. He also stood out because in the array of bright, light and damn near white people, he was the darkest one in the group.

It wasn't a huge crowd, it was small and intimate, but too many for the courthouse. As the sunset and the time drew near, Annette noticed that Horatio wasn't there. She leaned to her left to whisper to Tonya, but the strangest thing happened. An older very handsome man emerged from the building. He was average height, he had thick dark hair with flecks of gray, and his beard was the same. But his eyes were his most captivating feature, they were a startling grayish-green.

A hush fell over the courtyard when he appeared. Cecile stood and greeted him with a hug. He hugged Grandmére Luisa, and glanced at the uncle before he swept to the other side. Family members scrambled and rearranged, so that he could sit in the front row closest to the aisle. He only acknowledged the older people and Marisa. He spoke quietly to the woman beside him, who rolled her eyes, but rose. The row rearranged again and he motioned for Marisa to sit at his side.

Annette saw Jay and Carl when they entered. She had hoped that he had decided not to come. When he arrived, Omar and Xavier stood with the minister at the front. Annette's heart sped up because there was an empty seat beside her.

Please don't do it, Jay. She begged silently. She heard Damita snicker and she could tell by Xavier's expression that he saw them too. Annette jumped when someone slid in the seat beside her.

"Was anyone sitting here?" She looked into the eyes of Horatio.

She shook her head and expelled a long breath. When he noticed Tonya and Damita he said hello. Damita glowed like a damn lightbulb! Annette reconsidered their reconciliation after her antics today. Since things were about to start she looked straight ahead. Xavier caught her eye and winked. She smiled broadly.

"Whew! For a minute, I thought he was winking at me." Horatio whispered in her ear.

Annette stopped laughing once the music began. "After All is Said and Done," by Beyoncé and Marc Nelson played. Everyone stood and with the sun setting, the mood was perfect. As Bianca came in view tears blurred Annette's vision. She blinked rapidly in succession and as she looked straight ahead, she stared straight at Jay.

As emotions welled in her chest an apparition of Elaine hovered over his head. Standing straighter she looked back at Bianca. She looked beautiful! Her hair was swept up and held by baby's breath flowers as curls cascaded down her back. Sonny looked nervous as he held her arm and walked her down the aisle. Annette teared up again.

Tonya passed her a tissue and held her arms. They both stood in awe and happiness for their friend. Tonya openly cried, while Damita smiled, but all eyes were riveted to the couple of the day. As Bianca approached, Omar stood, his love openly shone in his eyes. Xavier lightly pushed him forward.

The ceremony was sweet and simple. They did traditional vows and it was obvious that for that moment no one else existed. Tonya had gone through five tissues and even Damita looked teary eyed. Annette's tears finally fell, some for happiness, some to release the adage of looking back. Before they knew it, the strains of "This is For the Lover in You" by Shalimar broke through each person's emotions. Omar and Bianca were still locked in a kiss. Xavier looked at them with a smile and the minister finally nudged them. They broke apart, smiled and moved down the aisle. Confetti was thrown and everyone reached out for them.

As the family lined up and the small crowd went through, Annette stood with Tonya as they waited to sit down and eat. She stiffened when Jay approached. He looked good in his tan suit and as he came closer memories assailed her.

"Stay strong." Tonya whispered in her ear.

"Hello Tonya, Annette." His eyes penetrated hers, and it made her sad to think that not too long ago, this man had been her future.

He grabbed her hand, "You look amazing, Annette."

"Thank you." There wasn't much more to say. So many things had gone wrong, but he stood in front of her and reminded her of how much he once meant to her. The smell of cologne and his aura reminded her that there wasn't one inch of him that she hadn't known. And loved. He moved in close to her.

"I want to talk to you before the night is over. Okay?" He gazed at her intently.

Before she answered, the wedding planner interrupted and told everyone to make it to their tables. Tonya's eyes brimmed with curiosity but Annette stepped back as she looked for Xavier. He was still with the family engrossed in a conversation with Horatio and another man. He caught her eye right before the wedding planner made it to them.

Once they were seated, Omar and Bianca stood. They thanked everyone for coming and gave the floor to anyone who wanted to speak. Xavier fidgeted around in his seat and then he whispered in her ear.

"This is a damn setup! Look at who they put us between." He gritted out.

Uncle Luis was beside her and Uncle Geoff was beside Zay. Annette swallowed her giggles.

"Bianca did this on purpose! Why else put us between the two people that can't stand one another? If I give you the signal, duck under the table." He whispered urgently in her ear.

Annette looked at him to see if he was serious and saw his dimples. They looked at each other and laughed. She lightly punched his thigh under the table, to which he took her hand and held it. Under the table! Uncle Geoff had risen to speak, and Uncle Luis mumbled under his breath.

"This ass always wants to be the center of attention! Why can't he just let the kids have their day?"

Zay squeezed her hand and raised his eyebrows when she looked at him. She smiled but swallowed her laughter and became solemn when she was met with a glare from Jay. Damita, who sat beside him, didn't look very happy either. They were soon forgotten as Uncle Geoff's voice commanded her attention. His voice was rich, deep, and he spoke so eloquently that he received everyone's attention.

He spoke of Bianca briefly as a child with magical eyes, and he ended by welcoming Omar to the family. Once again Uncle Luis mumbled darkly.

"Who the hell does he think he is to welcome anybody to the family as if he is the patriarch?"

Angel covered his hand with hers, "Hush Uncle Louie, this is Bianca's day. You know anything dealing with Bianca, Geoff is involved." She spoke quietly.

"Humph!" Was all he said.

A few more people spoke and the last person to speak was Horatio. This time the mumblings came from both sides.

"Another showboat! I'm hungry." This came from Uncle Luis, who tapped his long fingers against the table.

"Xavier will you tell that old fart to shut the hell up? Somebody needs to put him in a nursing home." Geoff did not mumble or whisper.

"Nursing home my ass! Say another word to me and I'll beat your ass so bad you'll be the one in a nursing home." The man who had only spoke in quiet measured tones now roared.

Xavier's grip tightened on her hand, but she was too shocked to look at him. From the look on some of the guests' faces they were shocked also.

Horatio stopped speaking and someone exclaimed loudly, "Oh shit!"

Geoff had risen out of his seat, but before it went any further, Bianca's great-aunt Tess stood and spoke. "Wait just one damn minute! You boys better settle down over there. You might act this way at home, but I'll be damned if you ruin Bianca's wedding day! You ought to be ashamed of yourselves! Now sit back down and shut the hell up! Carry on Horatio. And Luis since you have so much to say, you can speak next."

There was a stunned silence that lasted a minute. Luis looked down and even Geoff looked properly chastised. Horatio cleared his throat and spoke again. He recovered nicely and his words about his sister left few dry eyes in the place. When he finished Bianca met him halfway and they rocked together as they hugged tightly.

Tess grabbed the microphone and spoke succinctly, "Louie, do you have anything else to say?"

"No, I do not, Tess. I will speak with the couple privately." He spoke loudly, then mumbled, "I don't have to show off."

"Then I guess it is time to eat." Tess had effectively taken over! She nodded to the wedding planner as she scrambled to get the caterers in place.

As they waited to be served Annette looked around. Right behind Damita was René! She sat looking shocked, but when she noticed Annette she smiled and waved. Annette waved back, and she felt uncomfortable until Zay squeeze her hand.

"Didn't I tell you these damn folks were crazy?" He whispered in her ear. It always amazed her that as deep as his voice was he could lower his decibels so drastically.

She chuckled as she glanced at him. "You did and I had no idea. I'm sure Bianca is mad as hell."

"Hmm, I don't know her aunt, but she should have been in Louisiana years ago. I've never seen anyone shut them down like that!" Xavier laughed.

Their food came and of course Xavier inhaled his and wondered aloud if there would be seconds. As she finished eating he gave her a rundown of the present family members.

He showed her Geoff's and Luis's sons, who surprisingly sat together. He then told her what he knew of the rumors and legends. Annette realized that Zay loved legends and was nosy as hell.

Bianca and Omar danced to their song, then Geoff led her out for a father and daughter dance. After that the DJ changed things with dance music. Almost all of Bianca's family got on the dance floor and did the 'wobble.' Annette noticed Tonya and Damita on the dance floor too.

She moved her shoulders while Xavier smirked at her, "Go ahead, I'll be out there in a minute. As soon as I take this tie off."

Annette left him and joined her friends on the floor. The next thing she knew Xavier joined them and she was surprised that he could dance. He brought the party atmosphere. After a couple of songs, the DJ slowed it down again and played "You and I" by John Legend. Xavier stopped her as she walked off the dance floor.

He held her close as they danced and even though she felt Jay as he stared at her, she was determined to have an enjoyable time. Xavier held her close as his hands dipped dangerously low on her back. Halfway through the song he kissed the side of her mouth which made her blush from the top of her head to the bottom of her feet.

"I can't wait to get you home." Xavier murmured softly.

When she looked in his eyes she forgot everything. His gaze swept her away to a place that held peace and safety. Things happen for a reason and she felt that Xavier in her life was no accident. Somewhere in the back of her mind a warning bell rang and cautioned her to hold on tightly to her heart.

Xavier kissed the tip of her nose, "Stop looking at me like that or everybody will know what's on my mind." He sighed deeply, "We will be stuck on the dance floor all night."

She laughed and they parted once the song ended. Xavier grabbed Bianca for the next dance. Annette looked around for Tonya and felt someone grab her elbow. It was Jay!

"Can I talk to you for a minute?" His voice was even.

Annette saw no way out as he led her outside.

Chapter 18

Jay was angry and hurting. He hated that bastard Xavier!
Annette had been decent enough and told him that she spent
time with him. She actually said she was "with" him, but he
never expected to feel the hatred he felt. Deep in his heart
he felt that most of Xavier's actions at the reception had
been because of him. That guy wanted to mess with his
mind, and had damn near succeeded.

The wedding was okay even though he wanted to be
next to her, and it reminded him of what they had. And
needed to get back to. It almost killed him to see her next to
that goofball during the reception, and she looked happy.
That part hurt him more than anything. Or so he thought
until he saw her molested by that dickhead on the dance
floor. Carl had urged him to leave after the wedding, but he
hadn't listened.

Carl made things worse with his editorial of the
situation. He knew it wasn't intentional, but at one point he
wanted to deck him.

When they sat down at the reception Carl pointed out
everything. "Man, you might as well move on. She is at the
family table and dude looks like they have been together
forever."

Jay looked at him in amazement, "The last thing I will
do is hand her over to him." He said between gritted teeth.

"Looks like she is already there." Carl sounded
sorrowful.

"Just shut up, okay." Jay snapped.

"I'm just making observations." Carl glanced at Jay.
"Okay, okay."

Carl was quiet, maybe in shock after the blow-up
between the uncles, but once the dancing started, he was at it
again.

Jay watched Annette as she danced with Tonya and
Damita. He smiled as he thought of how she never minded

him as he stepped on her toes. Then Xavier joined the crowd, loud as hell of course, and jealously slithered through Jay's soul. He kept his cool because no one danced together. They did some line dance, Annette danced next to Tonya and Xavier danced between Bianca and her sister.

Then when the slow song played, Jay begged Annette silently to go back to the table. Instead she danced with the knucklehead and his hands were all over her. That's when Carl started up again.

"Damn it's time to go now. Even I can see where this is going to lead." Carl nudged his arm, "Come on man, don't put yourself through this."

"I'm not going anywhere until I talk to Annette. You can go." His words came out harsher than he meant, and Carl stepped away.

He should have left because Damita walked up next, with her own editorial.

"Hey! I thought you were gone." Her eyes moved to where he stared. "Damn! That's just how he had his hands on her at the restaurant!" Her tone softened, "I'm sure Annette is uncomfortable, but you know how she is."

"I'm aware that this bastard is putting on a show for me." Jay nodded and mumbled, "But he just doesn't know who he is messing with."

The song finally ended and when Jay saw Xavier move towards Bianca he made his move. Annette looked surprised, but not mad to see him. He led her outside, and he didn't stop until they were close to the parking lot. He had to wait for her because the gravel slowed her down in her heels.

He turned to her, "Annette what are you doing with this guy?"

She cocked her head, "What do you mean? I told you that we were together."

Jay wanted to pick her up, put her in his car and just drive far away. With her hair pulled back it brought more attention to her beautiful brown eyes and perfect mouth. He took a deep breath and tried another tactic.

146

"I know you did. I know that I hurt you and if I could go back in time I would, but I can't. I'm so sorry for the bad decisions I made. I just don't want to see you hurt again, especially from someone who won't make it up to you. I still love you." He grabbed her hand.

She looked perplexed as she gazed at him. "What makes you think that I will get hurt again?"

"Annette, listen, I don't know why, but that guy is with you to hurt me. I don't know what the hell I did to him, to make him dislike me so much, but he does." Her hand was still secured in his grasp. He wanted to touch her or kiss her but he restrained himself.

"What makes you believe that? I don't want to hear this." She tried to pull away, but he wouldn't let her.

"Think about it Annette. First, he tried with Damita, then when that didn't work, he moved to you." He saw the doubt in her eyes. "Even if that weren't the case, I wouldn't want to see him get hurt either." He figured a little lie wouldn't hurt, because he cared less if the guys heart broke in a million pieces. And he drove off a cliff.

This time she snatched her hand away and stood with her hands on her hips. "Now you are not making any sense. First you don't want me hurt because Zay is with me to get back at you. Now you are concerned if he will get hurt? How would he get hurt? You've lost me."

He grabbed both her hands and pulled her closer. "When you come back to me. If he really cares for you, I'm sure that will hurt him." Jay sure hoped it would, because he would love to rub it in his face. "I know it hurts me every time I think of him touching you, loving you…"

She narrowed her eyes and spoke softly. "How do you think I felt each time I looked at that picture and imagined you with her. The person I trusted more than anybody, not only allowed her to touch you, kiss you, and fuck you, but went back to do it again. And then looked right in my face and lied to me!" She stepped so close he felt the warmth of her body, "To know that as stupid as I am, I probably would have forgiven the sex part, but the lies, I can't do it. Did you ever think of what I went through?"

He responded softly, "Unfortunately, not enough. Everything I did was to protect you, because I love you." Jay heard the crunch of gravel. He knew it was that bastard Xavier.

"Jay, I gave us another chance. I begged you to tell me everything and yet you still lied to me! That's not love." She tried to pull away.

He pulled her close and raised his voice, "Can you stand here and tell me that you don't love me anymore? That you don't miss us?"

Annette leaned close to his ear, "I can tell you that when I think of us, Elaine is included. And I'm also pretty sure that I don't need a love that will intentionally lie to me and exclude me. If Elaine wasn't pregnant, you would have never told me that you had sex with her."

Jay's body responded to the feel of her body next to his and his fingers dug into her hips to bring her closer. "Once I straighten everything out, I will show you how much I love you and you will never have to worry about me again. I'm not giving up on us."

"You should have thought about that before you broke my heart. I doubt if it can ever be pieced together again." She pushed his chest and walked away.

Once again Jay heard someone walking in the gravel. He knew that Annette spoke too softly for Xavier to hear her, but he definitely heard him. Since this guy stood in the way of him and Annette, Jay wasn't going to make it any easier than he already had.

Jay walked back in to tell the happy couple good-bye. They sat at the table, with Xavier and Annette beside them. Xavier stared him down as he approached and Annette averted her gaze. Omar as usual, was cordial, Bianca tried but she glared at him while she thanked him for coming.

Jay looked for Carl and found him at a secluded table with Tonya. Jay approached cautiously. Carl had been miserable since he separated from his wife, mainly because of the lack of sex. He was so deep in conversation, he never noticed Jay until he cleared his throat.

Carl looked surprised, "Umm, are you ready to leave?"

Jay nodded, "But you can stay here. I was just letting you know."

Carl looked indecisive, "Give me five minutes, I need to talk to you anyway."

Jay hugged Tonya and walked outside. He lit a cigar while he waited on Carl. Five minutes turned into ten before Carl emerged.

'What's up man?' If Carl wanted to give more of his opinion, he would become the recipient of all Jay's pent up rage.

"Where did you disappear to man? The only reason I didn't come look was because I saw Xavier talking to Damita." Carl looked aggravated.

Jay gave him the condensed version of his conversation with Annette. Carl shook his head while he huffed and puffed.

"I told you this shit looked serious!" Before Jay cut him off, Carl held up his hand. "But it's a good thing I've been chatting with Carly." He snickered.

"Who's Carly?" Jay wondered about his friend's sanity since his separation.

"Omar's ex-wife? I looked her up on social media, we started chatting, then talking on the phone. And guess what?" Carl smirked.

His best friend had all his attention now and Jay was not in the mood for games. "What?" he questioned impatiently.

Carl rubbed his chin, "I've been boosting her up some, and she would like to see a brother. Face to face!"

Jay was irritated, "What the hell does that have to do with me?"

"I hate to break this to you, but the only way Annette will come back to you is if Elaine becomes a puff of smoke. That is not going to happen." Carl looked at him slyly, "That means that you need to find some dirt on ole boy that will make him a bigger douche to Annette than she thinks you are. Other than that, you are losing. Dude is shooting three-pointers all around your head."

Jay leaned against his car and thought carefully about what Carl said. It was true that he seemed to be fighting a losing battle, but all the dots weren't connected with the plan.

"Are you sure that it's the right Carly?" He pulled on his cigar.

"Hell yeah! Their daughter's picture is all over her social media." Carl pulled his phone out and showed Jay.

It was Liberty, but another problem popped in his head. "What makes you think that she will give you any dirt?"

Carl looked over his shoulder and lowered his tone. "The few times she has mentioned Omar, she hates him. Like real hate." He grimaced, "But we are going to see her. You need to be there too."

"If she sees two of us it might scare her away. Why don't you just sweeten her up and I'll tell you what to ask?" Jay thumped his cigar out.

"Nope! You need to go too. Once we get there if she looks like her social media, I mean I might try to hit it. But these women be fooling folks too much. They look one way on social media then when you see them in person, it's a different story." Carl shook his head. "I've worked it all out. But we need to head to your place to work out the details."

Jay looked back at the reception building with longing. Before he got in his car, Carl stopped him.

"Trust me, man, this will be the only way you have a chance. I know there is something dirty about that dude. We'll find it. We didn't make it to the top by being stupid."

Jay nodded and knew his friend was right. Nothing else seemed to work, and as he remembered the hurt along with the anger in Annette's face, he decided this was the course to take.

Chapter 19

Sexual frustration and anger summed up Annette's week. The fantastic love-making she expected after the wedding? Never happened! Xavier sulked on the way to his place and once they arrived he turned into an interrogator.

"Why were you outside with Jay?" He asked as he fumbled with the buttons on her dress.

"He said he wanted to talk to me. I didn't know we were going outside until he walked out there." She had hoped that she hadn't been missed, even though she planned to tell him anyway. Just not tonight.

She felt his sigh on her neck. "Okay. Okay."

Annette knew that he was upset, a blind man would have noticed on the ride. He was quiet and drummed his fingers on the steering wheel the entire way.

Once the last button was undone she turned and met his stormy glare. "Xavier, are you upset that I went outside to talk to him?"

Since she had never dealt with this type of behavior before she wasn't sure what to do or say. With Anthony, she was the one who watched who he talked to, and Jay never seemed to worry about casual conversation.

"Nope, not at all." Xavier rumbled and gave her a stony look.

"Then what is it? I can tell that you are upset about something." She hung her dress on a hanger and laid it on the bed. She knew that it would have to go in the guest room closet. Another one of Zay's quirks.

She felt him behind her as he pulled the hairpins from her hair. The feel of his hands in her hair made her stomach flutter with anticipation. Her head fell gently back as he softly pulled her hair. It always turned her on when he did that.

"But it did upset me to see his hands all over you." His breath was hot and delicious in her ear.

A heat sped through her body, it traveled at the speed of light. She had no problem with mad sex! Sometimes it was better than happy sex.

"But I will get over it. What did he want anyway?" Xavier stepped back and sat on the bed.

Chills covered her body when he moved. As he removed his shoes she saw that he wanted answers. Why couldn't he wait until later?

"Just the usual, he apologized, asked me why was I with you, and said…" She stumbled, not sure how to phrase the last part.

Xavier had taken his jacket and shirt off, but he stopped and glared at her. "Said what, Annette?"

She rushed through the words, "He said that once he straightened things out that we would get back together." She hurried to finish when she saw his eyebrows raised. "But that's just hurt talk, he will get over it eventually."

Xavier grunted, grabbed her dress and walked out the room. When he returned he pulled a tee-shirt out and gave it to her. When they finished their nightly routine, he laid in the bed on his back with his hands clasped behind his head. It seemed to her that he wasn't getting over anything.

"How did you know we were outside anyway?" She settled in the bed next to him.

"I was looking for you." He blew heavily.

She snuggled next to him and kissed his cheek. "Did you think I left you?" She teased.

"Yeah." He put his arm around her and drew her in close.

Xavier closed his eyes and as she pressed against him she let her hand wander to her favorite drug. He held her hand right before she reached her dreams.

"Nope not tonight, I'm not in the mood." Xavier looked at her and kissed her lightly on the corner of her mouth.

Annette was in disbelief! What the hell did he mean he wasn't in the mood? His body seemed to be as his magic wand pointed and beckoned to her. She peered at him to see if he was joking and he had once again closed his eyes.

An exasperated sigh tumbled out as she muttered under her breath, "I'm not going to beg for it."

"Good, because it wouldn't change anything." He said before he turned on his side, with his back to her.

The memory of that night and every night after still burned her panties, with anger. Ever since that night, although he came around he had been distant. The worst part was that she had not received her much-needed fix! He hadn't given her a real kiss since the wedding.

There hadn't been much time to talk this week, after his little upset episode. The day after the wedding they had spent most of the day at Bianca's, and the rest of week was busy with children and work.

To prove that a penis was her birthmark, she now rode with Xavier headed to Florida. Arrangements had been made with her children, and her time off had been approved, these were her justifications for being whooped. As they followed Bianca and Omar, she stole glances at him. His mood had improved and he seemed excited about the trip.

She slept most of the trip and was surprised when they pulled up at a beautiful villa. It looked like a resort!

"Whoa! Who lives here?" Annette unbuckled her seat belt and sat up straight.

Xavier looked mystified. "I have no idea."

As if they were overheard, Bianca's mother and brother walked out the front door. Marisa, Liberty and Cherise exited the truck and ran down the expansive driveway. Bianca and Omar exited slower and Annette approached them at the truck.

She looked in the truck window as they took their time. The back of the truck was completely filled as if Marisa would never return. She felt Xavier as he came up behind her.

"Is this where your mom and grandmother live?" Annette was still shocked at the villa.

"Hell no! This is my Uncle Geoff's place. We didn't know he had a home in Florida." Bianca looked upset as she looked around.

Omar and Xavier whispered to one another as they fell behind the women. When they walked in, Annette tried to act normal, but her mouth flew open as she looked around. This home was like an episode from the Rich and Famous. It was a palace. They walked to the gazebo (an actual gazebo!) where the family gathered. Annette saw Cherise out of the corner of her eye as she approached. Apprehension filled her stomach because after the way Damita had reacted, she didn't know what to expect.

"Hi Annette." Cherise said shyly. "I wanted to tell you that I don't care if you aren't with Jay, I still love you like a sister."

Annette exhaled a deep breath as she hugged Cherise tightly. "I love you too."

"And it's not just me. Momma feels the same way." Cherise whispered in her ear.

From the weight that lifted off her shoulders she knew that subconsciously this had worried her. She never wanted to lose the extended family that Jay's family had been to her. Cherise scampered off and joined the other girls.

After they sat around and talked, Xavier informed her that they would stay at a condo, instead of the palace.

Xavier glanced at her when they got in his car. "Are you okay? You've been awfully quiet."

"I'm fine." She answered before she looked at the scenery outside of her window.

The girls stayed at the palace, so it was just the two couples in the condo. Once they chose their rooms everyone retreated to them.

"At least there is a sofa in here." Annette murmured as she glanced around the room.

"I think each room has one." Xavier commented as he stripped off his shirt.

He jumped in the shower first and after her shower she donned on a shapeless duster that came past her knees. Then she wrapped her hair completely in a multi colored scarf, after she brushed her teeth and washed her face. Xavier came in and wrapped his arms around her.

"You are so pretty." He looked at her through the mirror.

Annette rolled her eyes. He hadn't noticed her subtle hint that she was not in the mood tonight. He felt so good. Xavier only had on his pajama bottoms and he covered her in his warmth. It took everything she had to remain strong. She sidestepped his embrace and peered in the linen closet. She pulled a sheet and blanket out, while he had an amused look on his face.

"What are you doing?" She heard laughter in his voice. "I think the bed has sheets on it."

She raised her eyebrow and walked out of the bathroom. In the room, she placed the sheet on the sofa and grabbed one of the pillows off the bed.

"I'll sleep on the sofa." She snapped.

"But why?" Zay seemed genuinely puzzled.

"Why? I figured you were probably still upset and not in the mood. I mean you have been mad at me all week, so please continue." She wanted to yell, but she didn't want the other couple to hear her.

"Mad at you? I haven't been mad at you." He sat on the edge of the bed and looked aggravated.

Annette jumped off the sofa and faced him. "Really? Well I couldn't tell. You have ignored me all week. So, if you aren't angry what is it? Have you gotten bored with me?" She thought about what Bianca had said once, how he would get bored with women and move on.

"Bored? Why the hell would I be bored? Where the hell is this coming from? Will you at least explain what you are upset about?" Xavier's voice boomed.

Annette stepped in his face, mad as a hornet. "Can *I* explain? If you can be mad for an entire week, I think I should be able to be upset for one day." She was almost nose to nose with him. "You have not touched me since before the wedding, you have barely talked to me, and you haven't even kissed me since then! And you want me to explain what I am upset about? Ha! That's freaking grand!"

As he reached for her, she moved out of his grasp and stood with her hands on her hips.

"Listen I was never mad with you. I let Jay get under my skin and I was upset with myself. I'm trying to work on some things and I didn't want you to see that side of me. That's why it might have seemed as if I was angry with you, but I wasn't." He looked down at his hands.

Another man who wanted to shut her out! His explanation only added fuel to her fire. She spoke quietly through her teeth as she squinted at him. "I thought you said you wanted us to be a couple?" He looked up in surprise as she rushed ahead, "If we are a couple we are supposed to work on whatever together. If we are a couple I need to know all sides of you, not just the good and fun." She punched each word into his chest with her finger. Xavier opened his mouth but she cut him off as she stepped back.

"I should have stayed at home! But no! I'm so used to riding down heartbreak highway I don't know how to get off the nearest exit. I finally agree with everyone, I am slow!" She bounced down hard on the sofa and jerked the blanket over her.

A shadow crossed over her as he stood. "Annette, look I can go sleep in one of the other rooms if you like."

The condo had two master bedrooms, one on the first floor and the other on the second floor, but it also had three smaller bedrooms. Two upstairs and one downstairs.

She jumped back up to a sitting position. "Don't you dare! We are not airing out our problems to your brother and Bianca! Just go to bed!"

"Then let me sleep on the sofa." His voice softened.

"No! I'm fine, and anyway you slept on my sofa last night and you drove here. Get some rest, goodnight." She laid back down, once again she snatched the blanket over her.

She felt his breath in her ear, "Then get up, I'll sleep on the sofa with you."

"No, I'm not in the mood." She didn't turn around.

The lights went out and then before she knew it, she was picked up as Zay settled on the sofa beneath her. She squirmed but could not escape his embrace. He had placed her between his legs and she felt her need as it flourished through her body. He rained soft kisses on her shoulder and with each kiss her defenses weakened. She settled down when he spoke softly in her ear.

"Annette, I wasn't mad at you, nor was I trying to hurt your feelings." He paused, "The way I feel about you is a new experience for me."

She tried to turn, but he held her in place and continued to speak into her neck. His breath sent shivers down her spine.

"When Damita told me you left with Jay, I felt," she heard him swallow. "I felt fear, then when I walked outside and heard what he was saying, saw how he touched you; yes, I became angry."

She was floored that Damita tried to set her up! That extended family sentiment would not include her! Annette thought back and remembered how Jay had spoken louder when he said certain things. He must have known that Xavier could hear him. Her body relaxed against him as her anger at him ebbed away.

"When Jay told me that he never doubted how much you loved him, I thought he said it to bust my chops. But when I overheard him say it to you, I knew he spoke the truth. To know that no matter what happens that a person loves you, I don't know about anything like that. I wondered how much of a chance do I stand? I don't have anything to offer that can top that type of love. I was upset when I saw him touch you, but I was more upset because I thought I needed to let you go. And you are right I have been slightly ignoring you, because I wanted you to walk away. But you stayed the same Annette, until tonight that is, and I faced the truth. I don't want to let you go. I wasn't trying to be hurtful, and you are not slow. I think you are as close to perfection that I will ever find, for me."

There were no words that described the emotion that flowed through her body. What he said left her momentarily speechless. His hands cupped her breasts as his kisses moved from her shoulder to her neck. It felt so good to have his hands back on her that a small moan escaped from her.

"Xavier, I feel like each time I pull you to me, you push me away. I'm far from perfect, but I meant it when I said that I wanted to be with you. Zay, I'm not going to lie to you about how I feel, but I need you to be honest with your emotions. If you are mad, even if it is at me, I need to know. At least let me defend myself or accept responsibility for my wrongs. I need to know that we are in this together."

His hands had stopped but when she finished, he pressed her body deep into his hardness. After a minute, his hands went back to driving her crazy as they tugged and teased her nipples.

"Annette, you are so good, I don't want my ugly side to scare you off." He nipped at her neck.

She finally managed to turn over, his eyes were slits, full of desire. "Even your ugly side looks good to me." She ran her tongue down the middle of his chest until she got to his magic wand. She released him from his pajamas and as she stroked him with her hand she ran her tongue down his length.

"Ahh, Annette, can you unwrap your hair? I like to feel it against my skin." He ran his fingertip across her lip.

The look he gave her, along with the sensuous storm he had created inside her she would have peeled her skin off if he asked. She took her hair down and captured his hardness in her mouth. Between his fingers against her scalp and the sounds he emitted from some deep place inside, she needed to be doused in water. Much too soon he tapped her arm for her to stop.

"Forget this sofa, we need to get in the bed." He stood.

Annette raised up, but remained on her knees on the sofa. Xavier looked down at her and pulled her head back softly with her hair. He swooped down and kissed her so lovingly, while he snapped open her duster. He ran his hardness down her neck and around her breasts. When his head grazed her nipples, her frustrations and heat came out in a sob, unable to hold it in, she burst out in tears. Xavier stopped kissing her and lifted her into his embrace.

"Annette, I'm sorry, I didn't mean to hurt your feelings. Don't cry." He stroked her hair.

"Zay, I need you inside of me, please." She wasn't too proud to beg because the fire inside of her could only be quenched by him.

After he stripped off her duster he laid her gently on the bed and covered her body in kisses. When he reached her love he gently licked her with the tip of his tongue. Her back arched and she grabbed his shoulders as she tried to pull him up. He was unmovable. He teased her unmercifully with his mouth, as he brought her to the brink then took it away. Annette wanted to slap him a few times as her body ached for release.

Finally, he stopped and mesmerized her as he kneeled over her while he stroked himself. The motion of his hand hypnotized and brought an untamed beast out of her. She caught him off guard as she sat on her knees and replaced his hand with hers. After she kissed his neck, she pushed him back and clambered on top of him. Her body sizzled as she slid down his magical pole and tears once again threatened to fall. Never in her life had she felt such an infusion of want, need, and relief. His hips lifted when he thrust himself deeper inside of her and watered the flames that burned through her body.

He flipped her to her back and he moved slowly as he crushed her in a kiss.

"Annette can I have all of you?" He whispered in her ear between moans.

In response, she crossed her ankles on his back and held onto his shoulders as she forced him deep. "You already do."

His fingers pressed into her shoulders as he caught her shimmers within his shakes. She held on to him for dear life as she continued to rock against him loving the feel of his hard pulsations inside of her. An unexpected wave caught her and she dug her fingers into his shoulders as she bucked uncontrollably.

The heat of their lovemaking left the room humid and the emotions they released crackled through them as they lay spent. Getting her fix seemed to have cleared her head. The earlier revelations from Xavier stuck with her and she realized that he had never received love. With that in mind she realized that they were both broken inside, him from his parents, and she from her past loves.

His breathing was even but she knew he wasn't sleep. Before she lost her nerve, she wanted to express what was in her heart.

"Jay was like a fairy-tale to me. Being with Anthony left me broken and no self-confidence. With Anthony, I always questioned why I wasn't enough for him, I wondered what was so wrong with me that I couldn't keep him satisfied." She paused as she felt his arm tighten around her. "When I met Jay and he showered me with attention and since I had never experienced that, I fell hard. It floored me and I wanted to make sure that he continued to feel that way, so I accepted things that I probably shouldn't have. I'm not telling you that we weren't happy, but I wasn't being true to me. Once again."

She stopped again as a lump formed in her throat. Xavier placed his chin on her head and she felt his heart as it strummed in his chest.

"Jay is a good guy and he was good to me. His biggest flaw was underestimating Elaine, I don't think he realized how crazy she is. Knowing myself, after I got with you, I had to question how strong me and Jay's bond was. Us not being together has as much to do with me as it does him." She took a deep breath. "Everything that happened has given me time to reflect and try to find myself. Granted had Elaine not put the wheels in motion, I would not be here with you. But when I think of that it makes me realize that I could have gone all my life and not known what I feel right now. Now that I have experienced this feeling, I never want to let it go." She snuggled closer to him. "Did tonight make you want to reconsider being with me? Did you think I never got mad?"

"No, I didn't think that, I didn't expect it to be that intense." Zay chuckled.

"Oh. Does that make you think differently about me?" Annette was ready to catch the bus home if he wanted her to be his 'Yes Woman.'

"Hell no! That shit turned me on. I was sitting here with my dick hard and feelings hurt." He laughed loudly.

Annette laughed too. Zay could be crude, but she realized that it was part of his appeal. She closed her eyes ready for sleep. She felt his words through his chest before she heard them.

He wound her hair around his hand. "If Jay was a fairytale, then what am I?"

She scooted up and kissed him on his lips, "You are real."

He looked at her in surprise and as he pulled her to him, and worked his magic.

Chapter 20

The humidity in Texas slapped Jay and Carl in the face. They had flown to Houston, then drove an hour into Foster, Texas. Jay slept most of the flight, he was worn out from his streak of bad luck. Although he felt as if this trip was a waste of time, he needed to get away. Everywhere he went he was plagued with memories of Annette. Elaine still worried the crap out of him, and all he thought about was wrapping his hands around her neck.

Since someone needed to be aware of his whereabouts, he told Damita. She surprised him when she was all for it. He realized then that her feelings for Xavier had run deeper than she admitted. The friend line she gave him was a ruse to make him realize how much she meant to him. Instead that prick decided to turn to Annette. Jay jerked his bags as he thought of Xavier. Maybe the tide would change and they would get some dirt on him.

Foster was a small town, not as big as Montgomery, but close. When they drove in, some similarities struck them, the town had many restaurants, a mall, and its downtown was very similar to their home. Carl talked the entire way, he made plans of how it should work, and of course gave his opinion about Jay's life.

"I was thinking. Just in case we don't find any dirt on Xavier, maybe you should leave—, or act as if you don't want Annette anymore. I think that will make Xavier leave her alone. He just likes the thrill of the chase." Carl munched on chips that he had picked up from the gas station.

He continued, "I also think that is how both brothers work. Remember Bianca was dating a friend of Omar's when he ran into her? He didn't blink an eye, he just stole her from him. And me."

Jay laughed, "But Bianca and Omar had something in the past, unfinished business."

Carl shook his head, "After that many years? No, dude was mad and he had a right to be. It's not as if they had broken up right before she hooked up with Greg. Neither one of them care about protocol or friendships. I'm telling you, I bet we find out they have been doing this for years."

Carl had a point but Jay knew that Greg was on a banana peel before Omar showed up. They checked in at the hotel, which happened to be Carly's place of employment, and once they were settled Carl called her.

Carl hung up and smiled. "She gets off at nine and said that we can meet her at the bar then."

"Did you tell her I was with you? I don't want her to see us at the bar and get cold feet." Jay stretched.

"Yeah, I told her, but she won't get cold feet. She wants to meet me and I think she is looking for free drinks!" Carl laughed as he rubbed his hands together. "I hope she looks like some of her pictures."

"Don't forget the purpose." Jay glanced at him.

"Ahh, there were two purposes, information and copulation, and I hope to achieve both." Carl pulled three condoms out of his wallet. "I have more in my room."

Carl left soon after and went to his room. After they freshened up and changed, they rode around town before they stopped at a bar-b-que restaurant. They arrived back at the hotel shortly before nine and sat at the bar. A few minutes later Carly approached them.

She was not what Jay expected. He saw her before she approached and she looked much better from a distance. As she came closer he saw that she was attractive, but the ravages of possible hard living or genes showed on her face. She was taller than he expected and darker. Carly wore her hair in a long wavy weave, she had full hips, a small waist and a bust line that looked fake, but overall somewhat attractive. The most prominent feature on her face was her mouth, she had a wide mouth and full lips.

It was obvious that Carl liked what he saw. He jumped up, pulled a barstool out for her and introduced her to Jay.

After he ordered her a drink, they moved to a table and made small talk, then Carl got right to the point.

"Carly, I have to be honest with you. When I contacted you on social media, my original intent was to get information from you about your ex-husband and his brother." She wrinkled her nose when he mentioned Omar. "But once we began chatting, I really enjoyed our chats and you."

Jay was impressed with his friend. While he 'confessed' Carl laid the hook down smooth. Her expressions went from disgust to a smile.

She looked at Jay then back to Carl in confusion. "Why would you need information on Omar? Is this about a job?"

"No, it's not about a job, we need more personal information." Jay saw that Carl was going to drag this out. But he let his friend do it his way.

Carly sipped her drink, "I was about to say, I know he hasn't run through all his money. Not with his stingy ass."

"No, it's not even about..." Carl started before Jay cut him off.

"All what money?" Jay wanted all the information he could get.

She looked pointedly at her drink and didn't open her mouth until after the server left with an order. "Omar got shot when he was a police officer. I don't know all the details but something wasn't right and the department paid him large. They kept it all hush-hush, and of course he wouldn't tell me, but rumor had it at ten to fifteen million." She paused at their reaction and to get her drink. "That was supposedly what he received after all the fees were taken out."

Carl and Jay were silent as they digested that. Certain things made sense to Jay after that statement. Like why Omar wasn't bothered that his brother might have messed up their business deal.

"Is he in some type of trouble?" Carly asked as she looked at the men. There was a slight smile on her face.

"No, he's fine. We really wanted to know about his brother, Xavier." Carl stepped in once again.

Carly's face crinkled in a smile. "Cray Cray Zay?" Her smile dropped and she looked at them suspiciously. "Why are y'all asking all these questions? I don't want to be involved in no mess with those two."

Jay decided it was time to take the reins. "It's not any mess for you. This is a personal matter about Xavier, and since we know so little about him, we were hoping you could help us out with his background. Just so that we can deal with him better."

Her eyes widened and she shot Jay a smile. "This must have something to do with a woman! It would have to for Xavier to be involved."

She cackled as she drained her tumbler, "Which one of y'all woman did he mess with?"

Jay decided right then that he didn't like Carly. She seemed to be the type of woman that enjoyed seeing the hardships of others. But in case she knew something he would answer her questions to keep her talking.

Carl spoke first. "Is this something he always does?"

She seemed less talkative when her glass was empty. Jay didn't know whether Carl had schooled the server or if they just knew her, but another drink magically appeared. Once again, she sipped before she spoke.

"No, he didn't do it, women just flocked to him and he didn't turn them down." She grimaced, "If Omar had been like that I might still have my daughter. Have y'all met Omar?"

As they nodded she became more talkative, that drink was magical in more ways than one! She stared into the depths of her short tumbler as she spoke.

"That bastard got the best lawyer he could find and took my Liberty away from me. Then when she graduated high school he moved her and I have barely talked to her since! And I haven't seen her at all. He should be the bastard you want some information about, but I doubt if any woman wants his mean ass."

The men thought she should be slightly tipsy, but she seemed to hold her alcohol pretty well. Since she threw the jab at Jay about Xavier, he decided to throw one back.

"Omar just got married." He watched her face closely for her reaction.

Her eyes widened, "Omar got married? Humph, I thought he was going to spend the rest of his life moping about that Baudoin chick. I guess the move helped him."

Jay and Carl looked at one another and when Carl gave him a slight nod he lowered the next blow.

"Carly, he married Bianca, is that the Baudoin you meant?" He waited.

This time her reaction was different! Her face mottled in anger and she looked at both men. "You have got to be fucking kidding me! He married that bitch? Well I'll be damned. No wonder he won't answer my calls."

Carl placed his hand on her arm, "You knew about Bianca?"

Carly gave an ugly laugh and Jay liked her even less. "I damn sure did. That bastard had my daughter around her and told me it was nothing, that they just worked together." She spat the last word out. "Then the next thing I know he tells me that he doesn't want to be with me anymore because he loved her."

She seemed transported to a different time as she spoke more to herself than them. "Liberty would come home and talk about her new friends. Bianca this, Bianca that, I knew there was something going on, because that's when Omar changed. He used to try to make things work better, then he stopped. He changed from the nice Omar, to the mean asshole he remains."

By now Carl rubbed her arm in a comforting motion, he spoke softly. "I'm sure that was hard on you."

"Oh, that was nothing compared to when Omar came home and told me he filed for divorce. He said that he and Bianca were getting married and that he would take Liberty off my hands. He didn't say that he would try to get with Bianca, he knew that they were getting married." She looked at them as a light gleamed in her eyes. "How could he have been so sure? Especially since she had a husband. But Omar was certain that Bianca's mean old husband wouldn't be an issue. If he hadn't been home that night, I would swear that he killed her husband."

The men looked at each other in shock. Jay recovered first. "Why would you think that?"

A nasty gleam came into her eyes. "Bianca was married to an old man, I can't remember his name, but he was a mean drunk. And for a while I tried everything I could to change Omar's mind. But he wouldn't touch me, wouldn't talk to me unless it was about the divorce, so I got fed up! I told Bianca's husband about them." She nodded her head, lost in the memory. "He was mad as hell! Then the very next morning I heard he was dead. A car accident."

Everyone was silent, soft music played and the clink of glasses could be heard. Jay wanted to leave but the story enthralled him, he couldn't move. He remembered that Annette told him some of Bianca's history, but obviously he hadn't listened.

"Does Omar know that you told her husband? Or Xavier?" Jay tried to pull her back on track. As interesting as the history was, he wanted dirt on Xavier, not Omar.

"I'm still living, aren't I? Hell no, I didn't tell him, he would have killed me and telling his brother is the same as telling him. They tell each other everything." She slurped from the bottom of her glass.

Carly gave Jay an interested look. "It's your woman, isn't it? Maybe he will get tired of her, he usually does. That's the only advice I can really give you. Just let it play out and then I'm sure she will come back home."

Jay was suddenly tired. Nothing had been gained by this trip. The only new information was that he couldn't force his hand with money, because they didn't need it. He looked at Carl and threw some cash on the table. Carly's eyes grew big and she clutched his arm.

"I do have more advice to give you. Don't come at Xavier or Omar the wrong way. They are not what they seem."

Jay shook her hand off, "I realize that. But I'll be damned if I sit around and wait for him to get tired of my woman." He nodded at Carl. "I'll see you in the morning. Thank you for your help Carly."

She nodded somberly, "Be careful."

The next morning Jay decided that while he visited Foster, he might as well look around at some of the dealerships. To hell with the brothers knowing he had been here. If he brokered a new deal he wouldn't feel as if the trip had been a total failure. Before he called Carl, he heard a series of knocks at his door.

Carl walked in and looked refreshed. "Hey man, Carly is ready to talk this morning."

Jay looked at him incredulously, "Please tell me that you didn't hit it last night."

Carl grinned, "Hey I took one for the team. I didn't want the trip to be a total waste, so I got this monkey off my back."

Jay shook his head, "I hope you used a condom."

His shoulders shook in disgust. There was something about Carly that made him feel dirty, and this fool had laid down with the woman.

"Yeah, I used two in fact. If she has something good to tell us this morning, I think you might owe me one for this." Carl looked at him expectantly.

"I don't owe you a damn thing! I didn't tell you to have sex with the woman." Jay laughed.

"You are right you didn't. But you see after I put it on her, she is ready to sing like a jaybird." Carl took a bow.

Thirty minutes later they were at a restaurant two blocks away from the hotel. It was a mom and pop shop, with grease splatters and a server that called them sweetie.

After they ordered Jay gave Carly a good look. In the daylight, she looked worse for wear. He noticed that she had dark splotches on her face and her weave was due for a pick me up. He waited for her to speak. He told Carl on the ride over that if she started up on Omar again he would walk out.

"I figured I might be able to help you out, but I need something in return." Carly began with hesitancy in her voice.

"What do you need? Money?" Jay's patience was short.

"I want to see my daughter. I call Omar and he never returns my calls and when I talk to Zay he tells me that he's given him the message. I can't afford to get to Alabama on my own." Tears welled up in her eyes. "I just want to see my baby."

Jay felt a tremor of sympathy for her. "I think we might be able to manage that depending on what you give us."

Carly looked around, and even though the restaurant was nearly empty, she lowered her voice. "There are two men that live here, but only one is willing to talk to you." She took a deep breath and looked over her shoulder again. "Omar and Xavier messed them up really bad, they almost killed them."

Chapter 21

Moving day was hectic! Marisa's dorm room looked like a mini apartment. The men moved her things in while Bianca, Annette, Cecile and the girls decorated. Luisa directed the move and the decorations. Once everything was in place, the group, including the girls, headed back to the palace. Annette was worn out! She felt bad for Zay because he helped with the heavy lifting and she knew that he hadn't slept much the night before. A small smile crept on her face, neither one of them had.

Annette tried not to look green when they got back to Geoff's and realized that he had catered food for them. As in the caterers were present and served them! She felt totally out of her league! It wasn't pulled pork and baked beans, there was shrimp, oysters, calamari, lasagna, and a host of other side dishes along with dessert. And an endless supply of some white wine that was the best she had ever tasted. The only other people who looked shocked were Liberty and Cherise, everyone else took it in stride.

After they ate everyone dispersed. Bianca's mom and grandparents went to bed, Horatio left, Omar and Xavier went to the garage and left Bianca and Annette on the deck.

Bianca wasted no time, "I guess you decided that Zay was what you want?"

Annette looked for anger, disgust or judgment, but only found open curiosity in her friend's face. She shrugged her shoulders, "Yes, I thought about him, Jay, and most of all me."

Bianca sipped her juice, and her eyes urged Annette to continue. "I needed to be true to myself. And honestly after everything that has happened I feel more comfortable with Xavier, it's hard to explain. After being with him, I could not imagine not having his presence in my life." She gazed out at the landscape. "The only thing that kept me from making the decision sooner was Jay. I felt so guilty, as if I didn't love him enough to keep Zay away from my heart. Am I making sense or do I sound foolish?"

Bianca shook her head while she asked, "But how do you feel about Jay? Are you still in love with him?"

Tears stung the back of her eyes as an emptiness entered her spirit. "I think Jay will always hold a place in my heart. What we had was so special, but the drama and lies muddied it. When I'm with Xavier I don't yearn for Jay, but a part of me always yearns for Xavier."

In their silence the crickets chirped, frogs croaked, and the sunset looked like an ominous backdrop. To hear her innermost thoughts spoken aloud, freed some of her fears and put them to rest. It was as if long as they remained unspoken she could cast doubt to eventually make it untrue. She waited patiently to hear how Bianca felt about it. The wait lasted mere minutes.

"I understand and I hope it works out for both of you. Omar told me that he sees a change in Xavier since he has been seeing you. I didn't want to believe it, but it's true. I never dreamed that you and Jay would not be together, you seemed so perfect, but you know your heart. Are you in love with Xavier? Girl I almost choked saying that! It just sounds so wrong."

Annette joined Bianca in her laughter. "I don't know why you do him so wrong." She choked out between giggles.

"I just can't see it, he is so aggravating. But you didn't answer my question." Bianca took a bite of her dessert.

Annette chose her words carefully. "I can't call it love just yet, I don't know what to call it. But I am definitely in my feelings. It's a feeling that I have never experienced before, I can tell you that."

Bianca wiped her mouth with her napkin, "Well, tell me this: have you always turned into a werewolf at night?"

Annette turned her head as she spat out her drink. Bianca's shoulders rolled with silent laughter as she tried to keep a straight face.

"I mean Zay came downstairs this morning without a shirt and he had whelps all over his chest, and when he saw me he ran back upstairs. I didn't know what the hell had happened." Bianca cut her eyes to the side. "I never would have thought…"

"Damn you Bianca!" Annette could barely speak her laughter left her breathless. "I just get carried away sometimes."

"Obviously! If it's all like that I'm glad Damita didn't "sample" him, y'all would have fought. I hate to say this but I would have put my money on Damita." She grinned as she demolished the last of her dessert.

When she heard Damita's name she thought about what she learned the previous night. Bianca's face went from shocked to sadness as she shared it with her.

Bianca's head shook sorrowfully. "Damita cared more than she admitted to us. I understand she felt betrayed, but at the same time if she spent enough time with him to know that he wasn't for her, she shouldn't act like this. She told me and Tonya that she was jealous, but I didn't think it was this deep."

Annette was shocked about Damita being jealous but she saw it from a different angle. "I think Damita just wants to be in a relationship because she is lonely. Remember, she was looking at your brother, at your house and the wedding."

Bianca nodded, as she scoffed, "Right, she just went from bad to worse! Horatio? That's not lonely, that's damn near desperate."

Omar and Xavier looked at Geoff's collection of cars. He had the Escalade, a Hummer, and a nice Corvette. The brothers talked about the vehicles until Omar changed the topic suddenly.

"I see you decided to take the plunge with Annette." When Zay nodded he continued, "Do you think it's going to work?"

Xavier looked at him long and hard before he answered. "I think it will, but I'm sure you will tell me why it won't."

Omar laughed, "No, I'm not. I think if you do the right thing it might. Until you find something wrong with her."

Xavier stretched and smiled. "Nope, I don't think I'll find anything wrong with this one. She bathes regularly and she seems to be honest."

"Well at least you are easy to please." Omar smirked, "I hear she doesn't put up with your crap."

Xavier's brows knitted together in confusion. "What do you mean? I haven't given her any crap."

Omar laughed and could barely speak. "When I got out of the shower last night, Bibi was sitting on the bed and told me to be quiet. We heard Annette giving you the business, until I closed the window."

Xavier shook his head. "That damn woman is so nosy! Since you know that much, yes she did."

Omar watched as his brother smiled at the memory. He hoped that things worked out for him, because the Zay he knew would have stormed out of the room last night. The woman would have been on a bus home today. He didn't know who this man was!

"Are you going to do right? I mean it always starts out good, but later, I don't know what happens."

Xavier looked over his head and didn't answer for a few minutes. "Omar, I think she is the one. I don't know how she does it, but she makes me want to be a better person. I've never felt this way before. I haven't been mean to her, not really, and I've told her about our parents but she still sees the best in me."

Happiness flowed through Omar as he listened to his brother. He was mad at him at first for fooling with Annette, but now he was glad he did. He had never seen Xavier this peaceful.

He kept a straight face as he responded. "She sees the real you. Not what you choose to show people, but what is inside." He lowered his voice, "I'm happy for you, *ese*."

"If Jay would just leave her the hell alone, we wouldn't have any problems. He just keeps trying." Xavier sighed heavily.

"You would do the same. It will take some time, but it doesn't help that you are a complete ass around him." Omar liked Jay and he felt bad for him, but his brother deserved happiness too. No matter how much he respected Jay and thought he was a stand-up guy, no one could ever break the bond he had with his brother.

Xavier laughed, "I can't help it man. But I have to give it to him, he's messed with my head too. And you are right, but I would do it differently."

It was good to see Xavier laugh, but Omar knew that Jay would not give up without a fight. He believed that for Jay it was based more on principalities than emotions. Jay loved Annette, but he also didn't like anyone to get over on him. Omar had seen the way he handled business, he was ruthless if it came to cutting other companies out.

Once another company tried to underbid his original bid and claimed that they offered the same services. Instead of lowering his price, he presented the dealership with what he offered and showed them every flaw the other company had. Then he went to a few dealerships that the company served and took their business. That was his sole focus until he got it done. Jay had made some stupid mistakes when it came to his ex-wife, but he was no dummy.

"Just be careful, you know when emotions are involved anything can happen. Don't fool yourself that Annette doesn't care about him anymore. Emotions don't work like that." Omar's tone was serious. "I'm sure he still has hope, because if not I'm sure he would have repossessed her car."

Xavier's eyes narrowed, "What do you mean? What car?"

Shit! It was obvious that Xavier did not know that Jay bought Annette her car. He filled him in, but he didn't like the ugly glint that glimmered in his eyes.

"Just be cool. If it was a gift I'm sure he will let her keep it."

"And somehow you think that is cool? Don't worry I'll be cool, but he might as well give this shit up. I'm not..."

Geoff interrupted them when he strolled in. Bianca's uncle always made Omar feel uneasy, probably because he knew about his dirty dealings. He chatted about his cars, then he asked to speak with Xavier privately. Omar told Xavier he would see him back at the condo before he walked off.

*****

Bianca and Annette talked more, but Annette was tired and ready to go. Once Bianca paused she feigned a yawn and went to find Xavier. She ran into Omar on her way to the garage. He told her that Zay got caught by Geoff but probably wanted to be rescued.

Annette placed her hand on his arm before he walked off. "Omar can I speak with you for a minute?"

He got a strange look in his eyes that she thought was surprise at first, but realized he looked aggravated.

"Omar, I don't want to get too personal here, but can you call your parents sometimes?" Annette blurted before she lost her nerve.

That's when he looked surprised. "Why would I want to do that? I don't have anything to say to them."

Annette explained how his mother blamed Zay for him not calling and then she decided to lay it out for him. "Zay won't admit it, but it bothers him when your mother says that to him. I think it hurts him that when he did what was best all he gets is blamed and no appreciation."

Now Omar looked extremely aggravated as he wiped his face with his hand. "He never told me that the old lady treats him like that. I told him to stop talking to them! Damn!"

Annette frowned as she looked at him. "We both know that he is not going to stop taking their calls. That's why I asked you to call them. Please?"

Omar expression became tender. He held both of her arms and leaned in close, Annette thought he was going to kiss her cheek. Instead he whispered in her ear.

"I see why my brother is so crazy about you." He straightened and released her arms. "Okay I'll call them. For Xavier."

He winked at her and walked off. Annette walked into the garage and saw Zay as he stood with Geoff. Both men looked intense as they spoke and she caught a small part of the conversation.

Geoff looked intently at Xavier, "Do you want me to handle it?"

Xavier did the same thing Omar had just done and wiped his face with his hand. "No, it's not that serious, this is a personal matter."

Annette cleared her throat and both men glanced her way. Geoff looked at her, back at Zay then he smiled and nodded.

"I see. I believe I understand now. Let me know if you need me." Geoff walked by her as she approached and squeezed her arm.

Xavier put his arm around her and called out to Geoff. He spoke rapidly in Spanish and Geoff looked surprised.

Geoff smiled before he told him, "Don't worry I'll get Lil Geoff right on it."

When Geoff smiled, Annette felt a chill and saw the person that Xavier had warned her about. It seemed weird that before he smiled she couldn't conceive him to be a dangerous man. She crossed her arms as a chill hit her, but when Zay pulled her closer she felt safe and secure.

He walked out and Annette looked up at Xavier. "I didn't know you could speak Spanish!"

Xavier laughed as he kissed her nose, "Annette I'm Puerto Rican what did you expect me to speak? German?"

She elbowed him in the ribs. "Of course not, I just never heard you before."

"I didn't think you would understand me if talked to you in Spanish." He chuckled.

She pinched the inside of his arm as they walked out of the garage.

When they returned to the condo, each couple retreated to their room. Annette knew that Zay was tired and when he emerged from the shower she kneaded his shoulders and back. Her thoughts drifted to her children, they would have loved this trip. Guilt tapped her heart because she should have included them. She mentioned this to Xavier as his head lolled back from her ministrations.

"I was thinking the same thing. We can come back and bring them whenever you want."

Annette bounced on the bed. She kissed him on the cheek and hugged him tightly. "Can you get this condo again? Or one like it?"

"Umm yeah. This is our condo. If Bianca and Omar aren't here, we can use it." Xavier shrugged his shoulders slightly.

For some reason, she thought that they rented the condo, she had no idea they owned it! Annette shook her head as she realized she had a lot to learn about Xavier. Xavier spoke before she could question him.

"Can I get a little more? It felt so good." He gave her his disarming smile.

As she massaged his back she tried not to get aroused, but he felt good and his grunts were sexy. She maintained her composure a little easier because he kept cracking on crushed ice.

"You know Ant reminds me of Omar when he was a kid. His personality was just like Ant's, but the only difference is that Ant catches on quick when it comes to cars. He has an amazing mechanical mind. I think I might show him how to put a computer together, if he wants to learn."

While he spoke, Annette wondered why he didn't let other people see this side of him. It was as if he wanted people to think he was cold, uncaring and just about a good time. He leaned his head back on her chest and emotions overwhelmed her. She had been honest with Bianca when she said she had never felt this way before. With Anthony, it was pure lust disguised as love, Jay was her security blanket, if she needed it, he got it for her. Xavier was her lover, best friend, she felt safe and protected with him but she also felt so protective of him. There was a part of him that she sensed was so vulnerable that needed— hell that needed her!

Her fingers dug deep into his shoulders as he cracked on that ice and she thought of the other night. Even when she was angry she yearned for his presence, just to soak in his light. No wonder she was confused as to what to call her emotions! To keep her emotions at bay she jumped back into their conversation.

"I think Corey is more like his dad." She said in his ear as she nibbled his earlobe.

"Don't say that! I was thinking he was like you. He asks a million questions and now that I've seen your tantrum, I see the resemblance." Xavier chuckled and pulled her into his lap.

She kissed him hungrily while she ran her hand over his face as if memorizing every pore. His mouth was cold from the ice but that only intensified her heat. She stopped and felt selfish because she knew that he had worked so hard with moving Marisa. His muscles had been tense under her hands and yet she wanted to ravish his body.

"Let's go to sleep, I know you are tired." She murmured.

Once again, he crunched on that damn ice, but his hands worked on her body. "Ahh, Annette I am tired, but I doubt if I'll sleep much if I don't get a little bit of you."

He swept open her robe and if she thought that the chill of his mouth in a kiss made her hot, she melted as she felt the coldness on her nipple. A low guttural moan escaped her. A draft of air hit her body as he laid her on the bed and closed the window. She shook her head as she thought about all his quirks.

The bed dipped when he got on it. "Annette can I make love to you like I want to?"

A sliver of fear shot through her body along with an unexplainable rush of desire. If what she had experienced with him hadn't been his normal, she knew she was in trouble. Fear and excitement kept her from speaking so she only nodded.

She watched as he filled his mouth with ice and she almost screamed and came as he captured her breast with his frozen mouth. His other hand pulled at her nipple and she gasped as she felt water run down her body.

"Damn your body is so hot we might run out of ice." He murmured as she heard him rattle the ice.

With her eyes closed she tried to think of something that could hold off the volcano the rumbled in her body. She felt his cold tongue as it penetrated her heat before she heard him.

"Annette look at me." He commanded in a sexy damn voice.

She peeped at him as he ran his tongue across her sensitive lips. "Come on Annette open your eyes, I want to see your soul."

There was no way to resist that command! She opened her eyes as he found her center and released the ice inside of her while the heat of his tongue lapped her long and gentle. Her back arched and her body bucked as she lost it.

"Ohhh Xavier! Ahh…" Her scream was cut off as he entered her soul deep and hard. Even while her waves consumed her she could not close her eyes. He was on his knees and he gripped her butt hard as he gave her long hard strokes. At this point the only part of her body that remained on the bed was her head. On their own her legs drew up and her feet landed on his chest. Her body hummed with its upcoming release and he predicated it as his hardness increased. She saw stars first, then as he vibrated hard against her walls she saw the moon, and when he released his seed she saw the whole universe.

When the feeling in her limbs returned she was in his arms and he held her gently against his chest. When they finally laid down, she spooned her body against his and right before she nodded off she heard him whisper.

"Annette, you take me places that I never thought I would see."

Chapter 22

Jay and Carl waited in the bar for Leonard. Leonard was supposedly the guy who had information on the brothers. At first Carly wanted them to follow her to his house, but Jay nixed that idea. It could have been a set-up to rob them or worse. He didn't completely trust Carly, there was something about her that rubbed him the wrong way. Finally, this guy agreed to meet them at the hotel.

Jay sat up straight as an older guy walked in the bar area. He had a receding hairline, a long scar across his face and he walked with a noticeable limp. Carly appeared behind him and pointed out Jay and Carl.

"What the hell kind of info can this guy have? He doesn't even look like someone they would know." Carl whispered furiously.

Jay had the same thoughts and he almost reminded Carl that this had been his idea. Before he could say anything, the guy stood beside them.

"Are you the guys that wanted to talk?" Leonard's voice was gravelly, like a smoker.

"Yes, we wanted to ask you about Om…" Carl said.

Leonard cut him off when he quickly raised his hand as he looked around nervously. "I'm not talking in here."

He lowered his voice and Jay thought he heard fear mixed with anxiety. Since he was alone and looked as if they could take him down if necessary they went to Jay's room. Leonard looked around appreciatively before he sat down on the chaise heavily. Carl perched in the chair beside him and Jay pulled up the other chair.

"Listen I don't want to waste your time. Carly told us that you know about two guys that Omar and Xavier Rives messed up." Jay decided to get straight to the point.

Leonard let out a phlegmy laugh. "Yep, but I don't know about the guys, I am one of the guys."

Jay sat back, shocked. He took another look at Leonard. He was scraggly, his teeth were tinged with yellow, and the scar on his face was ugly. It went from his ear to the corner of his mouth. He and Carl settled in and let him speak.

Leonard was a former police officer, and spoke of his time on the force with reverence. He told of a time when being a crooked cop was like a job promotion. There was a feeling of de ja vu as Jay listened to him, because he felt the same dislike he felt for Carly. Leonard talked about how they skimmed drugs and drug money from busts. These kickbacks afforded them expensive houses, cars and trips. Then Omar came on the scene and found out about their dirty dealings.

"He was like this self-righteous prick who wanted to do everything by the book. I don't know how the hell he found out, but one of the high-level officers who was involved found out." Leonard looked out to the balcony.

After he asked for a drink and if they could move to the balcony so that he could smoke, he continued. Omar had gotten too much information and was about to release it. Leonard and his partner Thomas had received the order to shut him down. They got the opportunity during a high-risk domestic call. Their orders were to take him out and make it look as if he had been killed by the perpetrator.

Leonard blew his smoke out, "We botched it up. We got him and he was hurt bad, but he lived." He looked at Jay and Carl, "I never said I was an angel, and I didn't want to do it, but if I hadn't the guy who ran the show would have killed me."

Jay felt disgusted and once again there was no connection to Xavier. His leg jumped with impatience.

"What does this have to do with Omar's brother?" Jay snapped.

Leonard took a gulp of his drink. "He came to town after Omar got shot. When Omar was in the hospital we were still running the story that he had been shot by the suspect. We visited him in the hospital to keep suspicion down, and this guy never left! Thomas got scared every time he saw him, because most family members are happy to see that we care. This guy just stared at us with a blank look, never shook our hands or nothing. It was like he knew something. If he wasn't in the room there was another scary looking dude in there. I calmed Thomas down, told him not to worry because we had covered our tracks. I was so damn wrong!"

Carl refilled Leonard's drink while Jay shook his head. Leonard sipped and told them how emails and text messages had been uncovered. Shortly after, the brass fired him and Thomas while Omar received a settlement that was rumored to have almost left the city broke. Their boss told them that they were lucky that charges weren't going to be pressed. Both men found decent employment at a plant in a neighboring county, thanks to their co-conspirator, along with promises of extra work to keep up their lifestyles.

"Did he get fired also?" Jay found himself pulled into the story, but repulsed by the storyteller.

"No. We knew better than to mention David in any correspondence. We weren't crazy." He pulled on his cigarette. "We made bad decisions, but we were working, Omar was okay and fucking rich, so we moved on."

Jay said nothing but wondered how he had connected with so much slime in such a brief period. Leonard couldn't remember the exact amount of time but he said it had been long enough where he and Thomas felt comfortable. They left a bar one night and before they made it to the parking lot, they were picked up.

"I don't remember how they got us. One minute we were walking and the next thing I remember I was in a field getting the shit beat out of me."

Jay noticed how Leonard's hand had a slight tremor as he talked about that night. A tremor that hadn't been there before. Omar and Xavier had beat the men so badly, they both stayed in the hospital for weeks. Leonard's leg had been broken in three separate places, he had three broken ribs, his nose had been broken, a host of internal bruises and that ugly scar on his face. Thomas fared worse. Both of his legs were broken, along with his arm, hand, ribs, nose and jaw.

"I know you probably think that we deserved it, and maybe we did. But I was in debt up to my ass and David was crazy. But them Rives brothers? They got enough money that neither one of them have to work ever again. We were done with it! Thomas and I took the fall for everything! The shooting, the drugs, the weapons and the money, the case was closed." He shook his head, he seemed lost in his memories. "Since Thomas was the shooter, they fucked him up bad. That guy walks with a cane, will barely leave his house, and his scar makes mine look like a scratch."

His eyes cleared as if he remembered why he was there. "But that brother? That is the meanest motherfucker I have ever seen. I can deal with an ass whooping, but he fucks with you mentally. Poor Thomas has to go see a crazy doctor once a month." He traced his scar with his finger. "He held the knife up against my throat and started cutting until I gave him David's name. Then he cuts me and says some shit like "oops, it slipped." But I can't complain because he cut the top of Thomas' ear off."

Jay felt sick to know what these men had done and to know that Annette was caught up with such an evil asshole. Leonard was correct about one thing: it was over, they could have left it alone or pressed charges. The alcohol must have loosened Leonard's lips, because before Jay asked him anything he continued.

"That sick asshole came to the hospital once. My wife at the time thought he was a friend although he never smiled, never said anything to me, he only spoke to her. This bitch left me alone in the room with him! My kidney was bruised from the fight, so he walks over to my bed and pressed his big ass hands on my kidney. I couldn't say a word because that's right, my jaw was broken and wired shut." Leonard didn't look mad at the memory, he looked fearful.

The alcohol had run through his body so he got up to use the bathroom. Once he walked inside Carl looked wide-eyed at Jay.

"This is some crazy shit we are hearing! Two questions: Do you think it's true? And will it be enough to scare Annette away from that psycho?" Carl whispered.

Jay fiddled with his phone. "I think it's true, but I don't know if it's enough. She'll probably think he is some kind of hero."

"But man, that was overkill! Like he said they had gotten the money, and since the case was closed, Omar didn't have to worry about anyone coming for him." Carl glanced towards room as he whispered.

Leonard limped back to his chair and fired up another cigarette. Jay wanted to wrap things up, but he had some questions that needed to be answered.

"How did Xavier mess with you mentally? The hospital visits?" Jay asked.

Leonard guffawed, "I wish! No after it happened he left me presents every month, then it went to every three months, and now it's about every six months. But he leaves special gifts on the anniversary of Omar's shooting every year."

Carl's eyebrows knitted as he asked, "What do you mean he left you gifts?"

"Like dead rabbits or rats on my porch, sometimes a few scorpions and on the anniversary, it's always something big like a dead coyote. That's what did Thomas in, and why he barely leaves his house." Leonard held his head. "I just can't understand why he does it. We told the cops that we didn't know who did it. They thought it was someone we arrested or stole from when we were on the force. It's not as if we can try anything, hell you see how long it took me to make it the bathroom. The only thing I can come up with is that he is one evil bastard."

Jay silently agreed with him. He voiced the one thing that bothered him about this entire story. "Why didn't you tell the police the truth?"

Leonard's eyes bugged out of their sockets. "And end up dead? I've lost everything, my wife, my kids, and the only job I can get is at the grocery store where I work. I'm not losing my life behind this bullshit! It wasn't even our idea, we were just following orders."

Leonard's voice raised and he spoke rapidly. Jay smelled the sour stench of fear as it wafted off him.

He held his breath as he leaned forward. "If they were going to kill you wouldn't they have done it in the field? They made sure you got to the hospital, right?"

"Hell no, they dropped us on the side of the highway, and it's not a well-traveled highway either." He settled back in his seat and looked at the men through narrowed eyes. "You two really don't know what kind of men you are dealing with, do you?"

Jay and Carl looked at each other as they both shrugged their shoulders. That was all the prodding Leonard needed.

"While I was in the hospital I watched the news religiously. One day a special report comes on about a missing high-ranking police officer." As their eyes widened he nodded his head and continued. "Yep. Dear old David and he hasn't been seen since. And remember he was still on the force, missing without a trace. The only person that knew he was behind the entire operation was Omar's brother, Xavier."

Chapter 23

Jay and Carl sat forward in their chairs. If this was true, this was just the type of dirt he needed on Xavier. Jay restrained from the fist pump he wanted to do. When he came to Texas he thought the trip was a futile exercise, but he hoped to find something. He'd imagined that there would be a common law wife, or maybe a few children that Xavier didn't provide for. But a murderer? This was golden. If it was true.

"Do you think he is dead? Or did he just go underground so he wouldn't get caught?" Jay spoke urgently.

"Hell yeah, he's dead! There is no way David would go underground, that man sat on a goldmine. Plus, he was the golden child in this community, home-grown, star baseball player in high school and college, all that. Even if we had snitched on him people wouldn't have believed it." Leonard lit another cigarette and looked at them through the smoke. "You can pull up his name online and see what I mean."

Jay wrote his full name down and Carl finally spoke again.

"What happened when he went missing?" Carl's tone was hushed and Jay couldn't wait to hear his feedback when they were alone.

David had gone missing one night after he called his wife and told her he was going to a business dinner. His wife didn't know who he had dinner with or what the business was about. When she awakened the next morning and he hadn't made it home she became concerned when she couldn't reach him. After she called the police chief and explained what happened, every cop in the city looked for him. His car was found at an expensive restaurant in a neighboring county. When the sheriff in that town asked the workers and patrons that were there that night about David, no one remembered seeing him.

"Just like a that, he was gone. They asked the customers if they saw anyone strange, or if they remembered seeing his car. Nada. Some people thought that maybe he had another woman and had gotten caught up. No one ever came forward."

The sounds of activity around the hotel floated up to them and suddenly a small warm breeze slipped through them. Almost eerily. Jay thought about how the smallest towns hold the biggest secrets.

"You are sure he didn't orchestrate this himself?" Jay wanted to be sure.

Leonard grew animated and slapped his hand on the table. "There is no way! Once, before the shit hit the fan, I asked David why he stayed in Foster. He was smart as a whip and a born leader. He told me if he went somewhere else he would just be another cop. He knew he could rise in the ranks quickly here, and he did. Foster is a small town, but there is plenty of money here." He glanced at them with a light in his eye. "I'll tell you something else. David had offshore accounts and he told his wife about them, just in case he was killed in the line of duty. One of the few people that still talk to me, told me that when she finally tried to access them, the accounts had been depleted. Only the bare minimum was left."

"Wouldn't that show that he probably went off the grid? He just took the money and ran?" Carl sputtered.

Leonard gave him a hard look, "If he planned that, why would he tell her about it in the first place? You guys didn't know him, I did, but if it makes you feel better to think that your guy isn't a killer, then believe what you want."

"Did Xavier ever mention him to you after that night?" Jay wanted this nugget of information to be true.

Leonard snorted, then coughed. "That guy never said too much of anything to me after that night. If I saw him out— Do you know what he called me? Smiley, because of this scar, the scar he gave me! And that's all he would say, "What's up Smiley?" That would be that."

Carl opened his mouth, but Leonard cut him off. "That's one of the reasons Thomas stopped leaving his house. He would see Xavier and he would call him *pequeño lóbulo*, that's little lobe in Spanish."

They gave him blank stares, "He cut off his earlobe remember? That guy is a fucking lunatic."

After a brief silence Leonard pushed his chair back. "That's all I can tell you, I guess I'll go home now."

Jay looked at this man who he realized now was not as old as he appeared, he was just beat down. He needed one more question answered before he left. "Why were you willing to tell us?"

Leonard looked down at his clasped hands. "I heard that he moved, I hope it's true and I don't have anything else left to lose. My wife left me once the money dried up, my kids barely speak to me, I embarrassed them by being a bad cop and he can't make my life any worse than it is. I've gotten used to the dead rats, rabbits, coyotes and the spiders, so to hell with it."

Carl stood with his hands in his pockets but he caught him before he limped out the door. "What about Omar? Did he ever bother you after that night?"

"Nope. Omar became this rich, respectable guy to the public. He had been hurt in the line of duty, built up a security company, and raised his daughter as a single parent. For this small town, they had lost a golden child but gained another one. Whenever I saw him he just looked right through me." He seemed to notice their relief. "Don't let him fool you. While his brother fucks with your mind, Omar will kill you. I honestly believe if his brother hadn't been with him, I wouldn't be alive to tell the story."

Once Jay and Carl recovered from their shock, Jay got Leonard's phone number in case they had other questions. He had to give it to the guy, he didn't ask them for a cent.

Carl started as soon as he shut the door. "Do you believe that shit? Man, I never expected to hear anything like that! Who the hell are these guys and what the hell have Bianca and Annette gotten themselves into?"

Jay cocked his head at Carl. "Bianca? What the hell are you talking about?"

Carl blushed, "You know I still think she is the woman for me. We need to look out for her too."

Jay laughed, "I know you think Bianca is the finest woman on earth, and I hate to break it to you, but dude she is mean as hell! She probably would have been with Omar and Xavier if she had been here. I don't think we have to worry about Bianca."

They laughed and decided to go eat before they formulated a plan. Jay had a few plans in mind, but he would need help and fate to intervene for any of them to work. Unless he could twist the hands of fate. He smiled as they sat at their table.

"You are smiling as if we received good news. My mind is still blown, I thought maybe we would find out that he was a woman beater or something. But this..." Carl shook his head, unable to complete his thought.

"Yes, but once Annette finds out about the real Xavier, I think she'll leave him alone." Jay nodded his head.

"But will she believe you? After what she's been through with the Elaine fiasco. I don't know man." Carl looked skeptical as he gulped down his beer.

"That's why I recorded him. But I think I'll be a nice guy and give Xavier a chance to tell her first." Jay grinned.

"Jay! Did you not hear what I just heard? We just found out that he tortured this guy, keeps mentally torturing him and possibly killed someone. And you want to confront him? That doesn't sound like the best idea." Carl waited until the server left after she delivered their food. "Not a smart idea at all."

"Look, Leonard is scum. They tried to kill Omar and if someone tried to kill one of my siblings... I don't know man. I probably wouldn't have the stomach for what they did, but I would want to. Hell, I wanted to choke the shit out of Elaine for what she's done. I don't think he will get physical with me." Jay ate his food voraciously.

Carl looked doubtful. "Okay, but let me know when you go, so that I can be in the car or something. Do you think that is enough? Even if she does leave him, you still have the Elaine issue."

Jay took a generous gulp of his soda. "I'm hoping he will leave her and then by that time Elaine will have this DNA test and we can be back where we need to be. Xavier wants to be Annette's knight in shining armor, I don't see him wanting her to know how evil he really is. Even if she doesn't come back to me I don't want her with him."

"I hope you are right because they seem to be getting closer and closer. Luck has truly been on his side. At least now we know why he wasn't worried about pushing up on her. He doesn't need the business deal with you. Even if Omar just gave him a million, he is set. Now I see why they walk around all care-free, they don't have a thing to worry about it."

Jay grimaced because he had the same thoughts. Although it was Omar who got the settlement, as close as those two were, there was no doubt it had been shared. Carl was right, even with a million, Xavier was single, no kids, and could live quite comfortably. Jay had a Plan B, but he would wait until he mentioned it to his friend.

Carly met them in the lobby of the hotel when they returned. Jay was ready to research this David guy and now she wanted to talk! She led them to the bar and they sat at a table secluded in the back.

"Did he give you what you need?" Carly was straight forward as she looked futilely around.

They answered in the affirmative and thanked her. Jay was ready to go to his room but she stopped him.

"I've fulfilled my end what about your promise to me?" Carly bit her nail and looked at him nervously.

Jay told her that when she was ready to come he would book her flight, hotel and rental car. He refused to give her cash. The glance she gave Carl made Jay's stomach turn.

"Do you live in the same city?" She purred at Carl.

Jay saved his friend as he thought of something. "Carly, we are in a different town. You aren't trying to start trouble for Omar, are you? Because we don't have an issue with Omar, and if that is the case I'm not doing it."

Her gaze turned cold as she looked at him. "I don't give a shit about Omar. He has kept my baby from me for too long and I want to see her. Do you realize that I could barely see her when they were here? When he got custody, I missed one weekend and he took me back to court. They put me on supervised visitation!" Carly's voice rose.

She noticed a few glances and lowered her tone. With venom in her voice she told them how she could only see Liberty if Omar or Xavier was present. Once, she made it to the appointed spot five minutes late and they weren't there. When she took it to the courts Xavier was there and stated that he had come but she never showed up. They decided not to wait. After that the judge decided to give Omar sole discretion of her visitation rights.

"Liberty's graduation? I received an invitation just like everyone else and I wasn't allowed or invited to come to the dinner. He completely shut me out of her life! Do you know what she calls me? Carly! She won't even call me mom!" She looked down at the table.

When she looked back up she had tears in her eyes. "I know that I might not be the best mother, but they were wrong for excluding me out of her life. I missed proms, dances, and all the things that mothers should do with their daughters. If I don't try to establish a relationship with her now, Omar will make sure that I'm not involved in marriage or if she has children. My blood runs through her veins too!"

Jay still got a bad vibe from her, but she had a valid point. He gave her his business card and told her that whenever she was ready he would make the arrangements. Carly thanked him and her face was etched with raw emotion. He knew that it affected Carl too because he put his arm around her. Jay just hoped that he wouldn't go for round two with her.

Before she walked away Jay asked her a question that had simmered in the back of his brain. "Carly where are Omar's parents? Are they still living?"

Carly wrinkled her nose in disgust. "Yes, I guess they are. If you ever meet them you will understand why they both are so low-down and mean."

This was not what he expected to hear, so he asked her to elaborate. Carly had half-risen, but she settled back down. She told them how she had met them twice. Once when she was pregnant and the other time when Liberty was about two or three. The first time the mother was distant to her but fawned over Omar and his father was extremely quiet.

She smiled as she thought of the memory. "I remember that I wanted them to like me so bad, and I didn't feel disliked, but it was something. Omar dreaded going. We had put the trip off twice and when we finally went it was almost too late for me to fly."

"Fly? His parents don't live in Louisiana?" Jay had made this assumption, but he realized that neither brother had ever spoke of parents.

"No. They live in Chicago. The only reason we went was because Zay kept pressing the issue. Omar did not want to go." She smiled. "That's when things were good between us."

Her smile departed as she told of the next trip. Liberty was a toddler and when his parents saw her they adored her. Carly thought it was because Liberty looked just like Omar. On this trip, Xavier had come with them but spent very little time with the parents. Everything was cordial until they prepared to leave. Their mother cried about Omar and Liberty leaving, but when she hugged Carly she whispered in her ear.

"That lady told me to enjoy him while I could, but she doubted if I would be around long. Then she added that I wasn't good enough for him. I thought I misunderstood her but then she pinched me real hard on my arm and told me he only married me for Liberty. I was bruised for a week! I never went back." Carly got up suddenly and said she had to go. Jay reminded Carl that they needed to work and they went to their rooms.

When they got there, they began researching the missing cop. Everything was just as Leonard told them. He was highly regarded and no one had any idea what happened to him. One article mentioned his car and said that it was found in the parking lot but nothing was missing or disturbed. The only anomaly they found was when an employee of the restaurant was interviewed and he swore that the vehicle had not been there that night. It was very strange.

With the knowledge that he was a bad cop and person, Jay felt no pity for the man, but he agreed with Leonard. There was no discernible reason this man left a town where he had so much prestige. Jay stumbled across an article that featured David's wife. She stood in front of a statue erected at a local junior college in her husband's honor. Jay felt sorry for her and her children. He saved the article, determined to show it to Annette. Regardless of how bad this man was Xavier had no right to take his life.

Jay leaned back, he was tired. He hoped this worked out because he needed Annette away from that jerk. Damita text him earlier to inform him that Annette had gone to Florida with the guy. Damn! Jay needed to catch a break! An idea formed and as it took shape he smiled.

"Carl, I think I know how to beat this asshole at his own game."

Carl might have dozed off, but Jay's words brought him back to life.

Chapter 24

The rest of the Florida trip had been great. After Marisa was moved in, the next day Omar and Bianca went back to her uncle's house, but Annette and Zay stayed in. They went jet skiing, which scared her to death since she couldn't swim, but it was fun. Xavier swore he would save her before she drowned. Then that night they went to a club with the other couple, danced and had a wonderful time. Bianca was saddened their last day. Annette knew she hated to leave Marisa, but she seemed comforted that Marisa's father and Geoff were close by.

Annette noticed that when Mark, Marisa's father showed up for the move there was a shift in the atmosphere. Omar seemed uneasy and Mark seemed disgruntled. She reminded herself to ask Bianca about that later. Since it was just her observation and nothing went awry, it was a drama free weekend. Just what she needed.

When they returned, so did Xavier's sulkiness. She was getting tired of his mood swings! It wasn't long before she found out what caused it. Three days after they returned he invited her and the kids over for dinner. Given his apparent moodiness she was surprised and accepted. After they ate and the children went to the back to play, Xavier held her arm as she tried to leave the table.

"Let that sit for a minute. When are you giving Jay his car back?" He looked serious.

It was a relief when she realized that this issue caused his mood swing, but she wasn't quite sure how to answer. She decided the truth was her best option. "I tried to, but he wouldn't take it."

She thought that was the end so she moved to the kitchen to clean her dish. A smile crossed her face as she thought of how easily her kids clean their dishes at Zay's house. When she moved away from the dishwasher she stepped on his foot. She hadn't realized that he followed her in the kitchen.

"So, when are you giving Jay his car back?" He asked again.

"Xavier, I tried, but he wouldn't take it. And if I give it back to him I won't have anything to drive. I sold my old car when he bought that one." She appeased to his logical side.

Obviously, he left his logic in Florida. "Well, that wasn't smart." He raised his eyebrows as he glared at her.

It seemed as if he had just thrown her a little shade, and she didn't care for his smart attitude. "In hindsight, it probably wasn't. Since I don't have a crystal ball and couldn't see into the future, it seemed like a clever idea at the time."

He tapped his fingers on the counter and looked down. "Maybe you can come up with another idea on how to give it back to him, because that's not going to work."

Annette crossed her arms. "What's not going to work?"

"That you keep the car that he bought! There is no way that you are with me and driving a car that another man bought. Nope, that's what's not going to work. Why don't you give it back to him and get you another car? How hard is that?" Xavier had a mean glint in his eye.

Annette glared back at him. This man lived on Fantasy Island if he thought that she could just go buy a car. If he just dealt with women that had extra money lying around then she was not the one for him!

"Well excuse me Mr. Bright Idea, but you see my bank account is not set up that way. If I could afford a car now he wouldn't have bought me that one!" And if you don't like it then you buy me one, she added silently.

Realization settled in Xavier's expression. "Aw shit Annette! I'm sorry, I wasn't thinking. I forget how hard it must be being a single mother, and trying to make ends meet." He stepped closer.

Anger still sizzled in her. "That's obvious. Unless you want me scoping out a place to live I suggest you drop this issue." He wasn't the only one who could throw a little shade.

"I'm not dropping anything. You still need to give him his car back. You can just…"

"Just what? Catch the bus to work? Will that feed your ego?" She cut him off and shot back.

Xavier became still while he gazed at her. Then he showed his dimples and chuckled. "No, I don't think that you and the kids standing in the rain to catch a bus will feed my ego. I didn't even realize that my ego needed to be fed. But I do have a solution."

She rolled her eyes as he pulled her into the garage. Her car, his Dodge, and the mysterious car under the tarp were there, so she looked around for the bike he probably wanted to offer her.

"I have three working cars here. You can use one of them until you are able to get your own, or if we decide on a permanent arrangement, then I'll get you a car." He grinned at her.

As mad as she was, her heart still fluttered when he said permanent arrangement. That was the closest he had come to admitting any feelings for her. On the other hand, there was no way in hell she was driving a muscle car! He had the Charger and the Chevy Chevelle and an old mustang he was putting together. He walked over to the covered car.

"You can drive this one. It needs to be driven and I never drive it. It will fit you perfectly." He smiled.

"Why did you buy it if you don't want to drive it?" She was still a bit salty.

"It was a gift." He said before he pulled the tarp back.

It was a shiny black Mercedes CLS 550! Her heart stopped because if someone had given him this car he must have been a gigolo in his past life.

"A gift? Who the hell gives someone this kind of gift?" She had to give her gift back to drive his gift? This made no sense!

"Geoff gave it to me. I did some work for him and refused his check. A few days later this car shows up. He's not the type of guy that takes rejection well." Xavier looked embarrassed.

"Xavier this car is too expensive! I can't drive this." She thought of the French fries and chips in the backseat.

"Why not? I just need to add you to the insurance, I can do that online. Come on get in." He held the door open.

The leather seats cupped her butt, just like they did in her Audi, but she had to admit it was so nice. She ran her hand across the steering wheel and when she pushed the engine button, it hummed. She wasn't sure how much it cost, but she knew it was more than anything she had ever driven.

Xavier leaned in, "Do you like it?"

"Yes, I love it, but I can't drive this. It's too nice and I'll be too scared that I'll ding it or mess it up."

She looked imploring at him as she stepped out the car. With his arm around her waist he pulled her close.

"It doesn't matter, I don't care if it gets dinged up. It's not about my ego, but I'll admit it's mainly my pride. As a man, I am supposed to take care of your needs. It's a hard pill to swallow that are you are driving a car that another man gave you, as if I'm not able. Does that make sense to you?" He kissed the tip of her nose as she gazed up at him.

Annette sighed heavily, "Yes, but it makes me feel bad that I can't do these things for myself. I mean how hard is that?"

It was silly for her to throw his words back at him but they opened a wound that was barely healed. He closed his eyes but tightened his grip on her.

"I'm sorry for being a jerk. You make it look so easy and you never complain, so it didn't cross my mind how hard it must be. But don't worry your struggles are over. There is no way that you and your three will need for anything, not if I can help it." His voice was low.

She bumped into his car as she slipped out of his embrace. "No Xavier, I don't want you to feel as if you have to do that. I can take care of myself!"

"I didn't say that I had to do anything." He pulled her close again. "I want to make sure that you and your children are fine. It will make me happy."

She nodded because this man made her misty and hot all at once. He kissed her slowly which lowered her defenses. It stunned her how he could make her so angry, then dissolve her anger within minutes. She went from stunned to complete shock after his next request.

"Annette why don't you guys stay here tonight?" The look he gave was hard to turn down but she had to.

With great reluctance, she told him that wasn't possible since it was a school night and they had no change of clothing. The right side of her brain screamed that it wouldn't hurt for them to get checked in, but she shut it down.

"Can I come home with you?" His finger traced her cheekbone.

This was weird Annette thought. Xavier never asked, he just showed up and slept on the couch. "You know you can."

"Yeah, but I want to be with you, I need to feel your body next to mine. I'll get on the sofa before the kids rise, but it just seems as if it has been too long." He sighed.

It was hard to decipher the look in his eyes, somehow there seemed to be a sadness mixed with need. She realized it must have been her imagination when he opened his mouth again.

"It's not my ego that needs to be fed." He placed her hand on his hardness.

She laughed as she slipped in a few strokes. Xavier folded the tarp and put it in the trunk, then he explained that he would drive the Mercedes to her house and they would work out how to get the Audi back to Jay.

Before they walked in the house she asked him, "What kind of work did you do for Geoff?"

"I set up his network and security in a casino he bought managing partner rights to. I owed him one, so I didn't feel right accepting payment." Xavier looked pained from the memory.

Annette wracked her brain as she tried to remember if her house was decent when they left. On the ride home, she noticed in her peripheral vision that Jolisa kept glancing at her. When she asked her if she was okay she shrugged her shoulders and blew out her breath. It would amaze her if Jolisa made it out of puberty without being on a lifetime punishment.

Once they arrived home, after the kids bathed and while Xavier lounged on her sofa she began her nightly ritual. Her skin tingled with excitement as she washed her face. Jolisa scared her when she appeared in the doorway. She looked upset.

"What's wrong sweetie?" Annette immediately felt bad for her previous thoughts.

"Are you breaking up with Mr. Xavier soon?" Jolisa asked timidly.

Now her daughter thought that she and Anthony went through people like toilet tissue. "No, why did you ask?"

Jolisa shrugged her shoulders then blurted out, "I saw you standing with your arms crossed and you had that look on your face. I thought maybe y'all were breaking up."

In the back of her mind she realized it was possible that Jolisa missed Jay, since he had been in their lives longer. She felt guilty because it probably had been too soon to introduce Xavier to them as her 'man.' Her life would have a 'B' for effort, but her grade as a parent was sure to be a 'F.'

"Jolisa, do you want me to stop seeing Mr. Xavier?" She would do anything for her children, even if it meant sneaking around for a few months for them to adjust.

Jolisa's eyes widened in shock. "No! I like Mr. Xavier, we all do. At least with him we don't have to share you."

The last sentence was mumbled, but Annette heard it. Waves of shock sped through her and sadness crowded her heart. How had she missed what her children had felt?

"What do you mean share me?" Annette spoke softly because she didn't want Jolisa to think she was upset.

Jolisa slapped her hand over her mouth. "I didn't mean in a bad way. We like Mr. Jay, but with Mr. Xavier, he doesn't have any children so it's not as if we must share you with anyone. That's all I meant."

"It's okay, but I thought you all were excited about Malik becoming your brother?" Had she been so wrapped up in Jay that she missed important signs?

"We were at first, but he told us not to call him our brother. It made his mom mad, which I didn't understand. Daddy never got mad when we told him that Malik would be our brother." Jolisa looked at her mom with a perplexed expression.

If Anthony was a bigger person than Elaine that said a lot! A whole lot! Anger rose in Annette as she realized not only had Elaine messed with her emotions, she had also affected her children! Annette fixed her face as she faced Jolisa.

"I'm sorry I didn't know about this, I just thought you all got along well." Once again, she felt like a failure.

"It's okay Momma, we knew you were happy that's why we didn't tell you. We do get along mostly, Malik would only be mean sometimes. And that was usually on the first day he would come over, and mainly only to Corey." Jolisa clarified what she meant when she noticed the look on Annette's face. "He wasn't mean like a bully, you know how Corey can get on your nerves, he would just act aggravated. But now that you are with Mr. Xavier, we are all happy! Especially Ant."

Annette looked at Jolisa, her daughter was in the awkward stage. She was almost as tall as her mother but she was all legs, arms, and pimply skin. Her attitude was in the puberty stage but her body hadn't caught up. She listened as Jolisa told her how happy Ant was with how he was learning how to 'build' cars, and how the bullies had left him alone. Annette's heart stopped.

"Wait a minute! Bullies? What bullies?" She dragged Jolisa into the room and sat her on the bed.

"The bullies at school. It wasn't real bad, but Mr. Xavier stopped it all." Jolisa smiled dreamily.

"Ant told Xavier about the bullies? Why didn't he tell me? I would have gone to school and taken care of it." Annette cringed inside as she thought of the horror stories she heard and the sad news reports of young children who had committed suicide after being bullied. Children close to and the same age as her son!

Jolisa's voice brought her back to the present. "I told Mr. Xavier!" Her nose wrinkled, "I told Daddy too but he didn't do anything. He just told Ant that if he played football they probably wouldn't bother him. We didn't tell you because going to the school doesn't help, it usually makes it worse. But don't worry Momma Mr. Xavier took care of it."

Annette felt nauseous as she thought about kids at school picking on her son. He was so shy, that made him a prime target.

"How did Xavier take care of it?" She croaked out.

Jolisa relished in rehashing the tale. One day Xavier picked them up from school, because he promised Ant they would work on the Mustang. Xavier leaned against the car as Ant walked from the school with a gang of boys behind him. Jolisa of course pointed them out. When Ant approached Xavier asked, loudly, if the boys had bothered him; and of course, Ant said no. Xavier told Ant that if anyone bothered him that he would take care of them for him. He made sure he spoke loud enough for the bullies to hear.

Jolisa laughed so hard she looked as if she had blush on. "Momma you should have seen how big their eyes got. They tried to walk over all friendly and ask Mr. Xavier about his car. Ant hasn't had trouble since."

Part of Annette knew that it was wrong for adults to scare children, but the part wished he had beat their asses! She was sick of worrying about her children going to school! She took a deep breath, kissed Jolisa and told her to go to bed. When she passed the boy's room, she peeked in and saw them deep in slumber. Unable to help it she tip-toed in and kissed both of her sons lightly on the forehead.

Xavier lounged on the sofa as he chatted with Ashley. Annette was glad to see that her sister warmed up to him. Ashley wasn't that happy when she broke the news to her. But as usual she was supportive and she also knew of all the drama Elaine had created. But she still loved Jay like a brother.

They continued talking after she sat next to Xavier. Ashley's eyes lit up as they spoke about stocks, bonds, and retirement. Boring! After what seemed to be too long, Ashley retired to her room. Xavier's arm closed in on her as she soaked in his warmth.

"I thought you had gone to bed, it took you so long." He murmured in the top of her head.

She told him about her conversation with Jolisa and her concerns, but left out the part about the bullies. She hadn't quite wrapped her head around that one yet.

"You have completely won them over." She lifted her head as she spoke.

"They won me over, they are great kids. But there is something we need to talk about." He thumped his fingers against her arm.

He sure had become talkative lately! When they started seeing each other he would rarely answer with more than one word. It felt good that he expressed himself, but she wanted to wait until tomorrow. She sighed and sat up straight.

The look in his eyes startled her, she saw indecision, worry, and something akin to fear in his gaze. She raised her chin slightly as if to ward off any future blows.

"Annette, I told you before that there were some things in my past that aren't that great nor am I proud of them." He looked down, "Some years ago…"

"Wait a minute!" She grabbed his arm and stopped him. "I told you before I don't care about it. Unless you have a wife, ex-wife, or some children that you don't claim or take care of."

Xavier chuckled, "No, I don't have any of that. But I…"

"Then I don't want to hear it! If it was years ago, then I don't care. Unless it's something like…" She trailed off.

"Like what?" He looked at her quizzically.

"I mean you aren't bi-sexual or anything, are you?" The questions were now in her eyes.

"Hell no! Why the hell would you ask me that?" Xavier bellowed.

"I mean whatever it is, if it has no bearing on us now, then I don't need to know it. You have shown me what type of man you are. If you are telling me that what you have shown me is a lie or not the real you, then yes, I'll listen. Other than that, maybe I'll want to know down the road, but I doubt it."

Xavier took her hand and ran his finger inside her palm. They sat like that for a few minutes as he seemed deep in thought. When he looked up she ran her hand across his cheek.

"There is one thing I need to know." She kissed his cheek lightly as he raised his eyebrows. "Why do I have to park in the garage when I come to your house?"

Xavier laughed, "That's what you want to know?" She nodded her head. "I ask you to park in the garage because when you park in the driveway you block my security camera."

Now it was her turn to laugh. "Oh, okay I can live with that. So are we good with what we need to know."

Xavier gazed at her, his eyes trailing down to her mouth. "I might have a question or two, but they can wait."

Annette nodded as they walked hand in hand to her bedroom.

Chapter 25

Jay was frustrated, it took him three days to catch Xavier at the security office. He wanted the element of surprise in his favor. With Omar off on his honeymoon, he knew that Xavier would run the business. Carl had followed him each day still certain that he needed back-up.

The third day was the charm! Xavier's car sat in the parking lot between an old Ford truck and a Hyundai. Since the security office was in a business park it was hard to determine if any of the cars belonged to the security business or not. Jay hoped he was alone, because he wanted to get this over with. He gave Carl the thumbs up before he walked in the building.

The office was open but empty. Jay looked at the certificates and pictures on the wall as he waited for Xavier to come in. He was startled when Xavier clapped him on the shoulder. Jay noticed how large and heavy Xavier's hand felt.

"Jay! What's up man?" Xavier greeted him as if they were friends.

Jay turned and shook his hand off him. He waited for Xavier to sit before he sat across from him.

"You seem so uptight! That's odd, because usually after people see Carly they release some of their tensions." Xavier's voice boomed.

To say that he was surprised that Xavier knew about his trip was an understatement. When Jay realized how easily the brothers could get information, he had encrypted all his accounts. He brushed some imaginary lint off his pants to mask his dismay.

Xavier continued, "Ahh, I see. You didn't partake in what I know was offered. That's probably a good thing."

Jay sat on the edge of his chair and put his elbows on the desk. "Since you know that I was in Texas, you should know why I'm here."

Xavier looked at him coldly. "No, I don't. I can't think of one thing in Texas that would bring you here." Xavier rolled up closer to the desk. "I'm sure that Carly and old Smiley gave you an earful, but that shouldn't have brought you here. Unless you want us to investigate them?"

Damn! Jay wondered how the hell he knew that Leonard had talked to them. Xavier smirked at him and it took all Jay had not to wipe it off. Instead he took a deep breath and leaned back.

"No, what I want is to give you a chance to leave Annette alone, without her knowing about what type of man you truly are. I don't have to tell her if you choose to walk away from her." This time Jay smirked.

Xavier leaned back, closed his eyes and pinched the bridge of his nose. When his eyes opened he glared at Jay. "How do you know that I haven't told her?"

"Because she wouldn't still be with you." He held up his hand when Xavier looked at him in surprise. "Maybe if it was just Annette, but if she knew the type of person you really are, she wouldn't have you around her children."

Xavier leaned forward again, "Jay, I underestimated you. It never crossed my mind that you would travel to Foster to find something?" Xavier made air quotes and chuckled.

"Glad you think it's funny, but it's no joke. Annette and I have our problems but we could have worked them out, if you hadn't stepped in the picture. I refuse to let her be played by someone who just has some vendetta against me or just wants to get a piece. She deserves better than that." Jay refused to back down.

Xavier grunted before he spoke. "Whoa, man calm your ego down! Getting with Annette had nothing to do with you. Annette caught my eye from the beginning, but she was with you, so I respected that. But then I noticed a few things. Like how your ex treated her and how you did nothing to stop it. Then I noticed how you let your ex-wife lead you by your dick. That's what she deserves better than. You opened the door and I closed it."

Jay's neck became hot with anger. Carl was right! This asshole had been watching Annette all the time. He might not realize it but his gig was up.

"Whatever man. Like I said, I'll give you some time to figure out how to leave her alone. But if you decide not to, I'll tell her myself." Jay was tired of this conversation and he text Carl to let him know that everything was cool.

"Well I guess you should tell her then, because I'm not going anywhere." Xavier said dismissively.

His tone and attitude pissed Jay off, so he stood. "You might want to rethink that because when I tell her she will leave you alone. I'm trying to give you an option to save face."

"*Güey*, you can keep your damn options!" Xavier rose and sneered at Jay. "Even if she does leave me, I'm not going anywhere. It's not just about Annette now, I'm involved in her children's lives, so I'll always be around."

Xavier walked away and then turned around. "What makes you so sure that if I leave her alone that she will come back to you?"

This time it was Jay who smiled. "She might not, I just don't want her with you. It was dirty the way you got with her, and you know it. You don't care, just like you don't give a damn about what you did to the men in Texas."

Xavier stopped in his tracks and snarled at him. "Give a damn? Those motherfuckers almost killed my brother and you want me to feel sorry for them? Man, get the hell out of here!"

Xavier snatched the door open and Jay realized that the 'dead ass stare' Xavier gave people was normal. Jay admitted that he wanted to push Xavier's buttons, but it seemed as if he had unleashed the savage. He walked out with confidence, determined not to show his nervousness.

When the heat hit him, it was relief. Fall was around the corner but it was still hot as hell. Carl still sat in the parking lot, and relief washed over his face when he spotted Jay. Jay nodded and called him once he got in his car, he did not want Xavier to know Carl had followed him. It wasn't until after he told Carl that everything was cool, that he reflected on the rage he saw in Xavier. Jay would never admit to anyone that the look in Xavier's eyes unsettled him. Jay was just glad to get out of there.

Xavier's statement about the children shook Jay up. *What the hell was she thinking?* That's why she needed to be with him, she was too nice and naïve. She always wanted to see the best in people and took people at face value. What Annette needed was someone who would look out for her best interests, Xavier would not do that.

Once Xavier cooled off, Jay was certain that he would see that it would be best to walk away silently. He came to Alabama all suave, Mr. Romeo himself and he wouldn't want that image marred if people knew he was a psychopath. The only reason Jay was willing to give him some time was because Elaine's DNA test was next week. Jay was certain that the baby wasn't his because of the way she delayed it. He had to go to yet another appointment with her to make sure it was scheduled. Once the results were in, he would turn up his efforts in getting Annette back.

A small thought lingered in the back of his mind, what if she didn't come back to him? What would he do? He shook that idea from his head as he turned in to the parking lot of his office.

The day passed quickly since work had piled up in his absence. His office manager, Heather came in and sat across from him.

"What's up?" Jay barely looked up from his computer. Heather had been with him for five years now and she was a gem. He knew that the office would run smoothly if she was there. But Heather recently had some personal issues that made her absent more so than usual. Jay hoped that wasn't the reason for her impromptu visit.

"Nothing much, I just wanted to make sure that you are okay. I know that it has been hard since you and Annette broke up." Heather glanced around his office.

"Yes, it has, but work has to go on." Jay said lightly. He was not about to talk about his personal problems with one of his employees. He also wanted to give her a slight hint that she needed to do the same.

Heather stood suddenly, "I came to tell you that some man named Leonard, has been calling here insistently for you. He wouldn't leave his number, he said you knew it."

Jay thanked her and asked her to close his door on her way out. He had given Leonard his card, but not the one that had his cell number on it. In case Leonard decided he should have asked for some money, he didn't want the guy blowing up his cell. The phone almost slipped from his hands as he dialed the number.

"Hey Jay? Is that you?" Leonard answered the phone on the second ring.

After he assured Leonard that he was indeed himself, the man started going off. He was agitated and breathing hard which made it hard to understand him.

"Slow down man! I can't understand what you are saying." Jay almost screamed in the phone to catch his attention.

He heard Leonard gulp for air. "Who knows that we talked?"

"I didn't tell anybody. Why what happened?" Since he had just told Xavier, he didn't count him.

Leonard gasped for air. "Two days after I talked to you, he left a snake on my porch! A live one! Man, I couldn't leave my house, I had to call in to work and everything."

Jay was shocked and dismayed. He knew that Xavier had not left Alabama. Had Leonard given him bad information?

"Leonard, I don't think that Xavier has been back to Texas. Maybe the snake got on your porch some other way." Jay tried to reason with the man.

He heard Leonard as he sighed deeply, "I know it wasn't Xavier! It was the other guy from the hospital!"

After a moment of silence Leonard reminded Jay of the man who replaced Xavier at the hospital when Omar was injured. Then he explained that this mystery guy blew his horn until Leonard stepped out and almost pissed himself.

"He said that the next one would be in my bed if I keep running my mouth. I had to call a friend of mine to come get the damn snake." Leonard's voice trembled.

Jay sat in silence because he didn't know what to say. He finally told him to stay calm and to let him know if anything else happened. What he left unsaid was that there was little that he could do. Leonard hung up in a huff after he told Jay that if he needed more information, he would have to get from somewhere else.

Jay rapped his fingers against his desk. Xavier was crazier than he thought! What type of person waged this type of psychological warfare on another? He wished he had taped Leonard this time too, just in case Xavier decided to do the wrong thing.

Any hope that Xavier was going to leave quietly dissolved when he waltzed in Jay's office the next day and tossed the keys to Annette's Audi on his desk.

"It's in the parking lot." He gave Jay his 'normal' dead ass stare before he strolled out. Jay's blood pressure rose as he watched him walk out of the office.

After work, he went to his moms to eat. This would be the first time he had seen his mom since the wedding, so he was prepared to get an earful. And she didn't disappoint him.

Once he sat down to eat, or better yet before his butt hit the seat, she started.

"Jay why didn't you warn me before the wedding that Annette was seeing Omar's brother? I mean that would have helped." She rolled her eyes as she sat next to him.

"I didn't want to talk about it. That guy, I can't stand him. He..."

"I think the person you should be mad at is Elaine and yourself! I kept telling you that you were going to lose that girl if you didn't put Elaine in her place. But did you listen to me? No! You must have been thinking that Annette was an old crab cake like Elaine."

"Mom? Can I eat without you telling me what I already know?" He chomped on his now tasteless food.

The silence lasted for three minutes, then she started again, with a softer tone. "Jay, I know this has hurt you, just let it be a lesson. Maybe if things don't work out between them or if you meet someone else you will know what to do."

Jay swallowed his food and wiped his mouth. "This is not over. There is no way I'm going to sit by and let him use Annette until he gets tired of her. Hell, he was with Damita first or have you forgotten?"

René took off her glasses and looked at him sternly. "No, I haven't forgotten, but I wouldn't have called them 'together.' I hope you are not planning on doing something rash." She paused, then continued when he didn't answer. "I can't tell you what to do, but I can give you advice. Advice that was bought and paid for, not read or heard about. Sometimes you can push and try so hard that you get an opposite result from what you want. You can't make people do anything, especially when there are feelings involved."

"What do you mean? I haven't pushed anything on Annette, if anything he is the one pushing her away from me." Jay wanted his mom to understand how he felt.

"I'm just saying remember the purpose. You love Annette and you want her in your life, but sometimes when a third-party is involved it becomes more of a competition. Don't let the original goal get lost in your anger." She placed her hand on his.

Jay listened to his mom but he did not hear her. "But this guy came and messed up everything! He has Annette thinking he's this good guy, he hurt Damita's feelings, and doesn't care that he messed up their friendship. He is not who he appears to be."

René listened and when he finished she rubbed the back of her neck. "It will be up to Annette to see his true colors and Damita, her pride is just hurt. She will realize one day that she should look further than her physical eye when she meets men. If she would get over her pride, she and Annette will be fine."

Jay knew his mom meant best, but he also knew that she didn't understand. He got up and washed his plate, as he formulated a response that she would be satisfied with. So, he could go home.

"You are saying that I should just sit and twiddle my fingers while he runs off with Annette?" Jay stammered, as he tried not to curse in front of his mom.

"Xavier didn't create this mess, Elaine did. A scorned woman or man for that matter can be a terrible thing. But you can't blame Xavier or Annette for what has been in the works since you got divorced." René peered into his face.

"Mom he took advantage of Annette when she was hurt. Yes, if I had made better decisions she would still be with me." He knew he sounded like a petulant child but it couldn't be helped.

"Once again son, don't make this a competition. Yes, Annette was hurt, but you realize that you were the first relationship she had been in since her divorce. Maybe she needs to spread her wings." Her expression turned stern. "As much as you don't want to hear this, the Annette I saw at the wedding looked happy. I'm sure some of that happiness came from not worrying about dealing with excess drama."

"But Xavier doesn't mean her any good. He will do her just like he did Damita." Jay was sullen.

"Let her figure that out. As for Damita, she wanted something that wasn't there. I told her after the dinner we had with Annette's family that Xavier wasn't serious about her. A blind man could see that." René sighed. "I just hope you see you do not need to create any more bad memories. Because it is the memories that will bring her back."

She leaned closer to him, "Before we moved here, your dad tried to come back home. But each time I thought about it, the bad memories outweighed the good. And I created some of those bad memories by doing exactly what you are doing now. I wanted to make him be faithful. By doing that

I ran him off faster than if I had just sat and let him either hang himself or realize what he had at home."

This revelation stunned Jay. In his eyes, his mother was the best woman, mother and person he had known. He remembered arguments, but never anything that his mom had done wrong.

"How did you run him off?" The son Jay didn't want to know, but the man Jay did.

"When I found out about that woman, I made her whole life look dirty. I told him she was a whore because she had children by different men." She laughed, "It was a different time back then. I constantly threw it in his face, that and anything that seemed negative. The next thing I knew he moved in with her."

René's face showed no emotion, she just stated facts. "It all ended well, and I'm glad I didn't take that no count man back, but I played a part in our final demise. I don't want you to do the same."

"But if he tried to come back his memories weren't all bad. Right?" Jay wondered aloud.

"Of course not! But his plan was to do the same thing. I know because he cheated on every woman he got with. He wasn't looking at memories, he just wanted what he could no longer have. Don't you make the same mistake."

Jay loved his mom at that moment more than he ever had. He was glad she told him about his dad, but his situation was different. He hadn't run Annette off intentionally, he just made the wrong decisions. He hugged his mom tightly before he left, and as usual she had parting words.

"Don't lose the war trying to win a small battle." She smiled before she closed the door.

He thought of his mom's words, he had lost many battles lately, but he would win this war.

Chapter 26

The evening was muggy and remnants of raindrops sparkled on the streets like diamonds. "My Love" by Wale blasted from the speakers of the Mercedes as Annette drove to meet her friends. Her playlist was on a USB and every song made her think of Xavier. She purposely didn't put any of her old favorites on it, especially "A Couple of Forever's" by Chrisette Michele. That one brought back too many memories.

Things were going so well with her and Xavier, but an old habit remained, as she waited on the other shoe to fall. The corners of her mouth tilted as she thought of the past couple of months. The first night Xavier slept with her at her house, and that's all he did was sleep, because according to him she made too much noise. Since she was sexually frustrated that night she hadn't slept well and somewhere in the night she heard a whisper at the edge of her bed. It was Corey! He told Xavier in the loudest whisper that something was under his bed.

Xavier had asked before they went to sleep did anybody wake during the night and she told him no. Corey had gone an entire week without his under the bed story. She was embarrassed because she knew that Xavier worried about what the children thought of him. She patted his leg under the cover as Corey stood at the door looking frightened.

"I'll get it." She mumbled.

"No, go back to sleep, I'll check it out. Just in case something is there." Xavier said as he slipped out of the bed.

Corey gave her a triumphant look as if she had lied to him for many years. Annette laughed each time she thought of that night. No one seemed upset that Mr. Xavier had been in bed with her. That night apparently became the turning point.

After that night, there were some nights they stayed at his place and some nights he stayed with them. The first weekend after they moved Marisa, they went back to Florida and took the children. It was a different atmosphere, but it felt good, they felt like family. Annette heard all the rules that had been shoved down her throat all her life. She saw the frown lines and felt the displeasure of her family's judgments, but for the first time in her life she hadn't dwelled on it.

The children were with Anthony, so after dinner her plans consisted of a night of lovemaking. Xavier had given her his keys, in case he was sleep. It thrilled and scared her at the same time. On one hand, she felt as if they moved too fast, then it felt as if he had been in her life forever and she just hadn't known.

Everything was new but felt comfortable like an old pair of slippers. Xavier wasn't mushy affectionate outside of the bedroom, he didn't fill her ears with sweet nothings, nor did he crowd her space, even when they were together. But he didn't dissuade her from her affectionate nature or her silliness. The only requirement he seemed to have was his quiet time, the times when he needed to get lost in himself. She never had to leave the premises, she just had to leave him alone. Recently his moods appeared to have evened out.

The weird part was that he wasn't openly expressive, but everything with him was passionate. Their arguments were filled with passion, when they had fun it was tinged with passion, and the lovemaking exceeded all degrees of passion. But the differences in what she had become accustomed to were astounding. With Jay, she was treated like fragile glass and their alone time was spent in bed, shopping, or they spent time starry eyed with love. Xavier was the complete opposite. Their alone time was spent working around the houses, doing things like go-karting, movies, going to car races, working out and he held nothing back. If Jay was upset with her she never knew it, with Xavier she knew in no uncertain terms. She loved it!

This was the first time the friends had gotten together since the wedding. Bianca and Omar arrived back in town a few weeks ago and Tonya demanded that they go out. Annette wanted to see her friends, but she was apprehensive about Damita. She reached out to Damita a few times since the wedding to no avail. She finally gave up.

To her surprise Tonya and Bianca were seated and waited on her. Annette ungraciously looked at her phone and noted that she was not late. Then what the heck was Bianca doing here?

"It's about time you showed up! We were going to order without you." Bianca laughed as she stood to hug her.

Tonya shook her head and laughed. "This pregnancy is creating all new records. I almost fell out when Bianca walked in."

"At least I'm not last. Damita hasn't arrived yet." Annette laughed.

"Oh! Damita's not coming, she had plans. So, you are last!" Bianca chuckled.

Annette hugged her friends and noticed Bianca's bump. She had grown quite a bit since her wedding, but she carried it well. She mentioned it as she sat down.

Bianca blushed, "Yes, and if Omar could he would walk behind me everywhere with his hands wrapped around my stomach."

"Aww, that's so sweet. Especially since we know that he is catching hell with your hormones." Tonya smirked.

Annette looked around for the server, but Bianca waved the menu at her. "We ordered your margarita and water. You need to look at the menu, because when our server comes back we are ordering. I am starving!"

Annette laughed but followed her instructions. The server came with her drink and took their orders. Once that was accomplished Bianca settled down and shared pictures with funny anecdotes about each one. She looked relaxed and still had that serious glow. They were half-way through their meals when she finished regaling them with her honeymoon. She turned her gaze to Annette.

"We noticed that the house and condo still had food, so I'm assuming all is well with you and Xavier?"

Annette almost choked as her two friends gazed at her intently. "Yes, it is actually. We had a few bumps in the road, but we survived."

When she recalled the car incident Tonya stopped her before she went further.

"Girl shut your mouth! You gave Jay your beautiful car back? What are you driving now?" Tonya stopped eating and motioned with her fork for Annette to continue.

"If you hadn't cut her off she was about to tell us." Bianca snapped.

Annette smiled and continued, she left out the part about the car being a gift from Bianca's uncle. As private as Bianca was she assumed that she wouldn't want that part to be common knowledge. Curiously enough Bianca seemed unaware of it.

"I saw that car under the tarp and I wondered why he had it. It is not his style." Bianca looked thoughtful as she bit on her straw.

"What did Jay say when you returned the Audi?" Tonya spoke rapidly.

Since Annette wasn't sure how that went down, she shrugged, "Okay I guess, Xavier took it back to him." Bianca rolled her eyes upward, so Annette exclaimed, "You know if I had given it back to him, Jay wouldn't have accepted. Xavier said it went fine."

"Probably as fine as a ton of bricks falling off a building. But I understand. When the Rives men want something done, they take over. I'm not upset about you and Xavier anymore. You seem happy and Omar swears that Zay is happier than he has ever been in his life. I have no idea how he can tell, I just take his word for it." Bianca moved her head from side to side.

Tonya leaned back as the server took her plate. "Guess who has been calling me daily?"

"I hope like hell not Fred! And if he has, I do not want to hear about it." Bianca grimaced as she mentioned his name.

"Nope! Carl! After the wedding he called me sporadically, but lately he has been calling me every day!" Tonya smiled broadly.

As usual Bianca shot down her dreams. "Girl please! Carl? The last thing you should want is a man on the rebound and one who I'm sure is bitter. Just give yourself some time."

"Bianca! Carl is nice, he might be alright." Annette slipped into her role as peacemaker.

Tonya nodded her head. "He is nice and..."

"And he isn't even cute! His wife cheated on him as if he didn't exist. You don't think he has residual bitterness? Please! I'm sure at this point he is just looking to hook up. It just doesn't sound like the best idea." Bianca rolled over Tonya's hopes, dreams, and good news without batting an eyelash.

To lighten the mood Annette interjected, "I think your main concern should be if you have gone against Damita's friend code."

Bianca and Tonya gaped at her before they burst out laughing. Bianca had tears rolling down her cheeks as she tried to speak.

"That is the truth, she might curse you out because you knew she had a crush on that man when she was eleven!" Bianca choked out between laughs.

The table roared! Tonya fanned herself as she tried to stop laughing. Once Bianca wiped her face she turned serious again.

"For real Tonya, you have children and Carl doesn't. You need to think about them. He is used to being footloose and fancy free." Bianca dabbed at her eyes.

"Xavier doesn't have children and he's great." Annette told them about her conversation with Jolisa. Both women's eyes widened when she told them about the bullies and how Xavier handled it.

"Oh yeah, he's good with children. But that's different, Xavier has some experience with Omar and Liberty. Carl just doesn't seem kid-friendly. Just take your time with him." Bianca looked at Tonya innocently.

Tonya smacked her lips and turned to Annette. "It's really over between you and Jay?"

Annette nodded sadly and looked down at the water ring on the table. "Jay will always be special, he showed me that I can love and be loved. We both made mistakes, I tried to be perfect because I knew what he dealt with from Elaine, and I think he did the same. He wanted to show me that all men are not like Anthony, and he did. We were just so starry-eyed in love, everything was good, other than Elaine that is, but I don't think it was completely real. Not our feelings, they were real. Eventually we were going to have to take time to get to know each other, the real people. We probably wouldn't have done that until a few years into the marriage."

She kept her eyes downcast because she feared seeing disappointment from Bianca and judgment from Tonya. With a deep breath, she rushed on as she dabbed a napkin over the water ring.

"With Xavier, it's different. He's my best friend and I can talk to him about everything. Women issues, my children, my job, and even my family without worry that it will turn him away. For the first time in my life I can be myself and he seems to be alright with me. We haven't talked about the future, but I know that even if we don't make it he will always be there for me and I'll do the same for him." Annette looked up and was surprised to see both women's faces wet with tears.

"I think you guys will do just fine. It sounds as if he is the one for you." Tonya hoarsely remarked.

"I do too. But get ready because that man is going to want some babies. That's plural in case you didn't catch it." Bianca beamed as she dabbed her eyes for the second time.

Annette laughed, "I don't know about that, after dealing with my three he might change his mind. But we are just taking it one day at a time."

"Okay, don't worry I'll say I told you so." Bianca shot back.

"Speaking of making babies, I need to go." Annette beamed as her friends' eyes widened in shock, "What? It's been a rough week. He is so worried about me getting too…"

"Enough! Stop right there! I don't want to hear it! Bianca raised both hands as if she was in church.

Annette chuckled as she motioned for the server to pay her check. The night air hit her as she left, cooler than earlier but still too warm for this time of year. Before she got to her car, a weird feeling pricked her subconscious, she looked around because she felt watched. All she saw were couples and families as they entered or exited the restaurant.

The feeling remained until she pulled off quickly and made it to the main road. The weird feeling was forgotten as her panties jumped in anticipation. Xavier said he wanted to talk to her when she returned but he would have to wait until after she received her fix. The week had been long and torturous as they tried unsuccessfully a few times to sneak in some love-making. Xavier worried that she made too much noise and the children would hear, so he just teased her all week. Whatever he had to say could wait. Annette's smile faltered as she pulled closer to his house. Damita's car sat in his drive!

Her heart reflexively thumped hard and her hands shook. If Damita had other plans why was she at Xavier's? As much as she wanted it to be innocent she listened to her gut instinct. She parked in the drive instead of the garage and she took her heels off. Before she got out of the car she found the key to the side door, which led directly into the den.

Annette took a deep breath before she entered and fixed her face to smile. When she walked in her heart stopped. Damita stood buttoning her pants while Xavier held her shirt away from his body as he handed it to her. Damita saw her first and Annette noticed that her face was wet with tears. Good sex tears or tears of disappointment she wondered? Her vision blurred as she felt as if a hammer hit her in the chest.

"What is going on?" She managed to blurt.

Xavier dropped Damita's shirt and rushed to her. "Annette! Oh shit, it's not what you think! Please don't think that I…" He turned and looked at Damita. "Get your ass out of here!"

"Let me put on my shirt." Damita whined.

"I don't give a damn about your shirt, you need to leave. Now!" Xavier roared as he stepped towards Damita.

"Okay, okay." Damita passed Annette and murmured, "Remember no code?"

Annette felt dizzy and nauseous, Xavier covered her with his embrace, but she felt suffocated. She pushed him away.

"Annette, I promise you nothing happened. She asked for something to drink and when I came out of the kitchen she was standing in her underwear. You know I wouldn't do this to you." He pleaded with her.

Annette was too shell-shocked to speak so she looked around numbly. She saw a full glass of water on the table and Xavier's face was filled with anguish.

"Why was she here?" Annette snapped or tried to but it came out weak.

"Hell, I don't know. She called, but I didn't answer, I think I was in the shower, then shit!" Xavier rambled. Then he stopped and pulled his phone out. "She text me and said she needed to talk to me about you! I thought she was out with you, so I called her back. That's when she asked if she could come over."

Xavier shoved his phone at her and showed her the text. It was right there, but Annette needed to think. She believed Xavier, or she wanted to, but the fact that he wanted her to believe that Damita would do that to her boggled her mind! She knew Damita was upset with her, but they were friends, or so she thought. It was hard to connect the Damita she knew with the person he described. There were too many unanswered questions.

Annette walked to the door, with Xavier at her heels. He stopped her before she touched the doorknob.

"Don't leave. I don't know what the hell is going on, but just don't leave." He pulled her close once again.

When she relaxed in his embrace the floodgates opened. She sobbed, hiccoughed, and let it all out. Xavier picked her up and sat on the sofa, as he rubbed her hair away from her face.

"Annette if I had known that she would try something like that, I would have never agreed for her to come here. I never want to hurt you, not with any bullshit like this." He kissed the top of her head and she felt his body coiled with anger.

Once she settled down and wiped her face she looked at him. "Xavier, I just want to go home and think. I'm not saying that I don't believe you, but I just don't know what to think. I'll be okay and we can talk in the morning."

Xavier tried to persuade her to stay, he offered to drive her home, and he offered to follow her. She finally convinced him that she was fine and could make it on her own. She kissed him chastely on his cheek and left.

When she got home she wondered what she was doing there. She was drained but needed to talk to someone. It was too late for Bianca to be bothered, Tonya would get too excited and the person she wanted to talk to the most about her feelings, she had just left. The events of the night swarmed through her mind. Why were these things happening to her, she wondered? All the self-doubt, self-incriminations that she worked hard to rid herself of, rushed back. A single tear leaked from each eye as her self-worth plummeted. Before she reached the bottom of the pit, her doorbell rang.

Her heart lifted because she knew that Xavier had come to be her shoulder to cry on. When she peeked out the window shock and something akin to dismay hit her. It was Jay!

Chapter 27

The bad luck that had dogged him for months was finally lifted. Jay smiled as he left the doctor's office and formulated a plan to get back on track with everything. He sent Damita and Carl a text to share his good news as his heart soared because he knew that things were falling in place. It would only be a few days before the rest of his life fell into place.

Every so often he passed Annette's house and it angered him when he saw no cars or Xavier's car in the drive. That guy thought he was untouchable! Jay grinned as he thought of how soon he would find out different. His musings were interrupted when Elaine called.

"You are just going to leave me hanging in the parking lot? You didn't say good-bye or anything!" She screeched in the phone.

"What do you want me to say Elaine? You knew that baby wasn't mine, yet you used it to ruin my life. All I have to say to you is kiss my black ass!" Jay disconnected the call.

She called right back, Jay ignored it until she called again and he realized that short of getting his number changed there was no way to stop her.

He answered tiredly. "What do you want Elaine?"

"I only did it because I love you and want you back." She sniveled in the receiver.

"You had sex with another man, and got pregnant because you love me? That makes a lot of sense. Try that line on the other fella because I'm not buying it nor do I care." Jay snapped.

"You say you love Annette and you had sex with me. What's the difference?" Her snivels turned into sobs.

"You drugged me! That's the difference, an enormous difference and you know this." Jay was ready to disconnect.

"You weren't drugged every time and you know it! You just used me as your receptacle when it was convenient to you." She sounded hysterical.

"Whatever Elaine. What do you want? Because if this is all you want to talk about I'm hanging up and I won't answer your call again." Jay was tired of her.

"I want to get an abortion. I don't want to have this baby." Elaine moaned.

Jay stopped short of laughing and just chuckled. "Too late, now isn't it? I don't think that's possible now and it's not my concern. You need to blow up the other guy's phone."

This time he disconnected and decided to ignore her if possible. He had too much to do and a brief time to do it.

His excitement eclipsed because it seemed as if he would never get to share his news with Annette. Xavier seemed to be there constantly and there was no way that he would tell her with him in attendance. At the end of the week he and Carl decided to go out and celebrate. He celebrated his break from bad news and Carl celebrated the finalization of his divorce. Angie gave him the house and decided that she would do better in an apartment. This really put Carl in a celebratory mood.

"Man, she tried me once again." Carl moaned playfully as he downed his beer.

"Angie? What did she do?" Jay looked around the bar.

"She tried to push up on me about a week ago. After what Elaine did to you? Hell no, I got her out of there quick and in a hurry. I might have fallen for it if I hadn't been talking to a special lady lately." He smirked.

"I hope like hell you aren't talking about Carly." Each time Jay thought about her he itched.

"Hell no! Even though, Carly has been calling a lot since I put that thang on her. I'm talking about Tonya. You know she left her husband?" Carl looked at Jay slyly.

Jay looked at him in amazement, "You've got to be kidding me! Tonya? No man, she's not your type." Jay laughed, "I can see you with Bianca before Tonya. Man, you've got to move out of the circle."

Jay laughed so hard he had to set his bottle of beer down. He looked up and noticed that Carl wasn't laughing.

"We're just talking right now, but I like her. She has a great sense of humor. Speaking of the circle, have you told Annette about Elaine?" Carl filled his mouth with peanuts after he spoke.

"Nope. I hope to catch her tonight. I'll ride by there when we leave. I can't wait to get back on track with her, I really miss her." Jay looked down at the table.

"I hope you can get her back, but old boy is not making it easy. You better hope that he doesn't get her pregnant, you see how Omar did it when he took Bianca away from me." Carl smiled as he tried to joke.

Jay glowered because all he pictured was that bastard screwing Annette. He knew how enthusiastic Annette was while in the throes of passion. To know that Xavier had experienced it made his blood boil. Carl waved his hand in front of Jay's face.

"Earth to Jay, are you in there?" Carl clanged two bottles together which immediately brought the server to their table.

Carl ordered another one while Jay asked for the check. In case he caught Annette, he didn't want to be tipsy. He needed everything to go smoothly. Jay waited impatiently for Carl to finish his beer, while he rambled on about Angie, Carly, and all things female. Jay noticed he didn't say much about Tonya. Finally, Carl finished and was ready to leave. As usual he made Jay promise to keep going if Xavier was at Annette's.

Jay was happy to see that the Mercedes that she shouldn't have been driving was in the drive. As he walked by it he had to admit that it was a clean vehicle. His love of cars never wavered regardless of the owner. The Mercedes was top of the line, it was sleek and as he peeped inside it looked as if it had all the bells and whistles. He knew that this vehicle not only had 402 horsepower, but it was close to an eighty-thousand-dollar vehicle if not more!

When Annette opened the door, he saw that she was surprised, but he could also tell that she had been crying. The door widened but she stood in it.

"Hey, Annette can I come in?" He held his hands out.

She shrugged and stepped aside. She looked so good to him! He felt as if he had been on a deserted island and that she was water and a way out.

"Are you okay?" He stepped closer as she walked to the living area.

"Yeah, it's just been a long day. What made you stop by?" She looked at him curiously.

"I wanted to tell you in the person." Jay took a deep breath as he grabbed her hand and led her to the loveseat. "I got the results back from the DNA test and Elaine's baby is not mine!"

Annette's eyebrows furrowed together, "Wait, you mean she slept with somebody else so that she could pin her pregnancy on you?"

Jay clasped her hand tighter. "Exactly! But there's more, I talked to my attorney and he said that this might be enough for me to get custody of Malik!"

Annette's eyes lit up. "Jay that is great!"

She threw her arms around his neck in a hug and he held her close. Jay never wanted to let go, he buried his head in her neck, while he rubbed her back softly. When he began to nibble on her neck she pulled away.

"Baby, it's all going to work out like I told you. We won't have to worry about Elaine because we will have Malik and we can be the family we planned to be." Jay spoke softly and he still had his arms looped around her.

As Annette disentangled and stood, she bit her bottom lip. "Wow! It's hard to believe that we went through all this for a sham. How could one person be so evil?"

Jay stood and closed in the distance between the them. "I don't know, but that will never be a concern of ours again.

She did this to pull us apart, but we can show her that our love can overcome it."

Even though she didn't seem overwhelmed with happiness, she looked beautiful. Her hair was straightened, the blouse she wore made her breasts look fuller than he knew they were, and her pants cupped her ass perfectly. Jay adjusted himself because he had a hard-on from hell. Before he pulled her close she spoke.

"But her DNA test doesn't obliterate Xavier from my life. I guess you forgot about that?" She stepped away from him again.

The DNA test might not have, but I will. Jay thought. He pulled his phone out of his pocket slowly. He had edited Leonard's rendition of events. He didn't need Annette thinking of that psycho as a hero.

"Annette, I hate to tell you this but I found out some things about Xavier. He's not exactly what he seems." Jay looked at her expectantly.

Annette narrowed her eyes. "What do you mean you found out some things? How did you find out anything about Xavier?"

Jay wasn't comfortable with how accusatory she sounded, but he had an answer for her. "The California deals. Those guys are sticklers for everything being on the up and up and they didn't want anything to come back to bite them. So, I did somewhat of a background check on the brothers."

She still looked at him suspiciously, "And? What did you learn?"

That was all Jay needed to hear. He sat on the loveseat and patted the spot next to him. "Listen you can hear it for yourself. I didn't want you to think that I had fabricated anything so I recorded the guy."

As soon as she sat down he turned the recording on. Jay watched her face as she listened, and was inwardly glad when he saw revulsion and terror reflected in her expression. When she looked at him she shook her head, almost violently.

"No, no, that guy is a liar. Did he say why Xavier and Omar did those things to him? There is no way that they just picked up two guys and beat them almost to death. No, that can't be true." Her head still shook from side to side.

It hurt Jay to see her defend Xavier so vigorously, but he also knew that if he could get her to see that it was true, then her revulsion and terror would return.

He touched her arm lightly, "I think the brothers were working under someone else's orders, I believe it was about a drug deal or something. This Leonard guy, he's slime, but he is also messed up pretty bad, he can barely walk. The only reason he talked to me is because he's gotten used to Xavier terrorizing him and you heard him say he had nothing else left to lose. I'm sorry Annette, it shocked me too, but I had to tell you. I know that you don't want your children around a ticking time bomb." Jay noticed that she once again bit her lip and shook her head. He decided to go in for the kill. "These were just two guys, what if there are more? What if they want to get back at him for something he did? They could come after him."

There was pure terror in her eyes when she looked at him. "Are you sure that he was being truthful?"

He pushed her hair away from her face and kissed her softly on her lips. "Yes, he was telling the truth. I wouldn't have told you if I felt it wasn't true."

"Did they go to jail? If it's true, why didn't they go to jail?" Once again, she narrowed her eyes.

"Baby, like I said Leonard is slimy and was involved in something dirty too. That's why he lied about what happened to him to police."

He felt her body slump and he pulled her close. "It's okay Annette, I'm here for you. I'll always be here for you."

He felt her body shiver as his hands moved from her back to her sides. He wanted her so bad, and his hands flitted softly under her breast she pulled away.

"Jay, I just need to be alone right now. This along with earlier tonight, it's been too much. I am happy for you though, I don't want you to think that I'm not." Tears glistened in her eyes as she looked at him.

He leaned down and kissed her, she kissed him back briefly before she once again put her hands on his chest and pushed him back.

"Okay, I understand. But if you need me just call me. You know I'll always be here for you and I'm ready to do things the right way." He stood unable to hide his erection as it strained against his pants.

Annette noticed but she walked him to the door. Before he left he pulled her close again and kissed her on the cheek.

"By the way, you don't have to worry about a car, you know that your car is waiting for you." He told her before he walked away.

An indiscernible look passed over her face, but she nodded somberly. When he got in his car he looked back but she was gone. Jay wished he could have stayed with her, but he thought his visit had its intended effect. There was no way Annette would put her family in harm's way. Jay fist pumped as he drove down the street. Things finally looked up.

Chapter 28

Omar watched Bianca as she came out of the bathroom. Her hair had a part in the middle and two long braids swung past her chest. Her baby bump poked out of her short nightgown and he felt his nature rise as he watched her. She was his wife and his dream come true. Every night that he laid down beside her he counted his blessings. Not only did she carry his surname, she was carrying his child, a child created out of love.

"You might as well put your weapon down, I'm still sore from last night." She stood at the edge of the bed and pointed at his groin.

"I can't help myself. You do this to me." He tried to win her over with his sad look.

Bianca sat on the bed with her back to him. As she reached on the nightstand for the lotion, he grabbed it before she could.

"Let me do that for you. Come on get in the bed." He smiled innocently at her.

"Okay, but no funny stuff. I mean it, I'm tired. Just a tired, fat, pregnant woman." She moaned as she plumped the pillows behind her.

Omar started with her feet and worked his way up. Oiling her down made his condition worse. As he made it to her knees he tried to talk his hardness down.

"How was dinner? Were any blows thrown this time?" He kneaded her legs as he spoke.

"It actually went well. Damita didn't show, she called at the last minute and said something came up. I think she is still mad and jealous. But I did learn something interesting tonight." Bianca swatted his arm. "Are you listening to me?"

"Umm-hmm, you learned something new." Omar kissed her inner thighs as he spoke.

"Ome stop! I want you to listen to me!" Bianca clamped her thighs together and bumped his head with her knee in the process.

"Ow! Okay, I'm listening, you don't have to abuse me." He moved beside her and put his hand on her stomach.

"I didn't tell Annette that we found out we're having a boy, because I know she can't hold water. I'll wait until you tell Zay. But it's good I didn't because she made me and Tonya cry tonight!" she told him what Annette expressed to them about Xavier and she finished with, "I know my friend and I can safely say that she is in love."

"I had to stop making you feel good for that information?" Omar sighed.

"Ome, stop playing! Isn't that good news?" Bianca strained to look at him, before she turned completely around.

Omar grew serious. "Yes Bibi, that is good news because I'm pretty sure Zay is in love too. But you need to tell Annette that my brother is my best friend first." He chuckled.

Bianca gazed at him and touched his face before she spoke. "You laugh, but I think somewhere in there you are serious. You have me now Ome, it's time to let your brother go and live his own life."

Waves of shock reflected on his face. "What do you mean? I've never stopped Zay from having a life! That's bull! I was just joking, but he is my best friend."

Bianca sat up, "Ome, you and Zay depend on each other too much. One of the reasons he gets on my damn nerves so much, is when we first met everything had to be Zay-approved for you. I would tell you not to do something and you'd be hell bent on doing it until you talked to Zay. He feels as if he has to watch over you and just like you followed Liberty, he follows you." She kissed him gently. "I'm not saying you guys can't be close, but it's time to let me and Annette be there for the two of you."

Omar thought about what she said and there was a glimmer of truth in it. He wanted his brother to find the happiness he had, Zay deserved it. He nodded his head as he looked at her. The one thing he loved most about her was beneath that hard-outer shell, she was so loving inside. An inside he was determined to touch tonight.

"I was thinking that if you are sore, I could kiss it and make it feel better." He grinned devilishly at her.

"Now that sounds like a plan." She smiled as she parted her legs.

Before he made it to his primary goal the doorbell rang, twice in a row. Omar looked at Bianca as she groaned.

"Go let your brother in. He better not want anything to eat either!" She mumbled as she rolled out of bed.

Omar threw on his sweats and tried to walk his hardness down. It deflated as soon as he saw the anguish on Xavier's face.

"Man, they got me fucked up! Those bastards set me up! I can't believe this shit!" Xavier was loud and clearly agitated.

"Calm the hell down! Who set you up?" Omar sat at the kitchen island as Bianca padded noiselessly in.

"Jay and Damita! I can't believe those mother…" He trailed off as he spotted Bianca and sat down.

"Jay and Damita? What happened? And why isn't Annette with you?" Bianca talked as she opened the fridge and pulled out a grilled chicken breast, cheese, and mustard. She walked to the counter and pulled out a loaf of bread.

Even with his brother's agonized state Omar smiled and shook his head. He looked back at Zay and noticed that he seemed stunned by her actions too.

"Okay tell us what happened. And like Bibi said where is Annette?" Omar stood and went to the coffeemaker, but Bianca shooed him away. She mouthed that she would take care of it.

Xavier sat with his head tilted back and held the bridge of his nose. Omar hated when his brother did that because usually nothing good came after. He sighed and waited.

Xavier told them about Damita's calls and text, when he got to her arrival at his house, he looked down at his hands. Bianca turned from the coffeemaker, handed Omar his coffee and became an interrogator.

"She came to your house? Please tell me that you didn't screw her! Why does your story keep getting worse? Did Annette catch y'all in bed?" She squawked.

Xavier frowned at her, "Hell no I didn't screw her. She said she wanted to talk to me about Annette. I thought she was at dinner with the rest of you and something had gone down. When she got there, she talked about how she couldn't believe that I was with Annette instead of her. I tried to shut her down, but she kept talking. She said something about the friendship break was supposed to make me want her more or something. Then she tried to kiss me and I told her she needed to leave."

Xavier grimaced and grabbed his mug when Bianca sat it in front of him. He sipped his coffee and looked over their heads as he continued. "She apologized and I told her she needed to leave because Annette was coming. And I was tired of her. This…" He sputtered as he seemed to search for a word.

"This *novilla* asked me for some water and when I came back to the den she is standing in her bra and panties!"

"What!" Omar was distracted as Bianca coughed as if she was choking. Once she recovered she took over before he could open his mouth.

"No! Damita stripped in your den? *Bon mét*! What the hell was she thinking?" Bianca reverted to Creole when she was so upset or didn't want them to know what she said.

Omar covered his mouth to hide his smile and as he tried not to laugh. A year ago, this story would have had a different ending if Xavier had told it. As Xavier continued he only clarified one thing for Omar: Xavier was in love! Probably for the first time.

"This shit isn't funny man! Not at all." Xavier growled at his brother while Bianca glared at him.

"It's not Ome! Finish the story Zay." Bianca bit into her sandwich as she directed the conversation.

"I told her to get dressed, because it was not going to happen. She starts crying or something and took her time putting her pants on. I was handing her shirt to her when Annette walked in." Xavier closed his eyes and rubbed his forehead.

Omar chuckled, "You left the door unlocked *jefe*?"

Bianca kicked him under the island and Zay glared at him.

"No, I didn't I gave her my keys in case I was asleep when she came back." He growled.

Omar was stunned! Xavier had never given women keys to his place! This was more serious than he thought. Not only was his brother in love, he was whooped.

Omar wiped his face with his hands, "Did you explain to Annette what happened?" He loved his brother but why did he have to pull this story out of him?

"I tried, but she was upset. I was trying to tell her and get Damita out at the same time. Then Damita said something to her about a code or cold, and I felt Annette's anger." Xavier sighed.

"Damita said code? That jealous heifer! Why can't she get over this thing with you and Annette? Zay why aren't you with Annette? I am sure she needs to hear it again once she's calmed down." Bianca ended softly.

Omar wondered why his brother interrupted him with the first little spot of trouble he had with Annette. This could have waited until the morning, or better yet he should be at Annette's. He popped his neck as he glared at Zay.

"That's how I know this was a set up. By the time I get to her house Jay was there. So, I just came over here." He glanced at Bianca again.

This stopped Omar short. "What was he doing there?"

Xavier grimaced at him, "That's what I'm telling you *mi hermanito*. How else would he have known the right time to catch her? This was a set-up plain and simple."

They sat in silence for a few minutes, then Omar spoke. Now he was as upset as Xavier and when he started in rapid Spanish Bianca stopped him.

241

"Wait a minute. You know I only know a few words in Spanish and I need to know what you are saying. We aren't having any trouble." She glared at Omar.

"Zay man just go back over there. You and Annette are together now, you have rights. Bust it up! He doesn't have any business over there." Omar refused to let anybody get the best of his brother.

"Nope, I'm going home. If she wants to hear what he has to say, I'll let her. I need to know where she stands with that jerk anyway." Xavier stood and stretched.

Now that Xavier had calmed down, Omar was riled up. "Well what the hell did you come over here for?" He felt another kick to his shins.

"I just needed to vent *jefe.*" Xavier gave his brother a cold stare.

Omar threw his hands in the air. "Fine! Do it your way, but I'm telling you, if you want Annette you need to take your ass over there and let him know."

"No esé," He looked at Bianca. "No problems, I'm not starting any problems."

Bianca smiled at him as she gave him a hug. "You and Annette will be fine, I promise you." She said it softly, but Omar heard her.

"Zay! You are going to have a nephew man! We found out today." Omar wanted to give his brother some good news, he looked so dejected.

Xavier's eyes brightened as he hugged Omar first then Bianca. "I told you! A big boy at that."

But Bianca stole the show when she placed his hand on her stomach as he talked. Xavier's eyes grew wide as he felt the baby move.

"He's been doing that ever since you got here. He moves to the sound of your voice!" Bianca smiled.

Xavier smiled, but Omar noticed a sadness beneath his cheer. He walked him to the door and grabbed him once again in a bear hug. "It will all work out Bro, I promise it will."

Xavier raised his hand in a wave and left.

Omar felt Bianca as she wrapped her arms around his waist. "There is something that he is not telling me." He sighed deeply, "Why did you tell him that they would be alright?"

"Because they will. Remember I'm half witch." She pulled him back to the bedroom.

Chapter 29

Annette felt drained. The night's events had worn her out, but she wasn't sleepy. If she closed her eyes she saw Damita half-dressed with tears streaming down her face. Her expression had quickly changed to anger when she looked at Annette. When she arrived home that seemed to be the worst part of her night, until Jay came. Now she realized that Xavier was honest about Damita, and that Damita was no longer her friend. She was filled with hatred that stemmed from Annette being with Xavier. That hurt her because she loved Damita, but at least now she hadn't gone against a friend code. Because Damita had never been her friend, she only liked her while she was with Jay.

The next half of her night was spent hearing that man Leonard's voice as he told of unspeakable acts against him. For drugs? Xavier barely drank, but he almost killed a man about drugs? She thought of Jay's reasoning, as he spoke of the money Omar and Xavier had, and where it possibly came from. Something tickled the back of her brain but she couldn't remember it right now. She knew that there were things that did not add up.

When she couldn't sleep she rose and cleaned. As she scrubbed, mopped, and vacuumed she wondered why happiness always slipped through her fingers. Her soul was burdened with the stain of hurt that followed her with every step she took. Each time she loved without abandon, hurt waited around the corner, grasped her around the neck and choked it out of her. Whenever she decided to give her heart freely, pain imprisoned it for an undetermined amount of time. What had she done so wrong to never find peace in her essence?

She thought about the men she had trusted with her heart. Anthony was a serial cheater, Jay wanted to keep her safe with lies and fairy tales, and Xavier was a psychopath? Each one rang true except the last. The doubt of his truthfulness permeated her mind. The car that sat in her driveway, had it been payment for the infliction of someone's pain for gain? He told her that Geoff was a dangerous man, but he had also worked for Geoff. Had the work entailed evilness and destruction? Could she live with that?

She got in the shower and stood as rivulets of hot water splattered her body and rolls of steam invaded her senses. She scrubbed herself twice ridding herself of the surface dirt, but the inner turmoil remained. It seemed as if nothing could rid her soul of that awful man's voice. The shower discharged her by becoming tepid, not cool enough to soothe her soul, but cool enough to numb her body.

When she got in the bed so many memories came to her. Xavier as he tenderly loved her and opened his heart to her as he expelled his childhood demons. She felt his breath against her neck and cheek, that gentle reminder that he was beside her. The amaryllis crossed her eyelids, the first time he gave them to her and how he explained what they meant, a symbol of who she was to him.

Tears leaked past her lids as she pictured him as he played the game with her sons, their faces filled with excitement. Then there were the moments stamped in her brain of the time he took with Ant to bring him out of his shell. The memory that shattered her hurt, the one of Xavier sleeping on the floor in the boys' room as he made sure nothing was under Corey's bed. Corey on his shoulders at the beach, as Xavier kept him safe from the waves.

They had compiled many memories in a brief time. Although he wasn't an affectionate person, he dealt with her affectionate nature. The times she jumped on his back and planted kisses on his neck, or when she invaded his space to cuddle next to him, he embraced it all. Usually with a kiss on her hair or cheek, she had ridded him of his habit of kissing her forehead. Annette sat up unable to parallel the person Leonard described to the man she knew.

Vestiges of the sunrise peeped through her blinds and reminded her that this was a new day. A day to do things differently. She jumped up, peed, washed her face and brushed her teeth before pulling her hair in a ponytail. She grabbed a tee-shirt and cargo shorts out of her drawer. This was not the time to glam up, it was time to make decisions and set her heart on the right path.

Annette made it to Xavier's house in warped time. She nervously opened the garage, ready to use his keys to get in if necessary. The sunlight brazed the interior of the garage where he stood, as he glanced back before he went back to hitting the miniature punching bag. Annette pulled in and stepped out of the vehicle. She heard the banging and clanging and finally realized that this was noise she heard when he needed alone time.

He stopped and glanced at her without any expression, or so it seemed. She saw, no she felt a tremor of sadness. As the garage closed, the light was dim from the glow of a singular bulb.

"Hey." She stated as she sat on the hood of the Mercedes less than a foot away from him.

A sheen of sweat clung to him and his hair showed signs of dampness. Xavier wore a white wife-beater tee and shorts that looked as if they had once been sweat pants.

"Hey yourself." He said gruffly.

She was used to his varying mood swings, so she ignored him. "Jay came by last night."

"Yeah, I know." The punching bag flew back with his blow.

Annette waited until the clanging stopped. "Really? How did you know?"

Xavier looked at her, disbelief written on his face. "Because I came after you to make sure you made it home, and to explain to you that nothing happened. Did you think I would just let you leave thinking the worst?"

Annette fumbled with the words in her head, before she blurted out, "Jay told me about a man…"

Xavier's voice thundered as he cut her off. "I know what that son-of-a- bitch told you."

"So, it's true?" Annette felt something shift inside of her.

"Yep, it's true." He turned back around to the punching bag.

"Oh." That was all she thought to say. She looked at the muscles in his back as his repetitions hit the aluminum can was the only sound in the garage.

Annette stood and took a step closer to him. "Was this what you wanted to tell me that day? When you said that it had no bearing on us right now?"

Xavier stopped and looked at her with narrowed eyes before he nodded. The garage was quiet, warm, and filled with an uncertain tension as they faced off. Xavier stood stock still as his eyes searched hers.

Annette took a few steps, as she almost closed the gap between them. She inhaled deeply before she stepped off her cliff. "I don't care, I still love you anyway."

Xavier turned halfway, then he turned back to the bag, finally he turned and faced her. "Excuse me? What did you say?"

She took another timid step and was now close enough to feel the heat as it came off his body in waves. "I said I don't care, I love you anyway."

Xavier wiped the sweat from his brow as he stared at her. "Are you serious?" His voice was hoarse.

"I'm very serious. If you say that it has no bearing on us now, I trust and believe in you." Her voice cracked.

Xavier pulled the bottom of his shirt up and wiped his face. He mumbled a few words in Spanish before he looked at her. "Ahh, Annette, what did I do to deserve you? If I wasn't so sweaty…"

He stopped in surprise as she wrapped her arms around his waist and looked up at him. "I don't care about your sweat. I just need you, sweaty or not."

Xavier covered her in his embrace as his mouth consumed hers. His kiss was filled with so much unsaid emotion and she felt his tensions roll off his body. She absorbed it all and became so full, tears rolled down her face unobtrusively. Xavier paused and wiped her tears away with his thumbs.

"Why are you crying? I promise that I'll never do those things again, I'm not that man anymore." His hands rubbed her sides before he traced his fingers over her breasts.

The heat he always created made her cry profusely because her body ached for him. She caught her breath and tried to speak. "I'm not crying about that. I wasn't sure how you would respond to my feelings, I wasn't sure if it was the right time to tell you. I'm sorry I'm rambling, but I was scared and these are tears of relief."

While she rambled, he led her in the house. When they reached the bedroom, Annette sat on the bed and when she heard the shower she shook her head. Xavier was so self-conscious when he wasn't "perfect." The lack of sleep and emotional roller-coaster left her exhausted, so she undressed before she got in the bed. The sheets smelled like him. She drifted off as she became immersed in the scent of the man she loved.

Time seemed irrelevant as she slept, but she was awakened by hot kisses across her shoulders and Xavier's voice.

"Annette, there was no need to be scared. I know I'm not the best with expressing myself, but you are so special. Last night I was out of my mind because I thought our time was over. All I pictured was the time we spent and I also thought about the kids thinking I'd just dropped out of their lives. Then I thought about you thinking I was some monster. I know it hasn't been much time, but I don't want the life I had before. I can't imagine my life anymore without you and your family." He swallowed hard. "That's when I realized that I love you, because I've only felt a fear like that once before and it was about my brother."

When he mentioned her and her children, she lost it. Love blossomed and filled her pores while her panties became soaked. Tears ran down her face as she struggled to keep quiet. His nibbles went lower as his hands pulled her nipples and as usual gave her extreme hot flashes. Once she felt as if she could speak she turned over. Xavier suckled and nipped at her body as her words disappeared from her thoughts. As he reached the central vent of her volcano, his tongue set her ablaze as he alternated between nips and licks. She gripped his hair tightly as she begged him to stop.

Xavier sat between her legs on his knees as she opened up for him. Now that their hearts were aligned she needed a piece of his soul. His gentle caress of her inner thigh made her prop on her elbows determined to drag him inside of her.

"Annette?" He looked at her with a question in his eyes as she straddled him. She kissed him passionately, not wanting conversation but needing him in the worst way.

"Annette, I was thinking, and I don't mean right now." She stopped in surprise because it was so unlike him to stammer and stumble. She positioned herself directly above his magic wand, close enough for him to feel her moisture as she looked at him with raised eyebrows.

"Once we get settled I want you to have my baby. If you can't have my children, I don't want any." He bit her bottom lip before he inhaled in his warm mouth.

Annette lowered herself on his hardness before he stopped speaking. Their choreography was in time with the symphony their joined bodies created. Annette was swept away from the deep emotion she felt with his every thrust. She gave her love freely and without fear, which made her loving libertine in nature. There was no shame as she licked his sweat, sucked on every inch of him she could reach, and he did the same.

As her body closed in on his hardness she captured him in her gaze. "Xavier, I will have all your babies, if you want me to."

His eyes closed briefly as he grunted and his body shook as he released his seed deep inside her womb.

Later she cuddled next to him in bed. He was still enough to be sleep, but she knew he wasn't. She recognized that when he was still he was content, because when he was worried or agitated he couldn't be still. Hence all the work he did himself on his house.

"How much sleep did you get last night?" She murmured drowsily.

"None." He sounded half asleep.

"What did you build now? Or did you repaint every bedroom?" She giggled as she snuggled happily in his warmth.

"Nope. But I did look around my house and priced how much it would cost to put a wrought iron fence around my house. That way last night can never happen again, I can just talk to people at the fence." He chuckled.

"That sounds perfect. Because I can accept that you killed someone, but what you are not going to do is have women here undressed." She chuckled too.

Xavier sat up suddenly. "He told you that I killed someone? You mean to tell me that you have been thinking I'm a murderer?"

Annette sat up, lines of confusion on her face. "That's what the man said. I thought you knew what he told Jay. You didn't kill the man?"

Xavier had gotten out of the bed and looked at her through the dresser mirror. "No, Annette, I have not killed anyone. Although I have thought about it a few times since I've been down here." The last part was mumbled but she heard him.

Relief flooded her body as she fell back on the pillows. She told Jay that man was a liar! Annette was glad that for once she trusted her instincts and came to talk with Xavier. She stretched and realized that she hadn't slept since Thursday night and she was tired.

"Come on get up, we need to go talk to Omar." Xavier was at the bottom of the bed.

"Talk to Omar? I thought we were about to get some sleep? Come on Xavier I'm sleepy." Annette pouted.

He sat on the bed and looked at her tenderly. "No, I want everything out in the open. I don't want this to come up again and I want you to know everything. I'm tired of this old business hanging around my neck."

Another stretch was needed before she stood in front of him. She tried once again to get back in bed. "Xavier, it doesn't matter. You didn't kill anyone, there won't be anyone coming after you, and I don't care about the rest. I have seen the man you are and that's all I need to know."

"It matters to me *mi vida*. I don't know what you were told and I want you to know that I don't have anything to hide. And there are a few things that Omar needs to know." He kissed her forehead and turned her to the bedroom door. "I think you have some clothes in the other room."

"About that. Why do I have to put my clothes in the spare room?" She demanded.

"I'm not there yet. I have my closet set up a certain way, I can't change it right now." Xavier laughed as she stuck out her tongue.

Chapter 30

When Omar opened the door, a look of aggravation crossed his face until he saw Annette. He ushered them in and as the aroma of food and coffee hit Annette's olfactory, she realized that along with tired she was hungry.

As she walked in behind Xavier she heard Bianca from the patio, "Go ahead and eat. We knew you would be back this morning." She laughed, then jumped up when she saw Annette. They hugged and Bianca looked at Xavier with a smile. "You decided to go back last night, didn't you?"

Xavier looked down abashedly, "I did, but I didn't go in. I wanted to make sure Jay took his ass away from there."

This was news to Annette and she stared at him in amazement. "You rode by while I was inside crying my heart out?"

Xavier's head popped up and he looked at her with concern. "I didn't know what he told you, and I didn't know you were crying." He embraced her from behind and kissed her neck.

"All right now! That's enough, I do not need her to turn into a werewolf. Humph! Looks as if she already has. Y'all could have told us that you had made up by telephone." Bianca scrunched up her face.

"Forget you Bianca." Xavier growled good-naturedly.

Omar laughed as he brought his plate outside. Before they settled down with them Annette and Xavier fixed themselves a plate. There were eggs, French toast, Conecuh sausage, strawberries, watermelon and orange juice. Annette felt as if she needed to step up her breakfast game. They sat down and there was silence for a few minutes as they ate.

Omar broke the silence. "I know you didn't come here to eat, so what is it that you haven't told us?"

Xavier wiped his mouth with a napkin. "Jay went to Texas and talked to Leonard."

Omar's mouth set in a hard line and his eyes grew cold. "Leonard? How the hell did he find out about him?"

It was obvious that Bianca knew who Leonard was, because she listened but never stopped eating. Annette was about to explain about the dealership, but Xavier cut her off.

"Carly told him." Xavier spoke softly.

"Carly!" Bianca and Omar exclaimed at the same time. Annette sat in confusion because she seemed to be the only person who didn't know who Carly was.

Bianca explained that Carly was Liberty's mom, but Annette was confused as to what she had to do with a background check. Xavier cleared her confusion when he told her that Jay went to Texas specifically to find dirt to share with her.

"What the hell did he tell him?" Omar's brows furrowed together as he tapped his fingers against the table.

Xavier looked at Annette and asked her to tell what she heard. Annette recounted most of what she heard as she observed their expressions. Bianca looked down, but Omar and Xavier looked at each other in disbelief.

"Annette did Leonard explain that they almost killed Omar?" Xavier spoke softly.

Annette's head jerked. "No! The beginning of the recording was about how he was picked up after a night of drinking. He tried to kill you?" She looked at Omar in horror.

Omar and Xavier looked at one another before Omar explained how things happened. Then once he left the hospital Xavier had drilled him to recount exactly how it happened and to give him everyone's name that was involved in the shooting. Xavier found the emails that outlined how Omar was to be killed before he released his information to the state police. Annette knew that Bianca had heard this story before but she still dabbed her eyes as she listened. Once he recovered somewhat he and Xavier took the information they had to the chief of police and the mayor of the city. They decided to settle once the two crooked cops were fired.

"They were so worried about the news tarnishing their good name they preferred to pay. I took the money, gave half to my brother and…"

"You did not give me half." Xavier interjected loudly.

"It was almost half, and I know it was more than a quarter." Omar furrowed his brow as he looked at him.

"I know, but it wasn't half." Xavier refused to back down.

Omar looked at Annette, made a face and continued. "I gave my brother some money, enough so that if he chose to he would not have to work again, but I wasn't satisfied. These guys had almost left my daughter an orphan and I wanted them to pay."

Annette was amazed that Xavier wanted to quibble about the amount in the middle of Omar's story, but was riveted back to Omar's words. Omar told the same story that she heard Leonard tell, but with the knowledge of what had transpired before it didn't sound horrible. It sounded like poetic justice. When Omar finished he looked from her to Xavier then back to Xavier.

"I told you we should have killed those maggots. Then we wouldn't be sitting here talking about them." Omar stated calmly.

Annette's eyes widened, but Xavier voice calmed her.

"No *jefe*. Once you cross that bridge there is no turning back. I told you that." Xavier glared at his brother.

"I agree." Bianca spoke up. "With Omar. What if Leonard decides to tell everyone? He told Jay and my uncle always told me that dead men can't talk."

Omar looked at Bianca lovingly. "Your uncle told you the truth."

Annette looked at her friend as she calmly bit into her watermelon as if she spoke of the weather. Xavier shook his head at Omar and Bianca with a hint of a smile. Annette felt as if she had walked into a twilight zone.

"He won't talk anymore, I bet that he regrets telling Jay." Xavier glanced around nervously as he filled Omar in on the "presents" he left the men and the one that Lil Geoff had recently left. Annette reached out and squeezed his hand. She almost agreed with Omar and Bianca.

"Why the hell did you do that? Those guys aren't worth the effort." Omar looked at his brother quizzically.

Xavier looked up to the sky before he answered. "I wanted them to know that I would never forget what they did to you. Never." He then told them how Geoff had informed him of Jay and Carl's visit to Texas.

"Geoff? How the hell did he know?" Omar exclaimed.

"I don't know how he knows half the things he knows. But speaking of Geoff there is one more thing that needs to be cleared up." Xavier cleared his throat.

Xavier knew that Thomas and Leonard weren't the brains of the operation. When he coerced the name out of Leonard, he was lost. There was no way that he could touch the golden boy of the city, but he was fearful that the guy, David would have come after Omar later. Especially once he learned of his gofers misfortunes.

It was apparent that this was news to Omar. His eyes glinted dangerously as he listened closely to his brother. Bianca seemed enthralled by the news also.

"You are talking about the David whose shit didn't stink and he was missing shortly after..." Omar stopped as his eyes flickered with the ramifications of his own words.

Xavier nodded his head and continued. "Yep, exactly. But I didn't touch the guy, I'm not crazy, nor do I have a desire to meet Bubba in the pen. The only thing I did when I found out was call Horatio."

Bianca was about to sip her orange juice, but stopped with her drinking glass almost to her mouth. "Oh. Then Horatio told Uncle Geoff, and the guy disappears. It all makes sense now." She sipped her juice.

Annette held out her hand. "Wait a minute. You are telling me that your Uncle Geoff killed the man and took his money?"

All eyes reverted to her. "What money?" This came from Omar.

Once again, she recounted what she had forgotten to mention about the off-shore accounts. Omar and Xavier looked shocked, while Bianca nodded her head.

"That sounds like him. Xavier, you had to have told him about the accounts. Didn't you?" Bianca squinted at him.

"Hell no! I didn't know anything about any accounts." Recognition dawned across his face. "But I'm sure your brother would have been able to. After I told Horatio, the next time I talked him he told me that I could relax, it was all good. It's funny because we talked about some programming code that I was catching the devil with, and I thought that was what he meant. But the very next day I saw the news about David. I knew then that's what he was telling me."

They sat in silence while the birds chirped in the background. Then Bianca stretched and looked at Annette.

"To calm your nerves, Uncle Geoff does not 'kill' anyone himself, but he gets things done. You have now been introduced to an excerpt of the Baudoin dirty laundry. There is lots worse, but what can you do about family?" She stretched and stood.

"But I don't understand why Jay didn't tell me the whole story? Why would he act as if it was about some drug deal gone bad?" Annette looked stumped.

"Because he wants you back and he wants me out of your life. There's no way that Leonard didn't tell him the whole story! If he left out of the part about Omar, the story wouldn't have made sense and Jay wouldn't have accepted it. And when I mentioned it he didn't look surprised. Did you hear Leonard say something about a drug deal?"

Bianca sat down again as they all stared at Annette. She shook her head as she mentally replayed that nasty recording.

"No, Jay insinuated that, he said that was where your money came from. I was thinking that's why Geoff gave you the Mercedes." Annette giggled.

"Uncle Geoff gave you that Mercedes?" Bianca gaped.

Annette closed her eyes. Once again, her mouth ran wild! She looked at Xavier nervously but he grinned at her.

"Yep, it was payment for setting up the security system in his casino. Why? Are you jealous?"

"Hell, yeah I'm jealous! He probably bought it with the money from those off-shore accounts. According to Annette, there was enough in there for a few Mercedes." Bianca laughed.

They all laughed as they stood and walked in the house. All except Omar, he still looked upset. Xavier motioned to Annette that he was staying outside with his brother. Annette nodded and followed Bianca in the house.

Annette helped Bianca load the dishwasher as the men talked outside. The last two days had been so unreal, she felt as if she was part of a mirage. Bianca's voice broke her out of her musings.

"Zay told us about Damita last night." Bianca's face showed her concern.

The memory brought back the pain. The pain of losing not only a friend, but the respect for Damita. Annette nodded her head, "Yeah, that was something else. My first reaction was hurt because I thought something had happened. Then it hurt to think that she purposely wanted to hurt me. I might have been wrong for getting with Xavier, but I didn't do it to hurt her. She can call me thoughtless, but never malicious."

"I agree, she knew from my wedding that you guys were together. Xavier has not made that a secret. Last night was done out of malicious intent. Oh well, moving along." She glanced sideways at Annette. "I'll ask again are you in love with Xavier, or just whooped by the loving?"

Annette smiled shyly. "Both." She laughed as Bianca looked at her in amazement before she burst out laughing.

"Okay, I asked for that. Well I'll be damn! I guess there is someone for everyone." Bianca wrinkled her nose before she gave Annette a heartfelt hug. "He needed someone like you. I'm glad you guys found each other. Just don't tell Omar I said that."

ℰᏇᏣᏸℰᏇ

Omar lit his cigar as he looked out into the backyard. He felt his brother's gaze on his back, but he ignored it. He knew last night that Xavier wasn't telling him something and now he knew why. Jay had dug up old wounds, hurts and hatreds. Carly was one of them. Omar also knew that Carly didn't do anything for free. That worried him more than anything. How much money had Jay given her and what was she going to do with it?

"Good to see you and Annette have made up. She must love you." Omar decided to break the ice, since he knew that Zay wouldn't say anything until he did.

"I love her too. But that's not what's on your mind." Xavier's voice was deep, but soothing.

Omar and his brother had an unbreakable bond. His voice reminded him of the many hurts he faced growing up, and it was always Xavier who made things better. Then Bianca's words flitted through his mind. She was right, as much as Xavier had been his brother, father, and best friend, it was time for him to let go. He told Zay about the conversation and to his surprise, Xavier laughed.

"Man, you know I will always be here and have your back. I know it's the same with you. The women just add extra protection, especially Bianca."

Omar released the breath he hadn't known he held. "That's a relief I thought I'd lost my Bro-Dad. For real *hermano*, I'm happy for you. Do you think you can drop a word to Horatio about Carly?"

Xavier blinked quickly before he laughed. "Don't say that man. She's still Liberty's mom, no matter how awful she is."

"I was just joking." Omar chuckled briefly. "Speaking of awful moms, I talked to *Mamá* and *Papá*. They sounded half-way sober."

"Really? What made you call them?" Xavier looked surprised but pleased.

Omar told him how Annette confronted him and how he realized that he hadn't been fair making Xavier deal with them.

Xavier nodded thoughtfully, "I knew it bothered Annette, but I never thought she would mention it to you. Man, that woman is feistier than I ever imagined." Xavier laughed as he glanced back toward the house.

"Did you tell them that you were married?" Xavier's forehead creased with worry.

"Yeah *jefe,* I did. I also told them that you saved my life and that you are the only person that cares about them because I could give two shits about them." Omar gave a half-smile.

"You did not say that to Papá? Did you?" Xavier's voice rose.

"Calm down. No, I said it to mama and I meant every word. She asked me why I don't call and never come to see them. I told her they were drunks who never gave a shit about you or me. Stop looking at me like that." Omar laughed at his brother's look of horror. "Somebody needed to tell them the truth. You have been pacifying them with bullshit for years. She wanted me to call, I did, she cursed me out and told me to never call her again. The end."

He moved to the patio table and sat across from Xavier, who pinched his nose with his eyes closed. Omar spoke softly, "Let them go *jefe,* you don't need validation from them. Everything good you could get from them you have. The best thing they gave you was the ability to see that you wanted to be the opposite. We don't owe them a damn thing."

Xavier studied him for a moment before he spoke. "They are still our parents, but I see what you are saying. Thanks for that."

"*Jefe*, let go of your demons and go make some babies. You aren't getting any younger." Omar stood and clapped him on his shoulder.

"You are right about the not getting younger." He gazed through the door. "And you might be right about making some babies or at least practicing."

Omar laughed and followed his gaze. Annette stood at the glass door waving at his brother. Make-up less, with her hair in a ponytail and shorts on she looked so young, but very happy. Omar felt weak momentarily as gratefulness swelled in his heart for this woman who helped his brother become whole. When they made it in the house, Bianca looked at him sweetly, then immediately rolled her eyes at Zay.

He whispered in Annette's ear when he hugged her good-bye. "Thank you."

She looked at him in surprise as she tightened her grasp on him. "No thank you, for bringing him here. He is the man I needed."

Omar felt his eyes get wet as he released her. He jumped when Bianca came behind him. "What was that all about?"

He wrapped his arms around her as he led her in the house.

Chapter 31

Annette and Xavier slept well into the evening. When she awakened he was lying on his side staring at her. He looked more relaxed than she had ever seen him and the emotions in his eyes startled her. Before she spoke she reached out to put her hand on the side of his face and he nuzzled it.

"What are you doing?" She asked softly.

"Just watching you sleep." He drew her close and wrapped her in his security.

His warmth settled around her like a blanket. Annette felt so safe, secure and loved, she drifted off to sleep again. Xavier's voice rumbled through his body.

"I was wondering when you were going to wake up, so that we could eat." He pulled softly at her hair.

So much for more sleep! Annette chuckled as she rose and went to the bathroom. The food she cooked the day before was still in the refrigerator and a small reminder of Damita's shenanigans. Annette decided that she would leave that topic alone. Damita had been physically unfriended and would be avoided at all cost.

She studied him while they ate. Beyond his normal gorgeousness, there was a difference. He looked more relaxed and when he glanced at her the expression on his face took her by surprise. The guarded, blank look he usually wore was gone. He smiled at her while his eyes twinkled with an emotion that grabbed her heart and panties at the same time.

"Why are you staring at me? Do I have food on my face?" His dimples deepened as his voice rumbled.

She wanted to say something witty, but nothing came to mind. "I was just thinking that since we have our feelings out in the open, can we just be open with each other going forward? I don't care what it is, I want you to tell me any and everything, and know that my love won't change. Can we do that?"

He stopped smiling and scrutinized her before he nodded his head in agreement. "That goes for you too. I didn't like learning about the Audi from my brother."

How did that come back up Annette wondered? She nodded but couldn't resist, "I thought you knew. But anyway, you didn't tell me about Ant's bullies." She looked at him slyly as he blinked his eyes.

"That's different. Ant asked me not to. I took care of it, I wanted to smack that little fat kid, but I figured that wouldn't go over well."

She stared at him with a stern look. "Even if he asked you not to, I need to know. I won't let on that you told me."

He nodded seriously. "I was going to tell you after I accessed the situation to see if the bullies needed to disappear."

Once again, his dangerous dimples showed and she chortled after she crushed her napkin and threw it at him. The apprehension and worry of earlier was a far and distant memory. Later as she watched television she heard Xavier in one of the bedrooms with his drill. The corners of her mouth lifted as she shook her head. When he finally resurfaced he had bits of sawdust in his hair.

"What were you doing?" She inquired as he sat on the floor in front of her.

He settled between her legs before he answered. "Oh, I just put some shelves up in one of the rooms. Like the ones I put in your house, that way the kids can have their own rooms when they are here. But I need to go get a few more."

A wealth of emotions filled her heart. While she had been scared to reveal her feelings to him, she realized that he needed to hear it for security. Annette silently promised herself that she would never hide anything from him again. Since a huge lump occupied her throat she kissed the top of his head and ended with sawdust lips.

When she recovered she told him, "I can tell you that Corey will not sleep in a room by himself, I don't care how good it looks."

"We'll see. I'll find some way to make it comfortable for him, if not they can share." Xavier stretched. "What made you decide to be with me?" He turned his head and studied her.

Annette kissed his forehead, nose and when she got to his lips she answered. "My heart, soul, mind and body decided for me."

Xavier turned and rose on his knees, he gently swept her hair away from her face. "Damn Annette, there you go again. I've told you about my parents, explained the bond between Omar and I, and I even told you about the emptiness inside. All the things that have always made me an outcast, the odd man out." His hands moved to her thighs, slowing pushing her dress up. "I always believed that Horatio and Geoff let me in their inner circle because they sensed the likeness we shared. Even though they run that small town, because of their lifestyles and legends, they are outcasts too." He placed small kisses on each of her inner thighs and with each kiss her thighs widened. "You came into my life and filled the empty spots, with laughter, goodness, and family. When you let me in your life I felt as if I belonged. You saw the real me, no fronts or anything and you still accepted me as I am." His hands moved to her shoulders and he pulled the straps of her sundress down. "When I told you that I ran other women off, I gave them a little piece of the real me, the person that you saw and still gave me love. You make me want to be a better person, and anything I have is yours *Hermosa*."

He gathered her hair and pulled her head back before he sensuously licked her neck. She wrapped her arms around him tightly to scoot her body next to his.

When he released her hair, she licked his earlobe and whispered in his ear. "Then give me your dick."

His reaction was priceless. Xavier's mouth gaped open and his brows furrowed before he bellowed with laughter. "Annette what am I going to do with you?"

"Keep giving me what you have been, your love, patience, quirks and your…" He covered her mouth with a kiss before she finished.

She lost herself in the feeling as he tugged and caressed her. Unable to wait she pushed him back and slid on the floor straddling him. When she released him from his shorts, Xavier moaned as she leaned into him as she stroked him against her stomach. Xavier hungrily kissed her as he lifted her to his hardness and she encroached him with her heat. He slid inside her and it felt familiar yet new as she lowered her body slowly because she wanted to feel each nuance of his hardness. Xavier leaned back and she leaned forward to kiss him. Their bodies, as usual, moved in sync, but it felt different.

As he pulled her dress over her head, she wriggled out of it and heard him groan loudly. He sat up quickly impaling himself deep inside the recesses of her wetness. Her breasts ached with need and as if he intuitively knew this he nursed them gently. She gripped his shoulders hard as she fought against the heat that consumed her.

Xavier sucked at her lower lip as he moved in synchrony with the music they made. Her legs trembled as he stroked her slowly and sinuously while his eyes told the story of his heart.

"Xavier, I love you." She murmured breathlessly as the sensations tingled her soul.

She felt him harden more as he wrapped his arms around her to remain entwined in her blaze of desire.

"I love you too, damn I do." He mumbled as he submersed himself as deep as he could. "You *are mi alma e mi vida.*"

She felt him quiver inside as he released his seed deep inside of her. Her knees rammed into his back as their flames blossomed and burst together. Her legs tightened against him as her stomach contracted and her body shook. His seed entered her soul and quenched her insatiable thirst for his love. It was securely embedded in her heart, as secure as she felt in his arms. They held each other until their tremors diminished.

His lips were hot on her earlobe as she laid limply in his arms. *"Acabamos de hacer un bebé."* He whispered in her ear.

With no idea of what he meant, she nodded weakly. *"Sí."* That was the only Spanish word she remembered besides adios.

The barrage of foliage almost covered Bianca and Tonya as they sat on Bianca's patio. Since Tonya left Fred, she and Bianca formed a closer bond, that along with trying to keep up with Annette. It also helped that she wasn't constantly bemoaning about her trials with Fred. Recently she spoke more about Carl, which in Bianca's opinion was just as bad. Tonya was a master with a sewing machine and she came to Bianca's to look at patterns for the baby's room. As they looked at patterns for window treatments, Tonya brought up Carl.

"I'm going on a date with Carl next weekend." She grinned widely.

"I hope you don't think I'm going to cheese and grin with you about that nugget of information." Bianca pursed her lips together.

"I don't expect you to cheese and grin, but you know I need some advice. It's been ages since I've dated." Tonya whispered loudly.

"Girl why are you whispering? We are the only ones here!" Bianca laughed. "I'm not sure I'm the right person to ask. That sounds like an Annette question. Hell, she could probably tell you how to date him and get him to fall deeply in love. We always look at her as the naïve one, but lately I'm not so sure."

"Now you said a mouthful then! That is the truth! Forget I asked, I'll ask Nette." Tonya chuckled as she pulled some material out of her bag.

They pieced material together, and held the pieces against the paint cards Bianca held. Once they went through the first batch, Bianca turned her attention back to Tonya.

"Back to Carl, I still think that he is a bad choice for you." Bianca wrinkled her nose.

"Don't start on his looks! I think he is very attractive and we get along great. What is your problem with him?" Tonya seemed genuinely confused.

Bianca took a deep breath before she spoke. "I get a bad vibe about him. My mom always told me that I was like my great-grandmother, who supposedly had a 'third eye.' She told me to always trust my instincts because of this. Now that is probably an old wives' tale, but I do get vibes about certain people, and the one for Carl is not good."

Tonya eyebrows rose as she listened. "One day we need to have a long talk about your family! They sound and appear to be an interesting bunch. Does he make you feel uncomfortable? Is that the feeling?"

"No, it's not discomfort." Bianca moved slightly in her chair. "Okay I'll just say it. Carl seems like a pretentious asshole. He carries himself as if he thinks he is better than others and like he is all that. Which he isn't by the way, and I also don't see him as one that can move on." She continued as she saw Tonya's look of confusion. "After what Angie did to him, I can see him taking that anger and frustration out on the next person he gets involved with."

Tonya nodded, "I can see some of what you say. He does speak very negatively of his ex-wife, but I understand that. Other than that, he seems down to earth."

"Whatever." Bianca mumbled.

"You know Annette seems to be the only person you don't give grief to about men. You tried your best to keep Damita away from Xavier, and now me with Carl. I won't mention Fred." Tonya looked at her expectantly.

Bianca shrugged her shoulders. "Please don't. I just told you how I feel about Carl, you are free to do whatever you want. I knew that Damita and Zay wouldn't work, and contrary to your belief I tried to talk to Annette about Xavier. She wouldn't listen. But now, I'm glad she didn't."

Tonya looked surprised. "How did you know that Damita and Xavier weren't going to work?"

"She had to do too much. She always called, she always arranged for them to go out, and he was interested in Annette from the start." Bianca stood and stretched.

Tonya's eyes widened. "He was into Annette from the start? Does Damita know this? Y'all are going to mess around and that woman will have a new code, that includes Carl!"

"Speaking of Damita..." Bianca paused as she motioned for Tonya to follow her inside. Once they sat in the den she told Tonya what transpired at Xavier's. Bianca held in her laughter at the myriad of expressions that crossed Tonya's face.

"Bianca, we can't have her at anymore girls' nights! That would be too uncomfortable and to be honest, I don't know if I can consider her a friend anymore! That was scandalous for her to try." Tonya raised her voice and her arms flailed.

Before Bianca uttered one word, Tonya continued. "Annette was our friend first and I value her friendship more than Damita's. I mean Damita is alright, but this is the last straw. Did you know that she tried to cause a scene at your wedding?"

Bianca's foot stuck to the floor as Tonya spilled the tea. Damita antics spoke of immaturity and insecurities, characteristics that she hadn't noticed before. Tonya was in her element as she gave her the run down. Deep in thought about Damita's antics Bianca almost missed part of Tonya's colloquial.

"Hold up! What did you just say?" Bianca grabbed Tonya's arm to slow her down.

"I said that Carl doesn't speak highly of Xavier because of Damita. He didn't think that Xavier was good for Damita, and that she was hurting because of him." Tonya's tea became a slow dribble.

Bianca thought about everything she knew and it didn't add up. She glanced at Tonya and told her, "Here is what we need to do."

The women put their heads together and commiserated.

Chapter 32

The music blared in Jay's car, but it barely broke through his misery. Malik rapped along with whatever song played and usually this brought Jay happiness, but not today. A week had passed since he told Annette what he found out, and his plan had backfired. Annette still saw the guy and it seemed as if their bond had grown. He surmised this from the number of days through the week that Ashley's car was the only one in the drive.

It didn't take a rocket scientist or a blind man to figure out that she was spending weeknights with that jerk! Jay's calls went unanswered and weren't returned, his texts received the same result. When Omar came in the office Jay felt the hostility that he directed towards him. When Jay tried to talk to him he was greeted with a grunt and the coldest stare down he had ever seen. He saw the man that Leonard described and decided not to make any further attempts.

When he vented his frustrations to Carl, he told Jay to just let things play out. Jay was not satisfied with that answer. A week ago, it seemed as if his life was in a good place to get back on track, now it was filled with frustrations. Elaine bugged the devil out of him daily, Carly had begun to give him weekly updates, and Annette hadn't talked to him. To add to his misery, the security program needed a service patch that only Xavier could provide. His sugar had turned to shit quickly!

He and Malik were in route to his moms, because Malik wanted to see his Uncle Jermaine. Jay agreed but the closer they came he thought of ways to deter René from digging in his business. His heartbeat quickened as he saw a sleek Mercedes in René's drive! It looked like the car Annette drove. His vehicle was barely in park before he jumped out and raced to the side door. Annette sat at the table with René with their hands clasped together. René looked as if she had been crying.

Annette looked up as Jay barged in with Malik at his heels. Her smile lifted and slammed into his heart at the same time. Malik ran to Annette and she hugged him tightly as she kissed his cheek. René stood and grabbed Malik in a hug as she looked at Jay with an indistinguishable look. She walked to the stairway with her arm around his son.

Jay looked at Annette as she sat back down at the table. Her hair was in a ponytail, she was adorned in shorts and a tee-shirt, and she was the most beautiful woman he had ever laid eyes on. She smiled shyly at him as her eyes sparkled. Jay sat at the table, silent, because he was too scared to speak.

"Hello Jay." Annette finally said as she scrutinized him.

"Hey. I'm sorry I was just surprised to see you here. I'm glad to see you but surprised." Jay's voice was hoarse.

They sat in silence for a few minutes, which Jay enjoyed. He knew that whatever came next would not be good and he wanted it delayed for as long as possible.

"Jay, I came today to speak with your mom, because I wanted to clear the air, and frankly I miss her. I stayed longer than I planned because she told me that you were coming and I knew that we needed to talk." Annette cleared her throat as tears welled in her eyes.

"Don't." He stopped her. "I have a good idea what you are going to say, so you don't have to say anymore."

Annette surprised him when she grabbed his hand. "No, Jay, we have to talk about this! One of our issues was that neither one of us was as honest with the other as we should have been. You have been a major force in my life and it wouldn't be right for us to not talk about it."

Jay wiped his face with his free hand. He held onto Annette as if she was his life jacket, that one small touch soothed his soul. He glanced at her from beneath his eyelashes before he spoke.

"I know that you are going to tell me that we are done and that you are still with Xavier. I just don't want to hear it." It took everything he had not to spit that guy's name out.

Annette squeezed his hand. "Jay what went wrong with us goes so much deeper than Xavier and there is more to be said than we are done. I need to hear from you, the man I trusted with everything in me, why you did certain things. I don't want to look back two or three years from now and still wonder."

Jay cleared his throat, but his voice was still hoarse as his words slid over the lump. "Annette, I told you and apologized for the bad decisions I made. I can't think of many more ways to say it."

Annette leaned back but Jay refused to release her hand, he wanted this moment to last forever. Annette scooted her chair closer to him.

"Jay, you lied to me countless times. You lied about having sex with Elaine, you didn't tell me that she was pregnant when she told you, and you lied about Xavier." Annette's voice softened when she ended.

Jay's head jerked when he heard Xavier's name. He stared at her intently before he answered. "You are right I did. I lied to you about Elaine because I didn't want to see disappointment in your eyes, nor did I want you to look at me differently." He took a deep breath. "I didn't lie about him, I just didn't tell you the entire story. I did that because I was willing to do any and everything to try to win your heart back. It obviously didn't work."

Jay had lowered his eyes when he spoke, and when he looked back up his heart ached at the sight of the tears that streamed down Annette's face. With great reluctance, he released her hand and got a box of tissues out of the pantry. When he handed the box to Annette he grabbed her hand once again.

"Even with the things I lied about the one thing that remains true is how much I love you. And how much I will always love you." Tears stung the back of his eyes as her body shook with sobs.

Jay scooted closer and pulled her in his arms. He held her as she cried on his shoulder and he cursed himself for causing her hurt. He sniffed her hair as memories of the love they had for one another rolled like a carousel through his mind.

Annette pushed back slightly. "I'm sorry. I promised myself that I wouldn't cry and here I am. If both of us had been more honest, we probably wouldn't be sitting here now. Jay, neither of us revealed our true personalities to each other. You wanted to be the perfect man for me and I wanted to be the perfect woman for you. It's wasn't realistic."

"You are the perfect woman for me." Although Annette had moved out of his arms, he kept his arm around her chair.

"How can you say that? I never showed you the real me. I showed you what I thought you wanted to see. It's not your fault, but that's what I did. I knew what you went through with Elaine, so I didn't want to complain or second-guess your decisions. I thought if I did that you would think I was just like her. So instead I bit my tongue and held in how I really felt. I was too scared to lose you." She choked as she finished.

Jay listened, then he realized that she spoke the truth. He and Annette had been on a continuous honeymoon and each day they spent was filled with joy. He never put Anthony in his place because he wanted to wait until they were married. He continued to play Elaine's games to keep peace for Malik and Annette. He never expressed to Annette why he did the things he did, because he assumed she understood. He also never asked how she felt about the things they dealt with.

"I don't care what you showed me, I know that it wouldn't have changed my love for you. But you are right I wanted to be strong, fearless and your knight in shining armor. I thought that I was protecting you from Elaine's madness by trying to keep the peace. I also didn't want you to know how scared I was of becoming my father. Because there were many times when I wanted to just leave Elaine to fend for herself, but I couldn't do that to my son. In my mind if I made your life as comfortable as I could, I would never lose you and things would eventually even out. I made so many mistakes and now I'll never get a chance to show you that my love is pure and true." A couple of tears leaked out as he spoke.

"Jay, you can't assume the responsibility of what has happened to us. It was both of us. I wish I had realized then that I was strong enough to tell you how I truly felt. I wish I had expressed that I didn't want to deal with Elaine, because if I had, you might have done things differently. I know that you love me, and I will always have a special love for you in my heart. It will never die, but it is not enough to sustain us as a couple." Once again, her sobs forced her to stop.

"Annette, I feel as if you are and always will be the woman for me. Call me foolish but I can't imagine time healing the void I feel without you in my life. I just knew that the prospect of getting custody of Malik would be the key to us returning to normal. It never crossed my mind that I would lose your heart." Jay let his tears run down his face. Annette grabbed a tissue and gently wiped his tears away.

"Jay, Elaine will always be Malik's mom and as long as she has the hate in her heart for me, she would never accept me as his stepmom. What we shared will always be special. You showed me that love can be real and I'll never forget that." She swallowed as she paused. "You didn't lose my heart, I just finally grew up and faced the truth about myself. I'm not going to sit here and tell you that I didn't love you, because that would be a lie. But I treated the love we shared as a prize instead of a gift. I didn't express myself honestly because I wanted to win! I wanted to make sure that I ended with the prize. And that was a terrible way to think of our love."

The silence was heavy. Jay was happy to know that at least she did love him, but it hurt to think he had lost. She was his prize and he didn't care that he thought of it in those terms. He told her that. When Annette laughed it relieved some of the tension in the room.

"Jay, I'm no prize, I'm just me. I'm not mad about what we went through, because it helped me grow. I will always attribute that growth, to what we shared. The good and the bad."

"I understand. I also know that I took your love for granted. When I found out about Xavier, just from the little I knew about the guy, I couldn't imagine that he had anything to offer. I was wrong about that! He came and swept you away, right under my nose." Jay crumpled his tissue and threw it in the trash.

Annette clutched his arm. "Jay nobody swept me away. I can't tell you where I am going with him, but I am in a good place right now. He's been a major part of my journey also."

Jay turned away, "That's not what I want to hear. I don't care that you think he helps you, it was dirty what he did."

He felt Annette's hand on his back and her perfume assaulted him. "Jay, we were both wrong. Would you prefer to be with me while I have someone else in my – on my mind? Is that what you are telling me?"

He abruptly turned and captured her by holding her waist. "That would have eventually subsided, if he had left you alone. You were hurt and vulnerable and he had the choice plus the opportunity to walk away. He chose not to, for whatever reason."

Annette stepped back and hugged herself. She bit her bottom lip and he saw indecision in her eyes. She grabbed her chair and placed it directly across from him.

"Jay, I never meant to hurt you and I don't believe that Xavier wanted that either." She paused as he scoffed. "Xavier was willing to walk away, and he didn't because..."

Jay grabbed her hands and looked directly in her eyes. "He didn't because of what Annette?"

She inhaled deeply before she answered. "Because I asked him not to." She rushed on, "What began as an opportunity as you say for him, and a getaway for me became more complicated as time went on."

As Jay looked at her with disbelief and while hurt hammered in his chest, she continued.

"When I asked Xavier to stay, it was because I had become so dependent on his friendship. I couldn't imagine not having him as a friend. At least that is what I told myself. After I found out Elaine was pregnant, I was done, with you, Xavier, men period in my mind. His friendship never wavered and it wasn't based on who he thought I was, it was based on who I truly am."

"So, you knew from the beginning that you wanted to be with him?" Hurt and anger coursed through Jay's body.

"No, I didn't. I kept telling myself that I wanted things back with you, even with the drama from Elaine. But I realized that I lied to myself. I wanted to be happy and have peace of mind, but that was not going to happen with us." She stopped as his brows snapped together. "Not just because of Elaine, but because of what I felt for Xavier, it wasn't going away."

Jay looked down and thought of his options. Even though he didn't want to believe what he heard, he knew that she believed it. He looked at her and everything that he loved deeply about her stared back at him. The concern for him that he saw in her eyes, the nervous habit of biting her bottom lip, borne out of worry for him and her inner beauty that no clothing concealed. Disappointment washed over him as his throat became heavy with the tears that stung the inside of his eyelids.

"Are you happy baby?" He hated to ask but he had to know.

"Yes, for two reasons. I feel as if I have closed my circle. The circle of family that never quite closed with you because we allowed Elaine to keep a wedge in it. And also, because you proved to me today that you are still the man I admire, respect, and will always have a place in my heart. Those things make me happy." Annette pulled out another tissue, wiped her face and nose.

Jay leaned forward and kissed the tip of her nose. "Then I'm okay if you are happy. But I can't promise you that I won't keep trying to get you back in my life. I'll try not to, but you will always own my heart. Not a piece or a place, but all of it."

Jay stood and so did Annette. He pulled her tightly into an embrace as he whispered in her ear. "If you ever need me I will always be here for you. I don't care who is in my life or yours if you call, I'm coming."

Her body shook with her sobs and he held his as he rubbed her back. He kept her wrapped in his embrace long as he could to cover the emptiness he felt inside. Annette held him tightly before she broke free.

"Jay, you are one of the most amazing men I have ever met. I understand it might be awkward for us for some time, but I want us to build some type of friendship. Are you okay with that?" Her voice shook.

"Of course I am. And through it all, I never have been and I'm still not angry with you. I'm glad that we had this conversation and I'm glad that after everything you still see something good in me. One of the many things that I love about you." Jay ended wistfully.

Annette asked him to get his mom and Malik before she left. He called them down, his mom came quickly, too quickly for his benefit and Malik followed shortly afterwards. Annette hugged them both tightly and kissed their cheeks. Jay stood awkwardly to the side until she finished talking to his mom. When his mom finally scooted out of the kitchen, Annette looked sadly at him.

"I guess I'll leave now." She stuttered as she grabbed her purse from a chair.

Jay advanced slowly to her and opened his arms as he got closer. He breathed in her essence when she walked into his embrace. He wished silently that he could turn back the hands of time.

"Don't worry about me Annette. If you are okay, I'm fine. It's going to be hard, but I'm just glad I haven't lost you completely." He stroked her hair.

Annette pulled back and gazed at him before she stood on her tiptoes and kissed his cheek. "Don't ever think my love wasn't real, because it was and I wish you nothing but happiness."

Jay nodded as he released her and watched her walk out the door. "I love you too Annette, and I'll never give up until I have you back in my life." He murmured to the closed door.

Chapter 33

Annette felt drained but liberated as she drove away. When she cried her tears reflected how things once were and the loss of the future they had planned. It hurt her to see and feel his heartache, but she had to be true to herself. Elaine's craziness and her involvement with Xavier forced her to grow. The old Annette would have forfeited her happiness to make Jay happy and do what was expected of her. Her internal growth showed her that while she had loved Jay, it wasn't the love that encompassed her heart, mind, body and soul. That was the love she had for Xavier.

Thoughts of Xavier lightened her heart. No matter what he showed the world, he was a good person with a heart of gold. He knew that she was going to talk to Jay, he actually encouraged it. In his eyes that was the best way for them to have a fresh start. He explained to her that for years after Bianca left Louisiana, Omar remained hurt because he never knew why she left him. Xavier wanted Jay to have closure, so that he wouldn't have to hurt him. She chuckled as she thought about how she was so proud of his giving heart until he mentioned that last part.

When she pulled up at Xavier's house she saw Ashley and Liberty's car in the drive. Liberty was there before she left but she was surprised to see Ashley's car. Annette checked the time, because Bianca had called for a last-minute girl's night out. Annette was going but after the emotional turmoil she experienced she just wanted the comfort of Xavier's embrace.

She walked in and the house was quiet. The closer she walked to the sliding doors she heard the noise from the back. Marisa, Jolisa, Ashley, Liberty, and Cherise were on the deck in sunglasses and drinking lemonade. Annette was surprised to see Marisa, she hadn't known that she was in town. Xavier, the boys and Omar were in the back hunched over the Mustang. Xavier had extended his driveway to the back and added a portable carport for the car. Annette shook her head because Jolisa thought she was part of the older girls' club. Jolisa sat up straight when she noticed her mom.

"Mom! What's wrong?" Her screech made the others look intently at Annette.

Jolisa no matter how many attitudes she had was deeply connected to Annette's moods. Annette smiled at her brightly and hoped that it fooled her daughter.

"Nothing, my allergies are bothering me. Where's Bianca?" Jolisa's brows knitted together, but she didn't say anything.

"She's at home, she said that she was going to dinner with you." Marisa peered at her.

"Oh yeah, we are. I'm going to see what the boys are doing." Annette hurried down the steps.

Annette walked out to the carport and saw Omar directing Ant as he loosened some part from the engine, while Xavier and Corey looked on. There were streaks of grease on Xavier's arms and he was sweaty, but he looked good to her.

René's words came back to her. She told René about Xavier and how she felt about him. René became teary eyed but her response shocked Annette.

René peered over her glasses before she spoke. "Nette the only reason for me to be mad at you is for selfish reasons. Yes, I wanted you as my daughter-in-law because I love you. But I know how strong your feelings are for Jay. If your feelings for Xavier are stronger and put Jay on the backburner, you better embrace it girlfriend! There aren't too many people that find love like that. And I could tell at the wedding that he loves you too. That is too special to let go. I'm happy that you have not only found happiness but your voice."

René said other things about how she would always be there for Annette and how Jay would get over his hurt, because he was a "big boy."

Xavier noticed her and smiled. He walked to the entrance and gave her a once over. "Are you okay?" He inquired quietly.

His warmth beckoned her closer to him as she moved closer to him. He instinctively wrapped his arm around her.

"You talked to Jay?" He looked down at her as she laced her arms around his waist.

"Yeah, I talked to him. It went okay, considering." Her glance upward was met with a kiss.

"Okay, I know you will tell me about it later. Are you sure that you are okay?" His eyes shone with concern.

"I am now that I am here with my family." She looped her arms around his neck and pulled his face down for a kiss.

The original intention had been a smack but he engulfed her in a majestic kiss that took all her hurt and fears away. Omar's voice broke them apart.

"*Jefe!* Are you still working or are you done for the day?" Omar and Ant laughed, he thought he was one of the men, and Corey ran up to them.

"Momma, Mr. Xavier said that Uncle Ratio is coming over!" Corey's face was filled with excitement.

Annette looked at Xavier questioningly. "Horatio is in town?" She lowered her voice to a whisper. "And why is Corey calling him uncle?"

Xavier's laughter boomed across the yard. "Yes, he rode with Marisa and Horatio told Corey to call him that." He paused, "But don't worry, I'm not going to let him spend too much time with him, you know how that family is."

"*Ese* it's hot out here! I think we should call it day." Omar wiped his sweat with a towel.

"I'm coming! He wants me to do all the work." Xavier looked at her with a smile. "Go ahead and get ready for your girls' night. We will be fine, Omar said he would cook for us. He likes to do that kind of shit, but ask him about yardwork and you get a million excuses." Xavier whispered while he laughed.

Annette laughed as she walked towards the house. Her cloud had lifted and she looked forward to spending time with her friends. They were back to the original three, but after Damita's tricks she wasn't mad about it.

When Annette walked in the restaurant she was shocked as Bianca stood and waved her over. Since Bianca had been pregnant she arrived on time each time. Annette smiled but stopped short when she noticed Damita sat at the table also.

Bianca slid over and patted a seat next to her in the booth. Annette sat down with trepidation. After the day she had earlier, she wasn't sure if she wanted to deal with this. Damita gave her the side-eye and a dry hello when she spoke.

The silence was palpable until they received their drinks and appetizers. Bianca wiped her mouth before she spoke.

"I guess you know that we all know about the stunt you pulled at Xavier's. Tonya and I decided that it would be best that as friends we clear the air." She looked expectantly at Damita.

"How were you expecting to do that?" Damita looked between Bianca and Annette.

Annette kept her mouth shut, because she didn't need anything cleared. Damita a person non-grata as far as she was concerned.

"I thought instead of jumping to conclusions we could hear it from you. Exactly what were you trying to prove?" Bianca's voice was steady but firm.

"Nothing. I just assumed that if it was good for the goose it would be good for the gander. Annette, your actions hurt my brother deeply, but we need to clear the air about me? Humph." Damita showed zero remorse.

Annette finally found her voice. "I spoke to Jay earlier, and he understands, so don't try to make this about him."

Damita glared at Annette. "Of course, he is, he thinks you shit roses. Let's take him out of the equation. You slept with Xavier when you were supposedly my friend and you knew that I had been seeing him. You didn't care, but I'm supposed to care that your feelings are hurt?"

Their server gave Annette time to formulate her response as she brought their food and refilled drinks. Before she responded, Tonya surprised her.

"Girl go somewhere with all that! You told all of us that you had never slept with that man and that you guys had only been friends. At this point I'm wondering if you kissed him. Girl bye!" Tonya eyes sparked with emotion.

The outburst shocked them all. Bianca coughed (laughed) in her napkin, Damita's eyes grew large and Annette's hand went to her chest. She recovered and responded to Damita.

"Damita the difference is that you and Xavier were done plus you did tell us that you guys had only been friends. I was wrong, I admit, but I apologized and you said you were fine with everything. You did what you did purely out of spite. That's the biggest difference." Annette tried to keep her voice even, but failed at the end.

Damita ate in silence and they all followed suit. Annette's food tasted like grass. The previous friendship she had with Damita was done. The old Annette would have sat quietly until the end and just never spoke to her again. The new Annette needed to get her frustrations off her chest.

"Damita what you did was intentionally hateful and hurtful. I might have been wrong and if I hurt you, I am sorry because that was not my intentions. I never expected to be with Xavier, but I am glad that I am, regardless of how we got together. You knew that I was coming that night and you hoped that he would fall for your foolishness, so that I would catch you in bed with my man." Tonya snorted and distracted Annette, but she continued. "Yes, he is my man and since I can't trust you around what is mine, I don't see how our friendship can continue."

Damita had a mean glint in her eyes. "How do you know that his version is the truth? Of course, he will tell you that it was all me, so that you wouldn't be mad. But are you sure that it is the truth?"

"Damita! You…" Bianca stopped when Annette grabbed her arm.

Annette held her head high and looked Damita directly in her eyes. "Yes, I do believe him because I know he doesn't want you. If he did I wouldn't be with him now. Would I?"

"Whelp! I guess we can conclude this discussion." Tonya raised her eyebrows and looked down.

"I guess he'll have to learn just like my brother did. The first time he upsets you and you run to somebody else." Damita would not be deterred.

Annette had heard enough! "For your information, each time Elaine came by, or your brother had to run off at her call that upset me. When he left me out, screwed Elaine and lied about it, he broke my heart. That heartbreak might be how Xavier and I hooked up, but our friendship which turned into love is what brought us together. And it is what will keep us together. I just hope that one day you can find the same thing, maybe then you will understand."

Damita for once was silent. Bianca squeezed Annette's arm slightly. Then she turned to Damita, "Speaking of your brother, did he tell you to go to Zay's that night?"

Tonya and Damita looked confused. Damita broke her silence. "No, of course not. Jay told me to stay away from him." She looked down and mumbled, "I even offered to do something similar for him to have some dirt on Xavier, but he refused my offer."

Even with her anger, Annette felt sad that Damita was so bitter that she needed to lash out anyway possible. They finished their meal in silence. Annette was prepared to leave because she definitely needed her fix tonight. Even if it just came in the form of cuddling in Xavier's arms.

Damita touched her hand gently as she reached for her check.

"Annette, I know I was bitchy tonight, and you are right, I am jealous. I wanted Xavier to be the one for me because of my interest not anything he showed me. My mom says I'll never find a man long as I do that and she is probably right. He did not want me there that night and before you walked in…" She gulped before she continued, "He let me know that he wanted absolutely nothing to do with me. That's why I was crying, because he did not say it that nice. It might take me awhile to show it, but I'm glad you found happiness."

Annette was still a bit angry, but she realized that Damita was hurting too. This whole thing with her and Jay had taken a toll on many people. She sighed and acknowledged her apology and they all hugged before they left.

When she got to Xavier's, Omar was gone, Jolisa was sleep and her boys were in the game room with Horatio. She found Xavier in the bedroom closet.

She peeped around the door, "What are you doing?"

Xavier grunted as he rearranged his clothes. "I'm making room for the clothes you leave. But you will have to set them up right."

Annette raised her eyebrows. "Are you sure that you are ready for this big step?" She hid her grin.

Xavier's dimples showed. "I've never been surer of anything."

He stepped out of the closet and she lost herself in his arms.

Chapter 34

The last month had been trying for Jay. He faced the truth that Annette was lost to him. He hadn't given up hope for the future, but as usual he immersed himself in work. Xavier had provided the service pack and they were cordial to another. He thought about the day Xavier brought up their personal issues. Jay had asked him a question about the service pack and after he explained it Xavier looked him square in his face.

"It was never personal against you." His eyes went back to his screen.

Jay accepted the inevitable but he still thought Xavier was a prick. To make matters worse Elaine found out about Annette and Xavier. She threw it in his face every chance she could, which wasn't very often because Jay stayed as far away from her as possible. The weekends he spent with Malik, his mom picked him up. Elaine pitched a fit about that and the lack of extra money since Jay cut her off. He had no idea who her baby's daddy was, and he didn't care either. He might have learned his lesson late but he had learned it.

He returned to his task of scheduling his trip to California in a few weeks. That's when the deal would be finalized and he was on his way to spreading his wings. Professionally anyway. He was interrupted as Omar and Xavier burst through his office.

"Jay tell me you did not send for Carly to come here!" Omar was clearly upset.

Jay looked at the two men in surprise. He had stopped accepting Carly's calls a few weeks ago. Each time he had talked to her she brought up Omar and her hate flowed through the phone lines. Jay knew that if he arranged for her to see Liberty that she would bring trouble, so he stopped taking her calls.

"No! I haven't talked to her in weeks." Jay exclaimed. "Is she here?"

"Hell yeah! And I know that she didn't get here on her own. There is no way she stopped buying hair, dope, and too little clothes to save up." Omar looked at him suspiciously. "If you didn't then who the hell did?"

Jay shrugged his shoulders then it hit him! It had to be Carl. His friend had been secretive these last few weeks, Jay just assumed it dealt with Tonya. His first instinct was to not tell them but he thought about Xavier's computer skills. They would know by the end of the day if he started digging.

He sighed heavily, "It was probably Carl. But he didn't know any better."

Xavier looked at him knowingly, while Omar muttered in Spanish. Xavier grabbed his arm and shook his head. Omar just rolled his eyes.

Jay tried to ease their frustrations. "She said she just wanted to see Liberty. I'm sure she won't be a problem."

Omar leaned over Jay's desk and he noticed that dangerous look in his eyes. "Liberty doesn't want to see her. Carly doesn't give a shit about Liberty and her main purpose will be to cause problems. You and Carl went to Texas and stirred up things that had nothing to do with either of you. Now because of your meddling we, and I mean my brother and I will have to clean up this mess."

"Look, let me call Carl and he can have her back on a plane by tomorrow." Jay spoke hurriedly as he pulled his phone out.

"You tell Carl that if she causes one problem for me and my family this will be the biggest regret of his life." Omar snarled before Xavier pulled him back and then they left.

Jay's hand shook as he called Carl, he started in on him as soon as he answered the phone. "Dude what were you thinking by bringing Carly here?"

Carl sounded startled, "What? We promised her and she just wants to see her daughter. She said she couldn't get you, I figured I would help and take care of it. She also had

5

taken vacation and if she didn't come now she wouldn't be able to get any more days."

"Damn man, you should have talked to me first. Listen I'll explain later but you need to get her out of here tomorrow." Jay felt sweat cover his brow.

"Tomorrow? She's headed to Auburn, I don't even know if I will see her tomorrow." Carl sounded exasperated.

Jay explained to him why he had stopped taking her calls and relayed the events that occurred in his office. He almost saw Carl's eyes bulge through the phone.

"How the hell did he find out she was here?" Carl yelled into the phone.

"I don't know I just assumed Liberty told him that Carly showed up on campus." Jay felt the fear his friend currently felt.

"Wait a minute. There is no way she's made it to Auburn yet. Jay, she just got her rental less than an hour ago. Find out what's going on and I'll try to get her ass back here." Carl stuttered before he hung up.

Jay's curiosity got the best of him. He swallowed his pride and called Xavier versus Omar, because he still felt the heat from Omar's glare.

Mr. Personality answered on the third ring. "Yeah?"

"I called Carl, he's trying to find Carly now. How did Omar know she was here?" Jay got right to the point.

Xavier sighed, "She came by the security office this morning, talking trash as usual. Listen Omar will calm down, but she needs to leave. If Liberty finds out she is here and gets upset Omar will shit bricks." He paused, then murmured, "And then there's Bianca."

"Yeah, I got the memo. I told Carl, he thought he was doing the right thing. There was no malicious intent." Jay wanted to hang up because he was hit with an inexplicable urge to ask about Annette.

Xavier chuckled. "I know. What are you scared your homeboy might disappear?"

Before Jay answered Xavier hung up. What Annette saw in that guy was a mystery to him. Once again, his thoughts drifted to what he lost. This guy had possibly killed someone and she was still with him! Jay knew he would never find another woman like her.

Carl burst through his office door with a wild look on his face. "Man, she won't answer her phone! I don't know where the hell she is."

Jay told him what he learned from Xavier and Carl groaned while he held his head. "Calm down dude. We will get in touch with her and back on a plane."

Carl's eyes rounded, "Do you not remember what Leonard told us? About Omar? Shit man, I'm fucked!"

Carl paced in front of him as he tried Carly again. When his call went to voicemail, he sat down and cradled his head.

Jay laughed, "Man, calm your ass down. How much trouble can she cause? Auburn has a huge campus and hopefully she won't find her. Don't worry as soon as she needs some gas money, she'll call."

Carl mumbled incoherently. Jay wanted to laugh again but he knew that Carl was scared. "Look, let me call her. Maybe she will answer."

Carl looked hopeful as Jay looked for the number he had avoided for weeks. He gave Carl the thumbs up when she answered.

"Hey Carly? This is Jay." He spoke pleasantly as possible.

"I know who this is. It's funny that you can call me back now. I knew you were full of shit when I met you." Carly laughed.

A feeling of dread crossed Jay's spine. Carly sounded comfortable and she also did not sound as if she was driving.

"Carly, I meant what I said but there is a lot going on right now. I don't think this is the best time to see Liberty." Jay kept his voice lowered as he tried to placate her.

"That's okay. I can wait. I have a little unfinished business with her dad anyway." Carly smacked her lips.

Carl had invaded Jay's personal space as he tried to listen to the conversation. When he heard what Carly said he bounced around the office on the balls of his feet.

"Carly, you promised me that you wouldn't cause any problems for Omar. Do you remember that?" Jay's voice had risen with anger.

Carl scribbled on a post it and as Jay tried to read it he almost missed what she said.

"Yeah, well, just like you lied about sending for me, I told a little one too. Omar came into all that money and instead of paying me to take care of his only child, he took her from me. Whenever I called that bastard and asked him for anything he told me that he wouldn't spit on me if I was on fire! Now this bastard thinks that he is going to set up house and make things easy for that Baudoin bitch? The one who caused all our problems in the first place? While I can barely pay rent for a one-bedroom roach infested dump? Hell no! If Omar wants me to leave he can pay me to leave." Carly seemed out of breath as she paused.

Jay looked down at what Carl had written: Remind her that they are dangerous!!!

Jay shook his head as Carly continued. "The best news you gave me was that he married her! Not only can I get his ass back, it will give me great pleasure to fuck with her! When I get finish with them I might not have to ask for the money!" Carly cackled.

Jay tried one last time to rationalize with her. "Carly, I think you are making a big mistake."

There was silence before her voice returned with a hard edge. "I don't. I'm not scared of Omar nor his brother. I've been waiting for this day for a long time. Once he figures out that it will be easier to pay me, then I will disappear from his life. Forever. I want to see how many zeroes his spit has." She chuckled. "Jay? Tell Carl he can cancel that room reservation in Auburn, I won't be going there." She smacked her lips into the phone again.

"What about money? I thought you couldn't afford to come here on your own?" The feeling of dread Jay felt earlier intensified with each word Carly said.

"When you stay with a friend for some time and don't have to worry about rent and utilities, it's amazing how much you can save. Especially when you know that a big payoff is coming." She cackled once again.

Jay had turned his back on Carl and once he saw that his efforts were futile he told Carly good-bye.

Jay turned and saw Carl nervously sitting in the chair. "What else did she say?" He scratched his head. "Never mind, I know that she is not leaving. What are we going to do?"

Jay arched his fingertips together as he leaned back in his chair. "I don't know, but Carly sounds crazier than Elaine." He glanced upward, "We will have to tell Omar and his brother everything she's said. We can't do this alone, we will have to enlist the help of the brothers."

Excerpt of Insidious Sins – The Sin Series Book 3

Chapter 1

Annette felt like Cinderella. She dreamt of this time so many times and for it to become a reality was magical. The wedding planner had done her thing with the engagement party. The décor was classic. Each table was covered with crème cloths, and vibrant flowers were the centerpiece on each one. Behind the buffet table, gold balloons floated with pictures of the beautiful couple.

The engagement dinner was exclusive to family and friends which was still a large crowd. Annette and Jay's entire families were present; that included uncles, aunts, and cousins. Annette looked around her best friends, Tonya and Bianca were there with their significant others. Tonya's husband Fred looked dapper in his suit and tie. Bianca was gorgeous as usual, and her new-found love Omar matched her in dress and beauty. Omar's brother Xavier had shown up with Jay's sister, Damita, she looked magnificent and he did too.

Omar and Xavier had partnered with Jay in his business recently, but Jay seemed unbothered by Damita seeing Xavier. Annette sighed in relief with that thought, because she didn't want anything to spoil her special day.

Carl, Jay's best friend attended the event alone. He had recently found out that his wife had cheated on him, which sadly ended their marriage. To onlookers he seemed at peace, but the people closest to him knew that he wasn't. He had lost weight and tension lined his face, around his eyes. While Annette was happy he showed up she wished that he would soon find peace and forgiveness.

As she scanned the room, her gaze settled on the younger group of guests. The young adults were in their own world. Bianca's daughter, Marisa, hung out with Omar's daughter, Liberty, and Jay's youngest sister, Cherise. These three had become inseparable since they met. Marisa came from visiting her father in Florida for the event. Annette smiled as she noticed Jay's younger brother Jermaine as he glanced at Liberty every three minutes.

The younger children which included Annette's three, Jolisa, Anthony Jr., Corey, Jay's son, Malik, Tonya's three sons and a host of cousins seemed to all get along fine. The sight of the children happy made this day have even a more dream-like quality.

Annette and Jay stood at the front to give a preview of their vows. Their speeches signified the end of the dinner, and the beginning of the party. Annette knew that Jay was nervous about speaking. He had no problem when he spoke about computer programs and business, but matters of the heart was different. She squeezed his hand to reassure him. They both thanked everyone for coming and Jay cleared his throat before he began.

"Annette, the first time I saw you, a star twinkled at me all the way home. That twinkle always represented your eyes to me. From that moment until now, I have not been able to get you off my mind or heart. You are so special to me and I feel like the luckiest man on earth to soon call you my wife. Your love has been so joyous and I hope that I can give you as much love as you have given me. You have taken on so many challenges by being with me, you have stepped in and shared your love with not only me but also Malik. I can't find enough words to tell you what you mean to me, but I promise that I will love you and take care of you for the rest of my life."

Tears threatened to fall and ruin her makeup, she was so overwhelmed by his words, along with the love that shone in his eyes she couldn't speak. The words she carefully planned, were forgotten. Jay hugged her close and that simple gesture gave her the strength she needed.

She kept him close to her as she spoke. "Jay, my darling Jay, I want to thank you for showing me what real love is. Thank you for showing me that true love does exist, it exists in real life; and it exists between you and me. You have a heart of gold and to know that you want to share that with me, makes me the luckiest woman alive. Every challenge that we have faced, we have faced together and they have become triumphs." She paused, "The day you asked me to be your wife was one of the happiest days of my life. To know that you trust me to love and care for the most important person in your life, your son, is an honor. I can only say that wherever your love leads me, I will go, because I love you, I trust you, and most of all I believe in you. I can't wait for us to continue our journey as man and wife for the rest of our lives."

Jay leaned down when she finished and caught her in a passionate kiss, full of promise for what would come later. They were in a room full of people, but at that moment, no one else existed. The applause reminded them where they were, so they reluctantly parted.

Everyone rushed them with congratulations and hugs. Her family, of course, were so happy because they had researched Jay's net worth after they met him. Her true family which consisted of his family, her youngest sister, and her close friends, Tonya and Bianca. They were the ones she shared her true happiness with, because they understood, and loved her despite everything.

Tonya was in a full-fledged sob by the time she made it to Annette, she grabbed her tightly. "I am so happy for you and you look so beautiful."

Tonya kept it moving because it seemed as if everyone had risen to hug them. Annette hadn't realized how many people were there until that moment. Bianca approached her and she looked more beautiful than ever. She was always beautiful but since she had been with Omar, she had a glow. Annette whispered that she would be next and instead of a smart retort, Bianca just smiled.

She tried not to roll her eyes when her sister Andrea walked up to her, but that woman had rubbed her the wrong way all her life! Annette had two sisters, the youngest, Ashley, lived with her. Since she and Andrea were closer in age, people assumed that they were close. Not! Andrea had a jealous heart, and since she wanted to stay in their parent's good graces, she adopted their judgmental attitude.

"You look pretty Nette, and your dress looks so expensive! I hope you aren't trying to spend all of his money before y'all get married."

Annette looked around, Jay was busy laughing with Carl and Omar, her friends had disappeared, in other words she couldn't think of a nice way to escape this heifer.

"For your information, I bought my own dress, and I don't think you have to worry about me spending all of Jay's money."

"Humph, so it's like that? It must be nice." Andrea looked towards Jay with a scowl.

This was her day and her mealy mouth sister was not about to ruin it.

"It is very nice. Maybe if you loosened up some you could meet a man that wants to spend some money on you."

Annette moved to hug the next person in line while her sister stood in shock. Andrea and Annette's mom were so used to her taking their beat downs, Andrea didn't know how to respond.

Soon the DJ played their song, "A Couple of Forever's" by Chrissette Michelle, and Jay swept her in his arms.

"I can't wait to get you home Mrs. Soon to Be Darrington."

"That sounds so good. I can't wait to get you home. And since your mom offered to keep the kids we will have the house to ourselves."

"Let's go now!" He laughed as he showered her with kisses.

It felt so good to show the world their love. She couldn't have dreamt of Jay, not even in her wildest fantasies. He loved her, he treated her great, and he loved her kids as much as they loved him. They were so into one another, it took a minute before they realized that everyone's attention had diverted to the front door.

Annette's ex-husband, Anthony walked in with Elaine, Jay's ex-wife, and they were followed by Bianca and Omar's exes. What the hell?

They walked in as if they were welcomed, Elaine had on a burgundy tight beaded dress, and Anthony was in a black suit. Benita and Greg, were dressed in a similar fashion. As much as she hated to admit it, Elaine looked good. She had lost weight, her hair was still short but laid, and her make-up looked good. When Elaine spotted them, she gave a sinister grin.

"Just ignore them and let's continue to have a good time. Maybe if we ignore them, they will leave."

That was the last thing she wanted to do, she wanted them to leave right then. A few of Jay's clients had come in behind them, so she agreed. No need to have whispers of how he divorced the classy one and got with the ratchet one.

As she greeted the new guests, she stopped worrying as much about Elaine and her crew. But each time she glanced their way, Elaine glared at her. After the new people came, it became more of a party atmosphere. People danced, drank, mingled, and she was glad to see everyone have a wonderful time. Most of Jay's business associates only stayed a short time, and as the night went on, it was mostly family.

Anthony tore up the dance floor with Benita, Annette met him in a club so she was not surprised by his moves. What surprised her was how familiar he and Benita looked together, he was probably screwing her. The DJ slowed it down and Anthony swapped Benita out for Elaine. Annette noticed that Jay stared as he ran his hands suggestively over Elaine's body. When she looked back at him he smiled at her, and she guessed that her imagination worked overtime.

"It's time to shut this down, I'm ready to get you home." Jay murmured before he pulled her in for a kiss.

His kisses still made her weak, as well as his hand which caressed her thigh under the table. After they parted she hugged him tight and looked over his shoulder straight into the eyes of Elaine!

When Jay walked to the bar to tell the guys good-bye, her friends swarmed the table.

Tonya said goodbye, because her husband Fred was ready to leave.

"I don't know why you brought him! He has been looking bored all night." Bianca pursed her lips.

"Because he is my husband! You know that most men don't enjoy events like this." Tonya looked aggravated.

"Humph, it seems as if every other man had a good time." Bianca tried to look innocent and failed miserably.

"I am not here to argue with you. Annette, I think it was nice that Elaine didn't cause a scene."

"Here we go." Bianca muttered.

Annette sighed. "I'm glad she didn't either, but I wished she hadn't come. And with Anthony!"

Tonya glanced around, "Now that did surprise me. It's a small world."

"Small world? Misery loves company and that entire crew are the most miserable people we know. I'm not surprised. Elaine has probably learned everything she could about Annette and ran Anthony down. We all know that he is ready for mess." Bianca sounded disgusted.

Damita finally spoke up, "Tonya, I don't care what you say, they came to start some shit. There was no reason for any of them to be here. I'm just glad that Angie didn't bring her no-good butt with them."

Benita and Greg, the other couple with the interlopers, were exes of Bianca and Omar. Once Bianca and Omar got together they found out that Greg and Benita had been friends with benefits for some time. Angie was Carl's soon to be ex-wife, who had been outed for cheating. It was a regular soap opera.

They all nodded in agreement, and as they looked across the floor, Elaine stood with the men. Malik hugged his parents, as he left with Jay's mom. As soon as he left Elaine moved closer as she talked and laughed with Jay. Annette did not like the way she felt as she looked on. Her heart knew that Jay loved her, but he and Elaine had a long history. It didn't help that it was a known fact that Elaine wanted him back. Annette felt uncomfortable as she watched them.

She was snapped from her musings by Damita. "Girl, tomorrow we are going to give your sister a flowchart of who is available! She has been hanging around Xavier all night."

She was right! Andrea had moseyed over to the bar and batted her eyes at Xavier. Annette laughed at the look of frustration on Damita's face.

"I'll talk to her. I'm sure you don't have to worry about her."

"You might need to, because she doesn't seem to get the memo." Damita murmured before she broke into a smile as Jay headed their way.

All doubt cleared her head as Annette watched him approach. As he approached it was obvious that he only had eyes for her. Before he opened his mouth, Elaine had wobbled to the front and grabbed the microphone.

"Hello! I came here tonight to show that even though Annette slept with my husband and broke up MY marriage, that I wish you guys whatever you have coming to you."

Elaine's words were slurred, but understandable. Annette heard a gasp and she knew before she looked that it came from her family. Everyone was too shocked to move. Elaine went on.

"I have tried to move on, but it's harder when a skank comes and fucks your husband into foolishness. I just hope, Annette, that karma doesn't meet you and you have to go through what you put me through."

She paused for effect, and within that short amount of time Damita galvanized into action. She ran to the stage and snatched the microphone from Elaine.

"No, you are not going to do this here!" She gritted through her teeth.

After Damita acted everyone else came out of their trance. Carl, Omar, and Xavier moved to Elaine, but before they escorted her out, Jay approached her. Madder than a hornet.

"What are you trying to prove Elaine?"

Elaine straightened, and although she didn't have the microphone anymore, she spoke loud and clear. "What am I trying to prove? While you sit here like the royal couple all kissy faced, you seem to have forgotten that I am the mother of your only child! All of this money you have spent on this whore, while I was the one who was there when the struggle was real."

She gave a strangled laugh before she continued. "But you sit here like it is cool for you to marry your side piece and expect me to be fine with it. The real question is what are YOU trying to prove?"

"Let's not get this twisted sister." Damita got in Elaine's face. "When my brother struggled, you wouldn't lift a finger to help, and when HE made it you enjoyed all the fruits of his labor. And furthermore, Annette is not his side piece, she is his soon to be wife, a real wife; something that your ass doesn't know shit about."

Jay pulled Damita back, while Carl held Elaine.

"You bitch! You knew he was fucking around on me and never opened your mouth. You don't know what I went through while I was married. As a matter of fact, you don't know shit about marriage because no one will marry your ass!"

Annette stood four feet behind the fray, and she was so caught up as the drama unfolded in front of her, she hadn't notice that Anthony had slipped beside her.

"Are you sure this is what you want?" He was so close to her ear, she felt moisture from his breath.

"Yes Ant, this is what I want."

"You dogged me for having flings, then you turn around and break up a marriage? Nette I know you better than anyone, you won't be able to live with that."

By this time, Carl and Omar ushered Elaine out, Xavier came to cool Damita down, while Jay walked towards her. His stormy look grew stormier when he noticed Anthony beside her.

"Ant, I am not about to have this conversation with you."

"Maybe not now, but we will talk soon, sweetness." His tongue was almost in her ear as he spoke.

"You probably need to go take Elaine home." Jay didn't smile or pretend to have any pleasantries for Anthony.

"Yea, I will. You take care of my girl alright?" Anthony squeezed her arm before he walked off smiling.

Jay wrapped her in his arms and whispered apologies in her ear. Jay walked off to talk to her parents, and as soon as he left her friends surrounded her.

"I can't believe that heifer had the nerve to bring her ass in here!" Damita was still angry.

Bianca looked unconcerned. "She just wants attention. She brought that old news as if she was telling something that everybody didn't know. If she wanted to do some damage, she would have done it when more people were here. She showed out in front of family."

"Umm, my family didn't know." Annette spoke softly. Her friends gave her an incredulous look.

"Oops! You never told them Nette?"

"No, I didn't tell them about Jay until we officially started dating. Of course, I told Ashley, but she knew not to tell the rest of the family."

Bianca looked around slowly, "They know now. But I wouldn't worry about it, everybody has skeletons. It doesn't make a difference now."

"You don't know my folks." Annette said under her breath.

"There's nothing they can do it about now. You guys are together and headed to the altar. They will get over it." Damita reassured her.

"Yes, but I don't want them to look at Jay differently."

"They won't. Look at him now, throwing on the charm. By the time ya'll get married this will be forgotten."

Damita was right, Jay stood with her dad, and while he looked as if he understood; her mother tooted her nose, mouth, and forehead at him. Her mother was always so worried about what others thought, and tried to act so bougie, she would be a hard sell.

Tonya hugged her before she left and Annette read the admonishment in her face. She knew that Tonya would understand Elaine's rationale for what she did. Thankfully she kept quiet. Jay and Omar walked up together. It was time to leave and though she knew that she needed to approach her family, she cringed at the thought.

They walked to her family's table, and her sister stopped her as if she was security for the table.

"You could have told us the real story, so that we wouldn't have been so embarrassed." She hissed, while she glanced at Jay.

"Like I knew this was going to happen!" Andrea grabbed her arm when she tried to bypass her.

"You knew how y'all got together. With that in mind, you should have known something like this could happen. What were you thinking?"

"We will have this conversation later. Let me tell everyone good-bye, so that I can leave. I'm not in the mood for this."

"You are right. We will have a conversation. It's obvious that someone should have been talking to you when you hooked up with this smooth talker. You should be tired of making bad decisions, Nette."

Annette rolled her eyes after she snatched her arm away. She gave her parents a kiss and hurriedly told everyone bye. Her cousins were headed back to their perspectives homes in the morning, which left only her immediate family to be dealt with.

Damita stopped them at the door to remind them of the get together at the Darrington home. Jay's mom wanted both sides of the family to get to know each other better, but after tonight Annette's family knew too much. She was excited when the event was planned, but now it felt like a burden.

As they peeled out of the parking lot, Jay reached over and grabbed her hand. "I'm so sorry that happened tonight. I think your dad understood, but I don't know about your mom and sister."

She took a deep breath. "Jay, you don't have to apologize, it's not your fault. I should have had enough courage to tell them the truth, but I didn't want to hear their mouths. I just dread the backlash and I don't want them to look at you different. Whatever happens we will get through it."

Annette would reflect on that comment later.

Made in the USA
Columbia, SC
07 November 2022

70590545R00172